I0520112

Simbiosys – Ultimate Cyber Attack

This book is a work of fiction, and all events and characters are fictional.

Any resemblance to any actual persons or events is purely coincidental and unintentional.

ISBN - 978-0-615-35084-4

For Andrew, who encouraged me to write it down;

For Julie who still puts up with me;

For Jimmy who always challenges me;

For Chelsea who never asks for too much; and

For Lily, who stars in a cameo role.

Forward

Science fiction is usually the greatest predictor of the future. And the lines between fact and fiction are always blurred, but this one is just fiction.

Enjoy.

Chapter 1

The sound was shocking. Was it one hundred decibels? That's like standing next to a jackhammer; it can cause significant hearing loss. No, it was not that bad, but it was definitely loud enough to startle Jim out of his restless sleep. And for that fleeting moment, his re-entry into the world of the living was like the first moment a child enters the cold, hard world screaming and crying for comfort - Doctor Jim Andrews had no idea what was happening except that his ears had been assaulted. He surveyed his disheveled surroundings while coming to his senses. Jim was in his home office; it was a Monday morning in late September; and he had fallen asleep doing technical research, again. Lily, his pampered and entitled Chocolate Labrador, was forcefully insisting that it was time to *rise and shine*. That bitch was the culprit!

If dogs could talk, Jim was sure that Lily was informing of his duty to feed her. It was not a discussion, it was fact. The soft brown dog approached Jim's chair, nudging his leg with her snout, and in the excitement of seeing a life response, her tail moved like a helicopter rotor, shaking her butt and thighs at an impossibly high speed. Lily barked again, remaining firm in her message and purpose. She was taking control of the situation. Jim was not in charge, he never was.

"Hey girl, I know, I know, I know, it's time to get some food...c'mon, let's go." At his invitation, the impossible happened...Lily wagged her tail even faster than before.

Jim had been creating a software program to make digital music more rich sounding. In the rush and excitement, he must have dozed off. Perhaps sleep arrived when Jim was reviewing that PhD student's thesis – it was a little dry. He remembered his days of studying for his PhD, the endless research, the questions and the comments from his superiors. Seven years of paying his dues was the entry fee to become Dr. Jim Andrews. It was not easy work, but Jim loved it. The Stanford University bio explained that he was one of the foremost authorities in an esoteric field called auditory dynamics, which in simple terms was the study of the manipulation of sound. Jim's corporate consulting work paid well, and sensing the opportunity to improve his earnings, Jim had moved further from academia, spending half-time on corporate work and half-time at the University. The only wrinkle with this arrangement, as his wife continued to remind, was that Jim spent 12 hours on each job. It got so bad that Sally had recently accused him of having an affair with his laptop, she was convinced of it.

On his way to serve the dog, Jim stumbled across some books and papers that he had left scattered on the floor. He peered into the kitchen, it was old and it was ugly. The house had been renovated in the 1980's, and like everything else in the house, the kitchen was in need of either a military-style cleaning or a demolition job. With responsible homeowners, it would have been fine, but Jim's mind was distracted and Sally had been busy, so the house bore the brunt of neglect.

Jim looked in the sink. He forgot to load the dishes last night, something that Sally was constantly complaining about. He looked closer and concluded that there appeared to be more than one night's dishes stacked in the sink.

The dog food was in a bag on the counter, and the dog's metal dish was by the back door. He picked up the bowl and noticed that it was slimy. "Sorry girl…looks like your dishes are dirty too." Jim filled up the food dish and placed it in front of Lily. He smiled because she was immediately grateful and happy. "If only the rest of my life were that easy," he sighed.

Jim glanced at the clock on the microwave, it was 7:00am and he needed to get ready to go to the office. He felt like his schedule was determined by others, and because of that, he was out of control of his life. Jim left the kitchen and headed upstairs to see Sally. He figured she would probably be on her way out the door. Sally was a public relations consultant and she had been spending a lot of time with one of the larger manufacturing firms in L.A. Her client had faced layoffs due to the recent economic crisis and they had asked Sally to assist in making the firm seem to be as considerate as possible, despite the fact that they were closing down more than half of the operations.

Sally had been struggling on the project. But even before the job troubles, Jim felt that they were not really getting along. He felt like they needed some time to get back in touch with each other. Ever since her miscarriage last year, Sally had reverted into a shell and Jim felt lost. Gradually, he found that he could lose himself in his research and not be bothered by the demons that Sally seemed to be wrestling with.

Jim entered the bedroom and was disoriented at the scene. Perhaps it was the intense sunlight pouring in through the bedroom window. It illuminated the bed, highlighting to Jim that Sally was not at home and that she had not come home. He glanced at the clock on the night-stand to confirm that it was 7:00am. The bed was made and the closet was open, displaying the clothes which had been strewn about. As Jim took in the scene, reality sunk in. That's what caught his eye. It was the envelope with a simple *Jim*. As he fumbled with the letter, he felt a pit in his stomach and a dry throat. The letter was painfully brief:

Dear Jim,

I don't know how we got to this point, but I can't take it anymore. I need to do something different with my life and I don't think we're going to work. We've been married for 5 years and I feel lost. You're wrapped up in your work and I'm busy too. We gave it a good shot, but things don't always work out, do they? I've found someone new, you should do the same.

Sally

Jim crumpled up the letter and tossed it across the room. The letter was not really a surprise, things had been tough for years, but Jim regretted that his life had been focused on everything except his relationship with Sally, and now it had come home to roost.

Being alone was not a new phenomenon. Jim was born and raised on Long Island, New York, and he spent a good amount of time by himself as a child. Everyone knew that Jim was not *like* the other kids. As a freshman in high school, he decided that rather than be Jim Andrews, he should be Jimmy Page, the lead guitarist of his favorite rock music group, Led Zeppelin. He officially changed his name to Jimmy and saved his money to buy an electric guitar.

Thirty years later, Jim still could recall the day he plugged in the guitar to the amp and found that he had absolutely no musical ability, nothing, not a bit. After spending months practicing and growing increasingly more frustrated, he accidentally broke one of the sound pickups and had to take apart the guitar to fix it. The only guidance he could get for how to fix the guitar was from Dr. Roberts, his science teacher in East Hampton High School. Dr. Roberts inspected the instrument and showed Jimmy how the strings vibrated, and he explained how the magnets in pickups reflected that vibration, causing the electric current to be distorted which was transmitted through the amplifier to the springs in the speakers. That is what made music, he explained. Or in Jim's case, it made scratchy sounds which never quite resembled the music he so desperately sought.

"Wait a minute Dr. Roberts. Are you telling me that the electricity amplifies the sound waves which then travel through the air and cause vibrations in my ear?"

"Yes Jim, that's indeed how it works."

"But, doesn't that mean that somehow the electricity itself enters my blood? I mean, I can feel it in my brain and in my body. How does my brain convert these waves into emotions?"

Dr. Roberts smiled in a grandfatherly way and put his hand on Jimmy's shoulder. "Jim, I want to tell you two important things. First of all, the conversion of sound waves into emotions is a question for God, not me."

"God?" Jimmy questioned, sounding deflated, "God hasn't exactly had a lot of direct communications with me Dr. Roberts. What's the second thing you wanted to tell me?"

"Jim, you're going to be a great scientist."

From that day forward, Jimmy was hooked. He was addicted to the science of sound, and his thirst for knowledge was directed towards the laboratory of Dr. Roberts. It was filled with gadgets and tools, and Jim was blown away when Dr. Roberts demonstrated his newest tool, the personal computer. It was made by a company called Commodore, and Dr. Roberts showed Jim how the computer could produce sounds by typing commands into a simple program. Jim was captivated. "You see son, this is not just electricity causing sound waves. Technology has advanced to a point where digital information is instructing these processors to generate the waves. We have bridged the analogue-digital gap with a computer. I'm old now, but I can tell you for sure, the future is digital." Jim's eyes widened and his imagination was captured. He attacked this new environment with fervor. Jim Andrews did not have the natural talent to play guitar, but he knew that he could master the mechanics of making computers play for him. Math, physics and science became simple tools to be mastered for the sole purpose of improving his learning and supporting his passion for music. He was always tinkering with the computers and trying to create new sounds and new songs. And he hoped one day to make computers talk. Because if they could talk, they could sing; and if they could sing, he could turn them into Led Zeppelin, he just knew it.

Three years after his guitar repair session, Jim Andrews had placed his idol, Jimmy Page, back into the music bin and had entered Stanford University to study physics and computer science where he would spend the next 20 years of his life pursuing the science of sound.

Dr. Roberts passed away the year after Jim left high school, leaving Jim to grieve as if a part of his own spirit had left this world. It left a void. Research was lonely work, but it filled the empty spaces, and Jim became engrossed in his projects. He had spent so much time studying auditory dynamics that he did not hear the sounds of the world like most people. Jim's perception of sound had been altered. He analyzed every sound for clues to its origin and he mentally made notes of how the sound could be translated into computer codes and electronic signals. He advanced rapidly in the university department and became respected for his abilities. Each quarter, many job offers came in, but Jim liked teaching, and although he spent a lot of time in solitary reflection, he loved his lab at Stanford.

Just before he turned 38, Jim met Sally, and two years later they were married. Although the couple differed on thoughts of children, Jim agreed that it was time to get a job outside of the University. Besides, corporate life would offer more money and more free time. But Jim could never really get away from the University. The solitary workaholic effortlessly found reasons to work late at the office, or to be up late at home working. Sally was a companion, but she complained that she felt locked out of his personal space. Jim knew they had drifted apart over the past few years and now, as he sat on his empty bed, the truth hit home - she was gone. They made it to the altar, but Jim had jilted her in slow motion, like erosion. Jim was destined to be a loner. He was 45 years old, and he was alone, again.

As Jim was discovering his loss, Lily finished her meal and came upstairs to see what was going on in her house. Jim heard the muted staccato of her claws patting the hardwood as she slowly entered the bedroom. She was ready to go for a walk and was bent on convincing Jim to share her desire. "I guess it's just you and me now baby. Let's go for a walk." Jim's nose had begun to run since he was crying and he wiped his nose with his hand, and then wiped his hand onto his pants. He walked back through the kitchen which led outside, reached for a paper towel to wipe his nose, grabbed his jacket and a baseball-cap, and put on Lily's leash.

As he stepped out into the crisp, morning air, Jim looked into the sky and took a deep breath. At least it was a sunny day.

Yes, indeed, it was a sunny, shitty September day.

Chapter 2

The drive to the office was a bad omen. Traffic was jammed and the car was running on empty. Although the little yellow light had become illuminated, Jim knew that as long as traffic moved, he had enough gas to get to work. But he would definitely need to stop and fill up on the way home. Jim's latest gig was at a digital music company. The founder, Jake, was one of those 29 year-old know-it-alls who wanted to invent the next, best iTunes.

After 2 months on the job, Jim was named the Chief Scientist at Sound Fusion Factory. His job fit all of his short-list requirements – it was small, fun, and challenging. There were about 20 people in the company – Jim worked with 5 other engineers, and the rest of the people were in sales or marketing or some other area that Jim did not care to understand or learn about. While Jim did not really care about the overall business, he really enjoyed the stock options and he was enthralled with his project – to make digital music files sound better, while making the file size smaller. That kind of challenge was right up Jim's alley – he was king in that domain – no matter that his wife had abandoned him.

Jake insisted that the company be located in the swankiest part of town. Their office was a small 2 story building with every detail alluding to the company's future success. The foyer was grand, the receptionist was attractive, the company's logo was embossed in gold lettering on the front doors and fancy cars were in the parking lot. Looking at Jake, Jim knew that the dot-com bust had not touched this part of town. Jim was proud of his Company - he liked the identity it afforded him. He felt he had finally 'arrived.'

As Jim walked towards the office entrance, he saw Jesse, the CFO, standing outside talking to Ralph, one of Jim's co-workers. They were huddled close to the door and seemed to be fooling around.

"Hey guys," Jim yelled, "What's going on?"

"I guess you haven't heard," replied Jesse.

"Heard about what?"

"That jack-ass Jake has flown the coop. He's bankrupted us…gone…disappeared." Jesse spat.

Jim heard the words, but they made no sense to his brain. Then he noticed that there was a chain locking the front doors. Jesse and Ralph must have been trying to pull open the door.

"Dude," Ralph said, "Look at the door, man. It's chained up, we're screwed."

Jim shrugged, "I feel like a gloom-and-doom country music song today, what's next? As long as my dog doesn't die and my truck doesn't break down, I guess I should be okay. I…I can't believe it! My wife left me and I lost my job, *and* it's only nine thirty in the morning."

"Sorry man," Ralph replied. "That really sucks. Me and Jesse are going to go get drunk, you wanna join us?"

Jim smiled reticently and shrugged off the invitation with his shoulders. "No, I think I need some time to take it all in." As Jim tilted his eyes upward to the heavens, he made an effort to bring in the good air as he inhaled, and to release the bad as he exhaled. He commented, "Hey, did you notice how nice it is today? I mean…the sun and sky are really beautiful, aren't they? Look, there's not a cloud in the sky."

Ralph and Jesse followed Jim's gaze towards the sky and agreed with a tentative pause.

"Yeah, it's true," commented Jesse, "Such a beautiful day to lose your job…Sorry Jim, we're outta here, man. Stay in touch."

Jim turned away from the chained-up office door and headed back towards his car. He pulled out of the lot, cranked up the radio and headed towards home. Jim was not so cavalier to expect that things could not get worse, but he was convinced that today was a day for the history books. Jim's FM radio was tuned to the local Rock and Roll station, KPRC 104.5, California's classic rock. Jim enjoyed the station because they used vinyl records so that the music was not missing the depth which occurs with digital conversion. He could always tell when a song had been digitally converted from an analogue recording. Jim liked new music, but for his old friends Robert Plant, Jimmy Page, John Bonham and John Paul Jones, there was no substitute for vinyl, not for Led Zeppelin.

Not everything was bad today, the weather was good, and it was Two-for-Tuesday on the radio. Finally, Jim had some good luck as he caught the beginning of Ramble On. Jim sang along in his consistently off-key voice, joining his boyhood friends in an anthem that somehow perfectly captured his mood. *Ramble On.*

Chapter 3

Lily stuck her wet nose onto Jim's face and rapidly, but precisely, placed her razor thin tongue so carefully between his lips that Jim felt momentarily violated. He sprang awake and wiped his cheek and mouth with his sleeve.

For the past 4 years, Sally had been the first one to wake up, and she was usually the one who fed the dog. Since Sally had left, Jim was now in a position of responsibility and importance, and subservience.

"Okay, Okay, Okay. I'm getting up." He grumbled, realizing that Lily was training him to be her new servant.

For the first time in his life, Jim had the one thing that Sally had always asked for and he had been unwilling to give - he had time, and lots of it. Jim believed that he had too much time on his hands. He needed to get back into the swing of life. But first, it was about time Jim took a vacation. Sally and Jim had been so busy they hardly ever traveled…it was time to get out!

Jim heard Lily panting near his ear. Her breathing was a low bass whisper, with a scratchy hiss mixed in. He was momentarily captivated by the sound, but snapped out of it quickly. Yes, the dog would need to go to the kennel. Jim could not remember the lady's name that ran the kennel - he only remembered that she was a unique and quirky woman. He grabbed his laptop and googled 'Kennels and Boarding Los Angeles'. The list of results was mind-boggling, but he kept scanning the results until he found what he was looking for – Doggie Day Care. Jim clicked on the hyperlink and it brought him to the facebook page for Claire DeLuca. "That's right," he remembered, "Sally called her the Crazy Chinese Italian lady." Claire's facebook page had a link to her website, where her cell phone was listed as the contact number. Claire was a lively and gracious woman who happened to look and speak just like her pet poodle.

"Doggie Day Care this is Claire! How con I hep yew?"

"Hi Claire. It's Jim Andrews," he replied, but Claire's cell phone had poor reception.

"Hoo dis?"

"Ms. DeLuca…hi, it's Jim Andrews."

"Aaaah Docka Andews! Why, how ah yew dewing dear, I havin heard fro' yew in ages?"

"I'm okay…yeah it has been a while. Hey, listen, I need to go away for a while, and I was wondering if you could look after Lily."

"Miss Wiggles!" Jim had forgotten that Claire had a nickname for all her customers' pets, and he smiled when he thought of Lily as Miss Wiggles. It was true that sometimes she wagged her tail so hard that the back part of her body lopped around out of control.

"Why I wood luv to have uh. How lon' yew goin' for?"

"Well the thing is Claire, I'm not really sure."

"Oh," she paused, quizzically, "is every ting ok dear?"

Jim was astounded that Claire had picked up on his problems based only on the tone of his voice, and he marveled at the way some people could interpret moods.

"Yeah, it's fine Claire. Well…no…uh…it's actually…I mean…uh…I seem to have run into a little bit of bad luck, but it will be ok." He fumbled, "Aw shit, the truth is, Claire, Sally has left and I need to get away for a while."

There was a momentary silence on the line as Jim stopped talking, feeling awkward and embarrassed. He had not really accepted that his life was permanently altered until that moment on the phone.

"Ohhh, yew pooor thing! Now yew listen to me hon'. We all have 'em, bad times. Lord knows I have had my fair share. But our little furry loved ones like Miss Wiggles should not suffer for it. Look, yew know that I luv Miss Wiggles and I will meck sure she is hoppy as can be til yew get back home. Take yer time dear, and drop by annnny time, and ooh I am soooo sorry dear, oh yew poor, poor thing."

Jim hung up the phone and felt like a hurt kitten. His hands were sweating and he smelled like body odor. "Miss Wiggles?" he asked himself out loud.

Lily came running up to his side wagging her tail in eager anticipation. He mocked Claire's tone. "Come on Lil'. Let's go to camp!"

After dropping Lily off with Claire, Jim came to the stark realization that he was really alone. Jesse had left a voice mail for Jim a couple of days ago, so Jim decided to call him back.

"Hey Jesse, it's Jim Andrews."

"Hi-ya Jimbo! What's doing?"

Jim forgot how annoying Jesse could be, but he knew that he needed a favor, so he held his tongue.

"I'm good…hey, sorry for not getting back to you sooner. What's going on? I haven't heard anything from the Company."

"No, it's all fucked up, man. Jake just flat out disappeared. No-one has heard from him and his apartment is empty. I went by to see him and a moving company was carrying out his living room. The guy said that the furniture was being repo'd. Can you believe it? They repo'd his fucking couch, man."

"You've gotta be kidding me."

"No, I'm serious as shit. I couldn't make this shit up. Jake was a loser and he has spent all the money and skipped town. They're even selling all the office furniture."

Jim shuddered at the thought of all his valuable work being auctioned off to a 'vulture capital' fund like a second-hand piece of furniture. He had invested his heart and soul into his job, and Jake had left him swinging in the breeze.

"But that's not why I called you man," Jesse explained.

"What's up?"

"Look, a good friend of mine in New York was out visiting this week. He came to help me drink and smoke away the pain, if you know what I mean?"

"So?"

"Well, anyway, after watching Oprah all day, and sharing the peace pipe, I asked him what he was doing and he explained that he had joined a Venture Capital fund."

"A VC fund, Jess, those guys are ass-holes."

"I know, I know, you're a scientist not a business man. But hear me out. His firm just invested in a company outside of New York City that is working on some telephony stuff."

"Telephony stuff? What the hell are you talking about Jess?"

"Look man, you're the scientist, not me. I'm just a CFFO, a Chief Financial Fucking Officer. And I'm unemployed like you are. But you and I both know that you are much more employable than I am, even if you are a son of a bitch." Jesse joked. "Listen man…Give the guy a call, his name is Rob. He told me that this company is hiring like crazy and he was really curious to know where the engineers from Sound Fusion Factory were going."

"Where are we *going*?" Jim replied caustically, "We're on a highway to hell, man, and you know it." He sang, "*Highway to Hell*."

Jesse laughed, "You're a sick, son-of-a-bitch, head banger Jimbo. You must've had too much AC/DC as a teenager. Look man, my friend Rob's a survivor. He's a smart guy, like you, and I trust his judgment. I'll send you a text message with his info. Give him a call."

"Thanks Jess, I will."

Jim hung up the phone and immediately started dreaming about New York. It had indeed been years. New York was far away, it was on the opposite coast, it was the opposite of California. Jim was mesmerized. A few minutes later, Jim's phone buzzed as the text message arrived. Jim stared at the number for a while, and decided to call. He left a voicemail and hung up, then came back down to the reality of his life.

It was 3:00pm and he was sitting, in his pajamas, in his home office, staring at the computer screen…nothing at all, no news, no messages, nothing, boredom. Jim walked over to his record collection and pulled out the *Dark Side of the Moon*. He popped on the stereo and relaxed as he lost himself into the sounds of 1968.

The phone rang somewhere in the middle of the '*Great Gig in the Sky*.' Jim faded back into reality slowly.

"Hello?"

"Uh Jim…I mean…Dr. Andrews, this is Rob Benson from Culliver, Stewart Ventures, sorry I missed your call."

"It's okay…I was calling you because Jesse gave me your number."

"Yeah, I know. I spoke with Jesse for a while last week about Sound Fusion Factory... hey, listen, we were hoping to invite you out to New York to meet with a client of ours. You might have heard of them, it's a new firm called Audacity Frontier?"

"Nope, never heard of them, what do they do?"

"No…Oh well...uh…I'm not really the technical person, you know. I can't explain it very well, but they are actively involved in the mobile telephony and music space. Anyway, our client is looking for a Sound Scientist, and we heard that you have recently become available?"

"*Available*?" Jim chuckled. "Yeah I guess you could put it that way."

"So, you'll come?"

"Sure, when did you have in mind? I'm pretty open these days."

Jim hung up the phone. The fantasy of free time and his blossoming dreams of a vacation quickly evaporated, but Jim was relieved because, in his heart, he knew that work was his passion. It was his distraction from the cares of ordinary life.

The next morning, a FedEx package arrived at Jim's door. He was surprised, but accepted the mail, thinking that maybe Sally had decided to quickly file divorce papers. He examined the unfamiliar mailing address, it was from Connecticut, and he opened up the package. It contained an itinerary and an invitation letter. Big spenders - Maggie had booked a first-class ticket and had reserved a suite at the Tribeca Grand hotel. Jim was pleasantly surprised and felt a rush of self-importance. Yes, he was valuable, and, yes, he was worth it.

On the agenda, Jim noticed that the first meeting would be a dinner meeting in Manhattan, followed by a casual day at the Greenwich office. They had made reservations at an exclusive French restaurant in downtown Manhattan, *tres chic*. Jim set down the letter and felt happy, wanted, and appreciated. A few minutes after opening the package, an e-mail arrived from Maggie with the same itinerary. Jim clicked the <OK> button and noticed that his calendar was updated, and that an eTicket confirmation was delivered to his email.

"Nice," he exclaimed, and headed towards the bedroom to shower and pack his bags.

Yes, a change would be good.

Chapter 4

The hairs on the back of his neck stood on end and a chill streaked its way down his spine, making the tops of his ears numb and momentarily distorting his vision - such moments of panic-ridden ecstasy are rare.

It's not easy to be a computer programmer – you spend long periods creating mundane infrastructure and, despite the fancy new gadgets, most of the work is still based on 1970's technology and it requires primitive tools and cryptic computer languages…and yet, it is addictive.

Addiction is not too strong of a word, because the attention and effort involved in creating programs is intense. You can lose days and even weeks to the outside world, and you can get "buggy eyed" from staring at the screen for so long. When creating and fixing a program, intense concentration is required, and some find that caffeine, nicotine or various other stimulants are tools of the trade to keep the mind working overtime. Sometimes you can feel your body rebelling at the sedentary discipline, but you keep at it, you keep working on the problem until it is fixed.

And for what? Why does he do it? It can't be only for money, because there are millions of people out there who will program for free. No, it has to be something deeper, it is a desire to tap into that godlike capability to create and to destroy – digitally. Programming is like that. It holds ultimate power for those who are literate in its mysteries.

But not all programmers are created equal – some are good, some are bad. And some are so brilliant that they do stupid things, especially hackers. What makes one a hacker? Is it the challenge of the unknown? Is it pride or arrogance which drives one to show their peers' weakness? Is there superiority in highlighting how someone screwed up in designing their own programs? Is it just another form of bullying?

Even in the world of hackers there are good hackers and bad hackers. Regrettably, some have an intuitive feel for the potential reach of distributing a program on the net, but they do not have the human skills to realize that an errant program can cause a lot of damage. They seem invisible, these programs, but people do tend to notice when they run amok.

But he was not a hacker, he was a respected technologist, and he was a brilliant programmer – his entire career spoke volumes about his ability to envision and craft elegant programs. *And, he had really screwed up this time.*

Usually, a bad program will crash the computer and you can fix it, but a good program will have redundancy built in. It will not crash, it should never crash - a good program is robust. And the seeker was robust, if nothing else – apparently it was too robust. As he realized that the seeker was still working, he felt pride…he had fathered true elegance…and then he felt like puking.

When wheels are put in motion, a vehicle takes on inertia - it needs to be stopped with force, like friction from brakes, or from the tires hitting the road, or the immovability of a brick wall. But in the digital world, there is no friction. All you need is electricity and a processor. Ever since the Internet boom, there is no shortage of processors; and unfortunately, there seems to always be a computer, somewhere, turned on.

How could this little bugger keep on ticking? What had he done?

He thought back about a story he once heard that God laughed after he had created the tiger. God liked the tiger, and with its creation, he decided that the world could be filled with chaos and intrigue. He reveled in his garden, pairing predators against prey, causing tension and suspense amongst the species, but as his kingdom spread, they threatened to run too wild. So, God created a man to be the referee and the steward. Man was endowed with a mind and a conscience to distinguish him from the animals, and he used his mind to tame the wild beasts. But there were some animals, like the tiger, that could not be tamed, and would have to be caged or destroyed. When God realized that man would destroy his peaceful chaos, he created a woman to balance things out, re-igniting the chaos and tension…and then he smiled, for it was good.

A man can't ride a tiger, he can only destroy it or cage it. As he stared at his computer screen, he wondered if he had created something worse, something that could not be controlled, and could not be destroyed…and then he laughed, for it was awful.

Chapter 5

Welcome to New York, New York.

Jim's driver was Anthony, a twenty-something kid from Brooklyn who was clean cut and wholesome looking – no tattoos or body piercings on this young man. Anthony was wearing a blue pin stripe suit, with sun glasses that made him look like a combination of a fashion model and a mobster, but his cheeks were ruddy and his complexion was fair. He was a tough kid, physically fit and disciplined - everything Jim was not.

"Hi Sir, Dr. Andrews," he said as he reached for Jim's bags.

"Thanks, and please, call me Jim."

"Yes Sir…uh, Jim," replied the boy and then paused uncomfortably.

"uh…Dr. Andrews, Sir, we're scheduled to go straight to your hotel, but, I'm here to take you to go wherever you need to go, so if you want to stop anywhere just let me know."

Anthony was speaking fast, with a tenor voice that vaguely resembled a smoky saxophone, but it was clear from Anthony's tempo that he was pure New York City. He spoke a mile-a-minute in a polite, almost military and street-smart accent. "Here's my card. My driving partner's name is Raul. He works nights, but sometimes we fill in for each other. Raul's number is also on the card. Just call or send a text message, we'll be there within 15 minutes to get you wherever you need to go, and we pretty much work 24 by 7."

Impressive…not only did the company have a black Range Rover with smoked out windows and shiny twenty-inch wheels to sport him around town, but they also had top-notch service to go along with it.

"Thanks," Jim replied awkwardly, "We can go the hotel. I don't have any other plans right now."

"Yes sir," Anthony replied, and they sped off towards downtown Manhattan.

The Tribeca Grand hotel has an atrium inside the building that soars 8 stories high, leading to a glass roof. The rooms overlook a bar in the center of the atrium, and the effect is like an enclosed arcade. The bar in the atrium is a swinging night spot and the music is loud, hip, and inviting.

Jim was welcomed in the lobby by the manager, who explained that he was staying in one of the Junior Suites and that all the details had been arranged by Maggie. Jim was escorted to his room by a hostess who, Jim was sure, doubled as a Ford model when she was not working at the hotel. The room was state-of-the-art and contained every gadget imaginable, a bathroom which looked like an Asian spa, a comfortable sitting room and a separate bedroom.

"This is a junior suite?"

"Yes Doctor," she replied. "I will show you how the entertainment system works, and on the desk is a menu of services in case you need anything."

"It's okay," Jim paused. "I'm pretty familiar with electronics. Don't worry about it." Jim was blushing. For some reason this beautiful woman was making him nervous. They all had a way of doing that to him.

"Thank you, Dr. Andrews," the hostess responded. "Here are your room keys and a couple of complimentary drink coupons for the bar. It gets hopping around 2:00am, so don't go to bed too early," she smiled.

Jim was uncomfortable and flustered. "Uh...yeah...thanks," he fumbled and stuttered, "thank you a lot."

Jim was relieved that the hostess left and he surveyed his new digs. Everything was modern, everything was clean, and it was all top quality. "Wow" Jim was impressed that Maggie had taken the time to set him up so well and he sent a text message to Jesse to let him know that everything was amazing. He thanked him for suggesting that he call Rob, and Jesse replied:

Good, now go get me a job there too you asshole ☺

Jim was exhausted from the flight and, even though it was early in the day, he decided to take a nap. He pressed a button on the night stand and the curtains automatically closed while the lights dimmed. He laid on the bed and fell asleep without struggle.

The ringer on the phone was electronic. It was a soothing buzz that gently brought Jim to consciousness. He had never heard a phone with such a pleasant sound, and he was initially confused.

"Hello?"

"Jim...hi, it's Maggie. I just wanted to make sure you were being well-taken care of."

"Maggie, this is wonderful, no worries, and thanks so much for helping me out."

"No problem, and remember, you have a dinner meeting at 8:00pm. It's 7:15pm now."

Manhattan in the evening, when the weather is nice, is perfect. Jim enjoyed watching people come and go, and the variety of sounds and activity stimulated his brain. He was alive! Jim entered the restaurant at 8:05pm, thinking that he should not be early. The maitre d' was formal yet inviting, and escorted Jim to a table that had been separated with Chinese screens to nestle their group in a corner with extra privacy. There were 2 men and 1 woman at the table, and they all rose to greet Jim as he arrived.

"Hi Jim, I'm Isaac Rubenstein. I'm the CEO of Audacity Frontier; and this Dr. Jeanine Wheatley, she's our CTO; and this is Dr. Shilesh Gupta, our Head of R&D."

They all shook hands and were seated. Isaac was in his mid-50's, with close-cropped hair, clean ears, aviator style glasses and a closely trimmed beard. He was finely dressed in a black Armani suit and had an open collar black shirt, with a gold chain that supported a small Star of David around his neck. Jim was immediately embarrassed at his own clothes, but was comforted that his new boss was elder to him – no more arrogant, spoiled rich kids like Jake. Although Isaac was very well manicured and well-appointed, there was a coldness to his demeanor. Isaac was looking right through Jim, not at him, and there was something about Isaac's accent that was unsettling. It seemed to Jim that English was not Isaac's mother tongue, but his accent was so perfect that most people would never notice. Not many people are so fluent in a second language.

Jeanine seemed to be the same age as Isaac, and was more freely flowing in conversation. Her hair was longer than most women's, and her clothes were professional and stylish. He noticed that Jeanine had a wedding ring, along with her Rolex and Prada bag. Her eyes and hair were brown and her skin was Mediterranean. Jim had a nice vibe from Jeanine and felt like she was polite and welcoming.

Then there was Dr. Gupta, or Shilesh, as he insisted on being called. Shilesh was at least 70 and he had long since lost most of his unruly hair. It was apparent that he attempted to tame his residual mane, with no luck, and stray strands of comb-over hair fell awkwardly out of place. Otherwise, Shilesh was well-groomed, and he had a mature grace that was reassuring to Jim. He could tell immediately that Shilesh was brilliant, and was comfortable with his talents without being arrogant or defensive.

"So, Dr. Andrews, Maggie tells us that your trip was fine?" asked Isaac.

The waiter arrived and explained that Maggie had arranged a fixed menu for the table. He asked when they would like the food to be brought out and Isaac succinctly and politely instructed him to keep the food at a moderate and comfortable pace. Jim could not figure out Isaac's speech. He was polite, and he was not condescending, but there was something very intense in Isaac's voice. It was not his tone, but rather the manner in which he stopped his speech. Jim felt like the sentences were well planned, almost as if Isaac had rehearsed them before the meal. Although Jim felt initially uneasy with Isaac, Jeanine and Shilesh made great strides to be welcoming and re-assuring. They talked about their backgrounds and interests. All were engineers or scientists and they all had attended top-league schools and post-graduate programs. Although Jeanine was married, she explained that her husband had died from leukemia about 5 years ago. The others were not married and did not freely speak about their social lives. The food was spectacular, and the wine pairings were true-to-form.

When the main course arrived, Jim was feeling a bit drunk, and he had finally loosened up with Isaac. Isaac was still intense, but was amicable and friendly and he engaged Jim in a wide range of conversation about his research and his interests. The dinner lasted for about two and a half hours, with six courses, dessert wine and a 'night-cap.' The conversation was completely casual, and Jim felt comfortable by the end of the meal.

At about 11:00pm, Jim sensed that, for his guests, the dinner was over and it was time to get ready to leave. It surprised him that there had never been any conversation about business or the Company, or really anything of substance. Jim guessed that they had all enjoyed the wine and did not want to spoil the pleasant atmosphere with business talk.

"Well Jim," replied Isaac, "It was nice to meet with you. Please feel free to look us up the next time you're in New York."

"Jim," Jeanine commented, "I'm sure that what Isaac means to say is that Maggie will give you a call tomorrow and set up a time for you to come to our offices." Jeanine smiled at Isaac as he meekly returned the smile.

"Would you like me to escort you back to the hotel?" offered Shilesh, "I don't live too far from there and it would be my honor to make sure you get home okay."

Jim suddenly realized that he was more drunk than the rest of the group, and he welcomed Shilesh's offer. They casually walked towards the hotel, enjoying the night life and the Manhattan scene.

"How long have you been working with Isaac and Jeanine?"

Shilesh was reticent, but explained, "I was running a laboratory at MIT. He made me an offer I could not refuse."

"Shilesh, I just got screwed at a start-up where the founder up and disappeared one day."

"I know," replied Shilesh. "I heard about it. Look, that was not your fault, now was it? You were doing good work there, but you got mixed up with a bad team."

Jim liked Shilesh and he liked what he heard. Although he was confused that there was no conversation of substance at the dinner, he was looking forward to finding out more about Audacity Frontier and the opportunities it might afford a top-notch scientist like himself. As they entered the hotel, Shilesh paused, "Well Jim, I will kindly take my leave now. See you soon."

They shook hands and Jim entered the lobby. It was close to midnight and the bar was starting to pick up - it was Thursday night after all. Jim remembered that the manager had given him some drink coupons, and he had a vague hope that he might locate that cute hostess from the morning. Jim sat down at the bar and ordered a scotch. He surveyed the scene. It was foreign. He was out of his element. Everyone at the bar was 10 or 15 years younger than he was, and they all were dressed like that guy he used to work for, that fashion model, Jake. Jim did not recognize anyone, and he did not even see anyone that he remotely wanted to talk to.

Rather, he sipped his drink and watched the DJ, who was doing a top-grade effort at mixing the songs and keeping the vibrations in the room to a sexy and provocative, urban hum. Jim finished his drink and headed back to his funky hotel room. He was drunk and desperately needed to get some sleep.

Chapter 6

At 6:30am, the phone by the bed rang, but this time the tone was not as pleasant as the day before. Jim woke up with a bad headache from drinking too much wine and he struggled to find the receiver.

"Hullo?" he whispered.

"Good Morning, Jim. It's Maggie."

Was she shouting? For the first time since he had ever spoken with Maggie, he was annoyed to hear her voice. She was like a bugle, "I'm sorry to call so early, but we've got a tight schedule and we need to have you here by 8:30, so I called to say *rise and shine*."

Jim was confused. There was never any note on his agenda about a morning meeting. In fact, the day was blocked out as a "general day" in Greenwich which Jim interpreted to mean a casual day meeting people for interviews. "Sure thing Maggie," Jim replied, "I will get dressed and head over."

"Great. I have briefed Anthony, and he will be waiting for you in the lobby at 7:00am. And don't worry about breakfast, I have arranged for it to be served in the car."

Jim shook his head in disbelief at the attention that Maggie showered upon him. He hung up the phone and headed towards the bathroom. He was unsettled that he would have to hurry along to get dressed. After showering, Jim paused and looked around at his suitcase and clothes. He had no idea about the dress code at the office, and he realized that he had not even unpacked or had any of his clothes pressed. Jim was going to make a typical appearance as a slob, typical. Normally it would not have bothered him, but Jim had noticed that Isaac, Jeanine and Shilesh were all very well appointed last night, and he still had a lingering memory of his most recent interview with Jake where he felt like a kid because his outfit was not appropriate, whereas Jake looked like he walked off the pages of GQ. Jim dressed in a suit that was older than his marriage and searched for a pair of suitable shoes which he knew did not exist. He did not bother to search for a neck tie, to do so would be foolish. He put on his beat up Sperry Top-siders and tried to close the collar on his shirt as much as possible. Jim had always been out of place at social situations, and today would be no different.

"Good Morning, Dr. Andrews," greeted Anthony, looking far too cheerful for this ungodly hour of the morning.

"Hello Anthony. Sorry I'm a little late."

The drive to Greenwich was pleasant. Maggie, in her typical form, had ordered a perfect meal for Jim. It was set up like his meal on the airplane, except Anthony was both steward and pilot. Jim ate his breakfast and took in the city sights while Anthony deftly maneuvered the New York traffic. It seemed hardly possible that an hour had elapsed as the car slowed down and they arrived at the Audacity Frontier campus. Anthony approached the entry gate and a guard stepped out to greet them. Oh shit, even the guard was well-dressed!

The office building was in the center of a large, rolling meadow. It was a rustic setting filled with long, wandering grass and a few trees sprinkled onto the landscape. At first glance, one would swear that this was what nature had developed when left to rule without man's intervention. But, upon closer inspection, the landscape was uncannily manicured. It had been carefully crafted to look like it was wild. In the middle of the meadow, there was a two story stone building with a slate roof and copper flashing. The broad meadow engulfed the building. Jim surmised that the property must have been about 30 acres and it was surrounded by a stately stone wall. But, although it looked like a Martha Stewart home, Jim noticed that the guard booth was high-tech, with a laser reader pointed directly at the license plate. He also noted that there were copious surveillance cameras everywhere, and they were artfully hidden to blend in with the scenery. Martha Stewart meets James Bond, he smiled. They slowly approached the office building, which Jim guessed to be about three hundred feet wide and the same depth. The walls of the building were a pale grey stone and the façade lent the feel of a stately building in the country, and yet every other architectural detail pointed to a brand new, state-of-the-art building.

The windows were tinted with a bluish-black hue like solar panels. The light reflected off them in a modern and simple style that somehow seemed bullet proof, if not eerily bomb-proof. The front doors, which were ajar, seemed to have been designed like a bank's vault door, they were sixteen inches thick, but had been accented with a matted stainless steel finish. The doors led into a small foyer with glass doors that automatically slid open to permit Jim to enter a vestibule.

The entry way was modest, but as he entered the building, Jim was taken aback by the sophistication of the lobby. There were two guards watching Jim carefully and standing next to an x-ray machine. This was not the TSA. These guards seemed to be actually looking for something, there was no fooling around or careless behavior like Jim encountered at the airport. No, these guys were serious.

Beyond the fortified entry, Jim glimpsed an impossibly attractive receptionist wearing a wireless head-set and seated behind a small, elegant desk. Her phone, computer and the lamps were sleek and her work area looked like Steve Jobs had dropped in to give some design hints. She rose from the desk, and Jim noticed that when Steve Jobs had finished decorating her office, Christian Dior had stopped by to adorn her in an appealing wardrobe. Jim could not help himself but to stare. Here, in the middle of the manicured wilderness in the Greenwich countryside, nestled within the foyer of a rustic, yet sophisticated building, Jim Andrews had seen a devilishly beautiful woman. She seemed to be perfectly proportioned, clean smooth skin, dark blue eyes and the hair, was it red? Or Auburn? Or Amber Sunset? Did she moonlight as a porn star? Whatever the exact color, it was not too long and not too short, perfect. Concerned that he might be unconsciously salivating, Jim tried to look around at the room instead of admiring Venus, who, he believed, was approaching him. Was it possible that she was approaching him in slow motion? Had Jim completely lost his senses? Inside and out, this was quickly becoming the best office in the world.

Anthony shattered the silence when he asked Jim for permission to send his bag through a scanner. Jim agreed reluctantly. "Don't worry," replied Anthony, "It won't damage any electronics."

The woman picked up her pace as she approached Jim and extended her hand towards him. "Excuse me, Dr. Andrews…it is a standard security procedure for guests to be inspected. Please do not feel alarmed." In the moment that the receptionist spoke, Jim realized that he was standing face-to-face with the magical Maggie. He was stunned and immediately felt embarrassed at how she must have seen him.

"Maggie?" he inquired.

"Yes, Jim, Hi, it's nice to finally meet you," she responded. "Now, if you would be so kind as to pass through our security machine, I would be very happy. Please, come this way."

Jim was escorted to a body-scan booth, where he was x-rayed and then waved through. Maggie was at the other side of the booth and welcomed him into their offices. "Welcome to Audacity Frontier Dr. Andrews. And, don't worry about the body scanner." She joked, "We can't really see all your private parts you know, but your package seems fine, if you know what I mean."

What? Did she say that? Jim blushed and headed in the direction that Maggie had indicated like a puppy drawn to its master. As he was walking, a guard handed him his bag and gave him a badge which affixed to his jacket. "It's an RFID chip," Maggie explained, "We want to make sure you don't get lost around here." She winked at him. "Now, I know you had a busy night last night, but I have a full day booked for you, Jim. First you will meet with Jeanine, followed by Dr. Gupta, and then you will meet with Dr. Rubenstein...I mean Isaac," she corrected herself.

"Sounds good," Jim commented, "Is there anyone else that I will meet?"

"No, that's it for today. After that we will see how things go."

Jim had spent all evening with this group of people and he did not think he had said anything intelligent or useful during their dinner. He had hoped that they were only a greeting crew and that he would be meeting with more technical people like himself during his tour of the company. Maggie must have sensed Jim's discomfort and she explained, "Dr. Andrews, I mean Jim, I am sure that you will find your day informative and useful. Relax, we're not a prison, but we do have high security as you can see."

Jim liked Maggie. There was no doubt in his mind that she was his type, but he felt woefully ill-equipped when he compared himself to her. He was back in high school hanging out with the nerd kids; and, all of the sudden, this hot and popular kid decided to be nice to him and he was walking with her. The brilliant professor could not find a word to say, and he evaluated the sound of Maggie's voice. It was pleasant, not at all bird-like, more of a low tenor, like a faint growl. And she spoke clearly and softly, without condescension or arrogance, putting Jim immediately at ease.

As they walked towards a conference room behind the reception area, Jim was not able to refuse the almost animal requirement to inspect Maggie's ass. He was startled when Maggie quickly turned around and made it immediately known that she was aware that he was checking her out. Oops, Jim was unable to hide his embarrassment and started to mumble some nonsense. But Maggie disarmed him. She shook off the situation and showed Jim into the conference room.

There was one window which looked out into the front parking lot, but otherwise the room was sparse. All of the walls were whiteboards and there was a giant flat screen monitor built into the front wall. The furniture was a matching Herman Miller set, with writing pads placed at each seat and a canister of yellow wood pencils at the head of the table. In the center of the table was a small vase with a purple orchid.

The room was about fifteen feet by twenty feet and had high ceilings. The room lighting was all LED fixtures, providing a soft, warm feeling in the room. And, the room was spotless, it even smelled new. Yes, the carpets were so new that there were not any shoe marks, and the walls did not have any smudges from the chairs. Even the whiteboards were clean, with markers and erasers sporadically placed, and held up by magnets.

But more than the furniture and decorations, Jim noticed that the acoustics in the room were unique. At first it was disorienting, but Jim realized that the room was strangely devoid of any background noise. He became acutely aware that there was some type of absorption system embedded in the walls and ceiling. He figured that there was a noise reduction program which was transmitting the inverse of any ambient noise so that his ears were hearing the background noise getting canceled out. The effect was stunning. Jim felt like he was in a recording studio since the sounds that he made did not echo at all and slowly absorbed into nowhere. The effect was to create a crisp silence in the room which Jim found pleasant, but at the same time it was spooky. Jim had never experienced an auditory sensation such as this. His mind began to contemplate the technical approach which was used to generate the silent, absorbed ambiance. Jim became lost in thought, overcome with a sense of wonder.

Chapter 7

"It's unique isn't it?"

Jim was startled at the interruption and turned quickly to find Jeanine standing about 3 feet away from him. Jim had not heard the door open, nor did he hear any sounds as Jeanine walked towards him. He jumped back.

"Hi! I'm sorry about that, you startled me." Jim excused himself.

"I know. It's pretty disorienting, isn't it? She pointed to some speakers in the ceiling and on the wall. "You see over there, and up there, we have installed a noise reduction system as a proof of concept. It ended up working beyond our modest expectations."

"What concept are you trying to prove?"

"We will get into all those details in good time, Jim. But first, I want to ask you more general questions. Let's sit down and relax. I want to give you a chance to talk about your background and your goals."

Jim allowed Jeanine to take control of the meeting. He followed her lead like an oddly matched dance couple. Jeanine was dressed impeccably, again, and she politely motioned for Jim to come towards the table. Suddenly aware that he was a guest, Jim pulled out a chair across from Jeanine and sat down. He leaned back slightly in the chair and then became self-conscious. Should he cross his legs? How could he make sure that he did not fiddle with his hands? Jeanine was putting Jim under the microscope and it was making him a little nervous.

Jeanine recognized that Jim was not ready to initiate a discussion, so she fired off the first question. "I read the paper you published on error reduction algorithms for compressed files Dr. Andrews. Your application of Shannon's Information Theorem of channel capacity was innovative. Tell me, how did you feel when you realized that the probability concepts that Shannon alluded to could be measured more precisely by applying chain theory?"

Jim was taken aback by the technical depth of Jeanine's question. "Well, it was not really new ground Jeanine. I was just tying together two previously separate approaches into a unified set. You see…Shannon's role was to realize that the wider the communication channel, the more likely that errors could, and would, arise. But, he was not thinking in a digital mode. His thoughts on sound and communications were based on analogue technology and theories, whereas the rise of digital recording created more discrete channels. In other words, there were new and different error paths. All I did was apply a more sophisticated probability method to the problem. I was standing on the shoulders of giants." Jim explained carefully.

"Jim," Jeanine said to slightly cut him off, "I know *what* you did. My question was how you *felt* when you realized the solution?"

"What do you mean, how did I feel?" Jim responded impulsively, "I was relieved. I was overwhelmed, I was *fired* up! You see…I had spent 6 months mulling Shannon's idea over and over and suddenly the solution just popped into my stupid head. And it happened when I was doing absolutely nothing - just getting a cup of coffee. I felt like I was struck by lightning! Smack! I nearly dropped the cup of coffee and ran back to my lab. I think I made a scene, because later I learned that the University cafeteria got quiet when I ran out. I was considered either a freak or a genius from that moment forward." Jim stopped talking. He had gotten emotional. How had Jeanine drawn the response from him? "I'm sorry," he said, "I'm not sure where all that came from."

"It's okay Jim. You answered my question. Thanks. By the way, was Sally in the cafeteria that day?"

Jim froze. He felt nauseated and irritated at Jeanine's question. "Who are you?" He quipped, "What is this place? What does my wife have to do with it?"

"Relax Jim," Jeanine reassured, "I was checking your references and I called up one of your colleagues from Stanford who I used to work with at LA Hospital. He explained to me that you married a woman from the University. Then, when I was speaking with Jesse, he mentioned that your wife's name was Sally, and that you two had recently split up. I'm sorry if my question was out of line."

"No…no, it's okay," Jim responded, "but remind me to send Jesse a thank you card when I get home."

Jeanine laughed and her pleasant demeanor erased the tension in the room. She had a talent for making Jim feel relaxed and open and he was grateful that she was working hard to make him feel welcome.

"Now Jim, I am sure you must have some questions for me? But I need to warn you that I can't answer anything detailed about our operations until after you meet with Isaac, okay?"

"Sure," Jim replied, "You mentioned that you worked at LA Hospital. How did you end up in Greenwich working as a CTO for a telecommunications company?"

Jeanine leaned back in her chair and smiled at Jim. When he absorbed her warm smile, Jim felt like he was talking to a family member who was being reunited after a few years' absence. Jeanine continued, "It is strange isn't it? I studied biology at Yale and then moved to the West Coast to get my PhD in Life Sciences. I specialized in infectious disease and viral transmissions. It was fascinating work, but you know how the life of a researcher can become." Jeanine was looking wistfully at Jim and he felt the same emotions she was alluding to.

"Tell me about it," Jim replied, "I'm not sure if I worked harder getting my PhD, or pursuing my lab work at the University. But, you know what? I liked setting up and running a lab. It was like having my own little start-up right there in the school. But I'm changing the topic. Please tell me how you got from LA to Greenwich, from a hospital to a telecommunications company."

Jeanine put down her pencil and explained, "I met Isaac at a research symposium in San Francisco. We started chatting during the cocktail break after the meeting and then he invited me to come to New York to meet the team. I guess I was instantly hooked when I came here. You know how Maggie treats you. Well, I guess we just clicked. Before I knew it, I was moving across the country and starting a new life." She snapped her fingers. "Oh, I am so rude, Jim. I did not even offer you a cup of coffee before we got started. Can I get you something?"

"Coffee would be great, thanks."

There was a deep allure to the opportunity of starting a new life, of finding a new beginning. He was drawn to the prospect of a fresh start. The rest of the meeting consisted of small talk and irrelevant topics. Jeanine asked about Jim's hobbies and the standard question about his personal evaluation of his strengths and weaknesses. After 2 hours of relatively pleasant conversation, she rose up and bid him farewell.

Jim was left alone in the room, wondering where the interviews were leading.

Chapter 8

This time Jim maintained vigilance. He kept a close watch on the door to the conference room. After the surprise entry from Jeanine, Jim wanted to make sure that he was aware when the next person entered the room. Jim surveyed the conference room. He approved of the pristine furniture and the advanced electronic display unit on the front wall. The Company spared no expense on top-of-the-line gear, and he peered into the LCD screen and tried to check his reflection. Out of thin air, a window popped up on the display panel and Jim was staring right at Maggie's image, a little too close for comfort. She had her headphones on, and was smiling.

"Hi Jim," she explained, "Sorry for the delay. Shilesh will be there in about 5 minutes. There are some snacks on the credenza, if you're hungry, and there's a bathroom behind the door panel to your left. Is there anything else you need?"

Jim smiled and replied, "No thanks Maggie, I'm fine."

"Okay, then see you later," and her pop-up window disappeared from the screen.

Jim had not seen the door to the bathroom because it was flush with the panels and was also covered in whiteboard composite. At the suggestive response, Jim indeed felt the need to relieve himself and decided to take advantage of the time between meetings.

A little after 12:30pm, Shilesh waltzed into the room and explained to Jim that sandwiches would be brought in for a working lunch. "I hope you don't mind working through lunch, but, as you can see, there are not a lot of stores around here."

Jim was happy to see Shilesh again. "Hey, thanks for getting me home last night Shilesh. I think those wine pairings really went to my head."

"No problem Jim. That's what I'm here for. I am the teacher, the guardian and the mad scientist, all wrapped into one." Jim could not help but remember Dr Roberts whenever Shilesh spoke. The patience, the clarity, the intelligence were all strangely identical. While Jim reveled in the experience, it was also an unpleasant reminder of all the traits that he had never been able to emulate and pass on to his students. Jim was a teacher and he liked to help people, but Jim was a loner, and because of a deeply embedded arrogance that he hid from everyone, he could never develop the patience that was required to elicit the intellectual fire inside of a novice. He had failed Dr. Roberts by not being able to 'pay forward' the gift of the love of learning.

"Well Jim? Is there anything you want to talk about?" Shilesh probed.

Jim was unsettled. This was the complete opposite of the discussion style he had with Jeanine. "Uh yeah," Jim improvised, "I was interested in Jeanine's unique background and wondered what you're doing here?" Jim's question was stupid, and now he felt self-conscious.

Shilesh smiled and spread his arms and hands out like welcoming wings. "Jim, I am not sure how I got here sometimes, but I do love what I do. You see, I am a computer scientist at heart. I have a passion for technology, and I love solving problems. So, my first instinct was to become a professor. And I was teaching a course in nanotechnology at MIT. That's where I met Isaac. He was auditing the class. Isaac showed a keen interest in the work I was doing. Sometime around that year, I invented the idea of microbytes. After the class ended, Isaac recruited me. I started as a part-timer, but I got sucked in."

"What in the world are microbytes?"

Shilesh leaned back in his chair. He gave Jim a second inspection and nodded with an approving glance. He continued, "Good question, Jim. That was a test, and you passed. As you know, nanotechnology is the study of controlling matter on an atomic scale. Since I am a computer science buff, I focused on the technology side of nanotech, and that is how I discovered microbytes. Where do I begin? Ok, I got it...Let's see, how about you tell me what you know about bits and bytes."

"Are you serious?" Jim wondered if this was another of the professor's tests, so he replied, "Each bit is a zero or a one. We connect 8 bits together to form a byte, and by changing the order of ones and zeros, we can manipulate and interpret the bytes. It's the cornerstone of computer science. But I have honestly never heard of a microbyte."

"Not many people have, Jim. It is just a silly term that I coined a few years ago. We are still not even sure that they exist. You see, the theory is there, but we cannot provide any empirical evidence."

"I'm afraid you've lost me Dr. Gupta," Jim replied feeling a newfound respect and admiration.

"Oh, don't be formal with me, Jim. I know it sounds a little far out there, but think of it this way. Under the traditional theory, all we have in a bit is two discrete states, 'on' and 'off', you know a 'one' and a 'zero.' It's a binary operation and we like the simplicity of that building block."

"Right"

"But Heisenberg threw a wrench into the whole mess with his quantum theory. You see, Heisenberg had to take the next step. He postulated that if I know exactly where a molecule is, then we cannot possibly measure its speed, and vice-versa. If it's constantly moving, it has no precise location. The Uncertainty principle, as he called it, when taken to its extreme would mean that I would never really know when the bit has been changed to a zero or a one. You see, he made us work in the quantum world of probabilities, not with binary exactitude.

"When we apply Heisenberg's logic into bits and bytes, we get altered states of 'on' and 'off.' We get partial states and transitive states and time slices of states. And, when we realize that bits have partial states, we can categorize and code them, we can generate the signals inside of a bit in what used to require a byte. It gets pretty complicated, but we break down the bits like we do atoms. You see, just like atoms have electrons and protons and neutrons, we can find the building blocks of bits and then we can work with them. The implication of using bits as building blocks instead of using bytes is enormous. It is much, much more efficient. It is smaller and faster. You see what I mean? Well, I coined these little critters *microbytes*."

It had been a good while since Jim Andrews had learned a brand new concept. He sat back in amazement and wonder when he thought about the potential impact of what Dr. Shilesh Gupta had said. Jim was lost in the moment; he was numb. Shilesh noticed that Jim's imagination was in full gear, so he gingerly interrupted.

"Anyway…like I said, I met Isaac and he shared my interest in nanotechnology."

"Microbytes," Jim replied in disbelief, almost smirking.

"Yes, the possibilities really are endless. Isaac and I shared a fondness for the applications of nanotechnology. You see, I'm an old man now, I'm almost 75. I have been lucky that the old brain keeps working, and I know that I am entering the final quartile of my life. When I started developing this effort with Isaac, I saw the future, and the future was nanotechnology."

Jim felt like he was sitting with Dr. Roberts in a high school classroom. Shilesh and Jim continued to talk about the usefulness of science, the Lakers, rock-and-roll bands, and even the stock market. Jim let down his guard and felt carefree in sharing his feelings and thoughts with Shilesh. In what seemed like the blink of an eye, Shilesh excused himself and thanked Jim for the time.

Jim shook Shilesh's hand. He swore that he saw the twinkle of Dr. Roberts in Shilesh's eyes. It was his spirit, it had to be. Jim felt like a teenager again. Working with Shilesh would let him start all over again. It was comforting and yet it was pure escapism. After Shilesh left, Jim felt his consciousness snap back into defensive mode. Who were these people? He wondered. Microbytes? Jim had met some of the smartest folks with whom he had ever come into contact.

He wanted more.

Chapter 9

Jim was fiddling with a yellow wooden pencil for lack of anything else to absorb his nervous energy. He took his fingernail and scratched a strip of yellow paint off an edge of the pencil, revealing the bare wood. Upon closer inspection, Jim realized that paint chips had now been scattered over the clean surface of the black granite table. He made a mess, just like the bread crumbs that he scattered on the fancy linen tablecloth at dinner the previous night. Great, Isaac would see that he was a slob. Confronted by the yellow dandruff, Jim swept the paint chips with his hand, moving the mess from the table top to his pants and onto the perfectly clean floor. There was no place to hide in this room. The meeting with Isaac would happen any moment now and Jim's paint chip mess was taking over the entire room.

Isaac was scary, he was intense. Jim stared at the LCD screen and prayed that Maggie would pop back into his life to save him from his nervous energy. But he had no such luck. Isaac soon appeared through the main door and Jim stood to greet him, letting the paint chips disperse to the floor. As they shook hands, Jim was painfully aware that Isaac now had paint chips on *his* hand. Jim had infected Isaac with his sloppiness.

"Hello Isaac."

"Yes, Jim. So tell me how your day was."

Did this guy get manicures? How can anyone be so clean and professional? Jim was convinced that Isaac was repulsed by his messy fingernails, the paint chips, and his casual appearance. It was hopeless. Jim could not compete in this world.

Jim responded to Isaac, "It was good. I enjoyed getting to know more about Jeanine and Shilesh, but I still do not understand what is going on at this company. What is it that you have in mind Isaac?" Jim inquired.

His question trailed off and lingered, unwanted in the air. Jim had again been too forward and clumsy in his speaking. Isaac showed only the slightest sign of annoyance, but quickly masked his irritation with a slight cough.

"Uh hem, yes," he stalled, "Well Jim, I started this company a few years ago and have only recently begun to expand it. That's how I eventually met up with your friend Jesse. You see, we're trying to reduce the digital weight of communications so that we can cram more capacity across existing phone networks. I know it sounds crazy, but if we can make inroads into more effective compression of communication, then I believe the phone companies can make millions, and in the process we can make our investors and employees wealthy. It is a challenging assignment, but I am looking for someone to set up a lab here and help us with signal compression and its error correction. Jeanine showed me your research paper and Shilesh verified its approach, so we decided to see if we could convince you to join us. Luckily, your old boss did us a favor by blowing up your company, so we decided to strike while the iron is hot as they say."

Jim was having a hard time believing his ears. He was being offered the chance of a lifetime and he did not know how to react. He wanted to mask his enthusiasm so that he could negotiate for a good compensation package, but he found it hard to hide that the opportunity to set up a lab from scratch and to focus on an area of research that he had invented seemed almost too good to be true.

"Well Isaac, that's a pretty interesting opportunity, but I am looking at a couple of other options." Jim lied, feeling hot and uncomfortable as he uttered the next words. "Um, can you tell me a little bit about the financial rewards?" Jim's lip began to sweat…oh man! I'm such an idiot…what's wrong with me?

Isaac's smile widened and Jim noticed that Isaac seemed to be looking down on Jim in an increasingly condescending manner. For the first time since he had arrived in his new world, it dawned on Jim that Isaac was doing all he could do to avoid revealing his arrogant and judgmental temperament. It confirmed his initial uneasiness at dinner the night before. Isaac was a snob. "Come on now Jim," Isaac joked, "we don't talk about money around friends, now do we? I mean, look, this is not really about money, is it? You and I know that it is much, much more than that, Jim."

Isaac whispered as he finished his sentences, causing Jim to lean in and expend extra effort to pay close attention. "You know, we're doing something here that is unique. This is the leading edge, Jim...it is the state of the art." Isaac launched a seductive promise, "Oh we will make a lot of money...don't worry about that. Our investors will cash in big time, and so will you. But, *please* Jim, let's let the administrators talk about those mundane matters, okay? I'm here to find out if you will bring your spirit and imagination to this team. So, do we have a deal?"

For a minute, Jim was convinced he had been dreaming - everything was too perfect. The distance between that Dog Day afternoon in California, and his New York trip seemed infinite. "I'm grateful for your consideration Isaac." Jim let down his defenses and gushed, "I would be honored. I...I...really can't explain how incredible this all seems."

"There we go! I knew you had it in you. Welcome aboard Jim! I'm glad you quickly came to your senses. Now look, Maggie will take care of everything, we'll see you back here in a couple of days."

"A couple of days? But Isaac, I have a lot of cleaning up to do in California. I think it might take me a couple of weeks."

"Jimmy, don't sweat the small stuff. All those things will be taken care of. Relax, it's different here. You'll see." Isaac stood up and left the room. The eerie silence returned and Jim wasn't sure what to do, or where to go.

And, he hated it when people called him Jimmy - only his Mom could do that and she was dead. Jim knew that Isaac knew it would be annoying to call him "Jimmy."

Chapter 10

"Hello stranger," she said, "I hear you're going to join the team. Welcome!" Jim was reflecting on the day and getting lost in the excitement when magical Maggie appeared in the room.

Jim and Maggie shook hands and he followed her out of the conference room, making every effort possible not to be caught 'checking her out' again. As they approached the reception desk, Maggie reached down and handed Jim his cell phone. "Oh, here, you can have this back now," she replied. Jim was surprised as he put his hand on his briefcase to look for his phone, almost not believing that she held it in her hand.

"I wasn't aware that you had removed my phone from my bag," he accused.

"Oh, sorry Jim," Maggie said as she pointed towards a sign on the wall which contained an icon of a cell phone with a red line through it. "I thought you saw the sign. It's a standard procedure for guests. Anyway, I am very happy you will be joining us. Anthony is outside and ready to take you back to the city. Tomorrow I will get in touch with you to discuss all the details. Maybe we can meet for dinner around 7:00pm?"

"Sure," Jim jumped at the invitation.

"Great…it's a date. I will pick you up at the hotel."

All during the ride back to the city, Maggie's response echoed in Jim's brain, "It's a date…it's a date." The mature man named Jim knew that Maggie was only figuratively speaking, but his adolescent ego and increasingly active libido was fantasizing that perhaps she meant it in a more personal way.

It was only when he returned to his hotel room that Jim realized the full extent of his jet lag and exhaustion. He fell in to bed without even getting undressed. What a day. It was crazy. It was like a dream.

Jim awoke at 10:00am. The phone did not ring and he was uncomfortable because he had not even undressed from the day before. Jim looked at his cell phone and there was a message from Maggie.

"See you at 7pm" M

Jim sat up in his bed and reflected on the prior day's events. He was genuinely impressed with Isaac's facility and the team was smart and driven. He felt reinforced and confident. Jim told himself that after years of hard work, he deserved this opportunity - especially after the fiasco with Jake, and after the let down with Sally. Jim had already started to project himself into his new role at Audacity Frontier. Sally and Jake were vestiges of a distant past. Jim saw the future, and he liked it.

As 7:00pm rolled around, Jim got dressed and went downstairs to the bar to have a drink and relax. There were some free spots on the couches in the lobby, so he sat down and ordered a draft beer. The effeminate male waiter looked at him strangely, giving Jim the impression that he had committed a faux pas. "I'm sorry, sir, we have bottled Stella and Amstel Light." Jim remembered that this was Tribeca after all and that draft beer must be too plain and simple.

"Right," he replied, feeling like a square peg in a round hole, "I think I'll have a Stella."

Maggie arrived as the waiter was walking away to get his drink. Jim immediately stood up like an erection. Jim felt like a school boy at the prom.

"Hi" he chirped, "Nice to see you." Maggie was dressed in more casual clothes, but still she looked like she was stepping off of the runway. Her shirt was impossibly low and Jim's spirit sank because he knew that he would spend the entire evening trying not to look at her breasts. It was not fair. He was not cut out for this kind of temptation.

Luckily for Jim, Maggie was wearing a scarf which, in an apparently unconscious and effortless motion, she positioned so that she was less revealing, immediately putting Jim and his budding hormones at ease. "I made reservations at a little Spanish place down the street. Are you interested?" Maggie teased. Jim panted. They headed out of the lobby. Meanwhile, the waiter was returning to Jim's table, but stopped and gently smiled when he noticed the couple was rising to exit. Jim saw the waiter and was grateful that he did not embarrass him. *First class*, he thought.

The restaurant was small and elegant. Consistent with the first dinner he had with the team, there was a table reserved in a quiet corner. Jim was impressed. They were seated and ordered cocktails and tapas, as they settled into making small talk and relaxing. Jim was falling for Maggie. He couldn't help it. And yet, he knew that this was a professional relationship. He was focused on business. If he made a personal approach, it could lead him to lose the job opportunity he had in hand. She was just a woman, he told himself, snap out of it. He re-doubled his efforts to let Mother Nature take a back seat and concentrated on seeing Maggie only as a human being in a business situation.

Maggie was carefree and casual. Jim could tell that she was highly intelligent, and he figured that she must have a photographic memory by the way she effortlessly recalled details of every subject they discussed. As he relaxed and got to know her mind, Jim realized that Maggie was like the others at Audacity Frontier, she was a genius in her own way. His appreciation for her intellect and talent grew deeper as they spoke throughout the evening. After dinner, they ordered coffee and the waiter brought out a small plate of cookies and chocolates. The evening had passed quickly and pleasantly. Maggie straightened up and lifted her stylish bag onto her lap.

"Okay Jim, now for a little bit of business, alright?"

"Sure," Jim also straightened. He had almost forgotten that it was a business dinner, and he was again feeling out of place.

Maggie's smile disarmed his awkwardness, and she continued, "I know this all came on quickly, but we would like you to help us set up your lab as soon as possible. Isaac is in quite a hurry to get things moving." She lifted an envelope from her bag and placed it across the table.

"Isaac asked me to give this to you."

Jim figured it was an offer letter, and he was not sure what to do with the package. "Aren't you going to open it?" she asked.

With Maggie's encouragement, Jim pulled out the letter and scanned its contents. For a moment he did not believe what he was reading. His base salary was $800,000, plus bonus, plus stock options, company car, expense account, living allowance, insurance – every perk imaginable. He continued down the letter, his title would be Chief Science Officer. His operating goals were exactly as discussed with Isaac in the conference room – set up and run a lab focusing on sound analysis and compression. Jim was silent. He glanced back at Maggie, remembering how beautiful her eyes were. He was pleased that she was also excited for him. He could feel her empathy for his happiness.

"Jim, is it good?"

"Yeah," he breathed. "You know this has been like a dream for me. I have never had such an experience. You're treating me like a celebrity, offering me a job that pays more than the President of the U.S. makes and I get the chance to do what I truly enjoy. Maggie, is this real?"

"Jim, don't be silly. You have very special talents and Isaac is the kind of person who wants to work only with the best and smartest people in the world. And *you* fit neatly into that category, Doctor Andrews. Now, we're going to need you to start setting up the lab as soon as possible. Oh, and this is a Non-disclosure form. Isaac is a stickler for privacy. It might drive you crazy, but that's just the way it is around here. Everything we do is confidential."

Out of nowhere, Jim remembered Lily and felt guilty. "What will I do about my dog? I have checked her into a kennel in California. She can't stay there forever."

Maggie smiled warmly, letting Jim know that she appreciated his care for animals, "How about this? You give me the details for the kennel and I will arrange to have your dog taken care of for a few weeks. Once you get things set up, we can go back to California and pack up."

"But I don't have any clothes," he countered, "I only packed for a few days."

Maggie flashed her devilish smile at Jim again. "Well now that we're onto that topic, Dr. Andrews, I wanted to tell you that you dress like a bumbling professor. And, thanks to our wonderful body scanning technology…" She winked, making him feel like she had indeed seen him naked, "As I was saying, thanks to our, uh-hem, our scanners, I was able to send a complete set of your detailed measurements to Barney's along with my personal comments on a style that would be more fitting."

"Anthony is having the hotel staff fill up your closet as we speak."

Chapter 11

Setting up a laboratory is a labor of love, and Maggie made the next few weeks of Jim's life seem effortless. She thought of everything, seemingly always one step ahead. Jim had been working non-stop for 2 or 3 weeks. He had lost track of time, just like before, but this was different, it was new. Jim was in his element and was having more fun than ever. But as the days surrendered to the weeks, he grew tired; really, really tired. Jim rubbed his temples as he sat down at his desk and surveyed his team. He remembered his first day in the lab. It seemed so long ago, but in a funny way he remembered it as if it were yesterday.

Jim's lab was on the ground floor of the office building, down the hall from reception. When he first entered the room, it looked like an empty warehouse. Jim estimated that the room measured 50 feet by 75 feet with three windows and one Herman Miller desk, with a laptop, lamp, phone and two chairs. The desk was situated in the middle of the gigantic room, like an oasis in an otherwise deserted place. Jim looked around at the naked walls, they were stark white and perfect, not a scratch, dent or wave; with perfect corners. The floors were a dark hardwood with a translucent white stain to match the walls, and the natural light coming in through the windows was refreshing. Although the room was empty, the same noise reduction system that Jim had felt in the conference room was installed. Jim was amazed that the technology could handle such a large space. He felt the privacy of a small room, but his eyes saw a large open area, the dissonance was exhilarating.

The windows framed picture-perfect views of the green and amber meadow. The landscaping was perfect, and Jim could easily forget that he was not in the middle of nowhere. Maggie explained to Jim that he did not really have a budget, but that there was not a lot of tolerance to re-do things. '*Get it right the first time*' was Isaac's message.

Maggie handed Jim a stack of resumes, neatly collated and ordered alphabetically. "These people are already working with us, and Jeanine thought you might want to consider using some of them to help you get things jump-started." She also handed him a blue print drawing of his current office, saying, "This is your blank piece of paper, okay? Fill it up. Design your lab. Tell me what you need. I will take care of all the ordering and logistics, but you, my friend, you need to give me the dirty details."

Jim felt a rush. He was literally beginning a new life, a fresh start. He was charting out his future on a new sheet of graph paper. His life was playing out like a fantasy novel. He was enthralled at the possibilities; then he picked up on a thread of conversation that Maggie had initiated. "Speaking of Jeanine, where is she? And where is Shilesh?"

"They're out of town for the rest of the week Jim. They're doing some field work in Paris, but they'll be back next week."

"Oh…okay, but where are their offices Maggie? I still haven't gotten the nickel tour of this place."

Maggie smiled at Jim and stuttered, "Yeah, uh right…okay," she paused, "Jim, I need you to sit down for a minute."

Maggie's tone had changed, and Jim sat down at the desk while she pulled up the other chair. Maggie lowered her voice and continued.

"Remember that I told you Isaac is a stickler for privacy, right?"

"Sure"

"Well, we had a security incident the night you and I were at dinner. Isaac was really shaken up by it. You see, we have our own private network here. Everything coming into and out of the office, including the connections to the Internet is strictly controlled. You must have also seen that we have guards and cameras everywhere. It's true, we're really strict. But, somehow a group of our working files were accessed that night. We know about it because we have a full control system to identify when files are opened or edited, sort of like an audit-trail."

Jim got the creeps, realizing that his every move would be tracked. He replied, "Sounds pretty serious."

"Yes, it is serious Jim. It was very serious. Isaac freaked out. I have never seen him so disturbed. He completely lost his temper. Within 15 minutes there was a whole team of snoops brought in to check for bugs, for access violations and to scour every inch of the place with a fine tooth comb. He even had people check for underground tunnels. It was spooky Jim. Anyway, we never did find out who it was, or how it happened. It is one of those unsolved mysteries, so to speak, and it is really eating at Isaac. He is still whacked out about it. And now he has changed policies to restrict the interaction of teams. It's kind of weird, I mean, we share our research data and we can have videoconferences, but the physical interaction between groups has been restricted. If you're not assigned to a lab or to a department, you can't physically go there. So, I'm afraid that the nickel tour will be 'virtual.' We're installing additional video terminals to accommodate the policy change. But we're in lock down mode. The only reason you and I get to see so much of each other is because I need to get you set up and operational. Otherwise, we would see each other when you entered the office, but other than that we would be video-conferenced. We would know each other only as talking heads on computer screens."

Jim felt a melancholy shudder at the idea of working without Maggie near his side. In a few short days she had found a way to get into his life. In a way, he hoped that it would never end.

His mind was wandering as Maggie clapped her hands. "Ok, as I was saying, Doctor, please design your lab. I'm supposed to start ordering equipment tomorrow."

"You want me to design this entire lab in one day?"

"No, you can do it at night too." She winked. "Come on Jim, no crybabies here, I told you we're in a hurry." Maggie stood up and began to leave the room. Jim was so stressed at the challenge in front of him that, for the first time since he saw Maggie, he did not ogle at her figure as she was leaving. Jim was busy. He had become very busy, lost in the details.

For the next 10 hours, Jim worked non-stop. He must have torn up his 'clean sheet of paper' about 20 times. His challenge was large. He needed computer servers, laptops, PDAs, scientists and data analysts. He needed tools for measuring sound quality, devices to test the compressed sound. He needed microphones, headphones, traditional hand-sets as well as media tools, and of course he needed a coffee maker. Jim envisioned a lab with 5 core stations. The teams would be split up functionally, two teams to focus on compression and two to focus on error correction – the fifth team would be the testers. If he had two teams on each subject, then he could create some friendly competition between the groups – *competition breeds excellence* - was the mantra of his day. The teams would need common workspace as well as private areas for research. It was mind-boggling.

Around 11:00pm, Jim called Anthony and asked for a ride home. Raul picked up the phone and said he would be right over. Jim sat in the car and immediately dashed off to sleep. Raul awoke him when they reached the hotel, and Jim stumbled up to his room.

The next day he was greeted by an architect who Maggie had invited to hash out the plans. For the entire day, Maggie, Jim and the architect discussed the detailed features of the lab, and then revised the plans over and over again. Once they were finished, Maggie looked at Jim and playfully teased, "Not bad for a scientist...hey, Isaac asked me to get him your staffing plan tomorrow. Have you had a chance to look through those resumes that Jeanine sent?"

"Well, not really, Maggie," Jim explained, "I have been a little pre-occupied."

"Come on now," she said, "Remember, Isaac hates crybabies. I will come by around lunch time tomorrow to pick it up." And she left.

Jim didn't even have a minute to savor the beauty of his lab design. He was like a lab rat, moving from one task to the next, guided constantly by magic Maggie. Jim's treadmill work pattern repeated over and over again – weekends and holidays did not exist in Audacity Frontier. Isaac was indeed in a hurry, and Maggie was making sure Isaac got what he wanted. There were no social lives, it was all-consuming. Jim's life consisted of working until odd hours, falling asleep in the car as either Anthony or Raul drove him home, then waking up disheveled and rushing back to work. Maggie had arranged for the rest of Jim's life to be fully attended to. His closet was always filled with crisp new clothes. There was always food - breakfast in the car, snacks in the hotel room and lunch and dinner brought into the office. Jim never had to do anything except set up the lab. He lost track of the days and lost himself in his work. It was an escapist dream for him.

The lab came up nicely and Jim was impressed with the team Jeanine had recommended. He interviewed each of them and found that they had impeccable credentials, good attitudes and strong work ethics. It was like a dream class for a Professor. Even though they came from all over the world, every one of Jim's team was young and single. Jim understood that Audacity Frontier was not a place that supported a work-life balance, and he wondered if this weren't a lawsuit waiting to happen. Jim dismissed the idea, figuring it was Isaac's problem, not his, and promptly got back to work. The lab was hard-driving and competitive. The team that Jeanine had short-listed fit perfectly into his plan for division of labor. Jim sent her a thank-you note and started parceling out the work to his associates. He assigned some background reading, asked the teams to start mapping out their plan of attack for research, and requested each team to elect a leader after the first week so that they could simplify communications. The teams were fired up and Jim was living gloriously. He had indeed arrived. Jim was king of his domain again.

Of course, Jim was still unsettled that he had never seen the upstairs floor and that, while his lab seemed to take up more than a third of the ground floor, he had never seen any other areas in the building. In the rush to get everything in his lab established, Jim had become so focused on his own challenge that the rest of the world took on a low volume, like a background noise. Jim seemed to be wearing blinders to the rest of the office and had even lost touch with world events except for the short time each morning when he could read the New York Times on the car ride to Greenwich. The day after Jim started working, the rules about cell phones tightened. Isaac's new policy was that there were no cell phones permitted in the office. Employees were instructed that violation of the policy was cause for immediate dismissal. With no cell phone and no easy internet access, Jim lost touch with his few friends in California. There was a public access room where he could do Internet research, but the transfer of data into the Audacity network was strictly controlled by a separate department. Jim was impressed that the data transfer group kept a service level that was consistent with the fast pace of the Company, but still it took some time to get used to coordinating with someone to move data around. Isaac was definitely a security and control freak.

Maggie sent Jim an email informing him that Isaac had called for a status meeting with Jeanine, Shilesh and himself on Friday at 7:00am. Jim looked at his calendar, noting that it was Tuesday, November 15th. He struggled to remember when he had left California - was it September or October? What had happened to Lily and to Sally? Jim felt a sense of guilt and made a note to himself that he had to get back to California before the end of the year.

During the remainder of the week, Jim began to get into a more mundane rhythm. After checking his calendar, Jim confirmed that he had been working at Audacity for 6 weeks. He was feeling that things were finally coming under control, and for Jim, it was like a fog lifting. He had set up the lab, he had oriented his people, they were motivated and the basic research had been parceled out to the teams. Jim had achieved his initial mission – thanks mostly to magic Maggie.

Occasionally, Shilesh or Jeanine would pop up on his video screen to chat, or he would see them in the public access room, but otherwise they were hands off. Isaac was a completely different story – he was completely absent. Jim had not seen or heard from Isaac since the awkward day of his job offer. Jim figured that Isaac was flying around selling or raising money because his only link to Jim was through Maggie. She was the 'central nervous system' of the company. It was Thursday morning when Jim finally sat down to prepare his status report for the following day's meeting. As Jim was thinking of ways to tell the wonders of his lab, a high pitched and piercing siren began to invade Jim's brain. He was startled and saw emergency lights in the ceiling flashing. Maggie's face popped up simultaneously on all of the video screens in his lab.

"I'm sorry to disturb you everyone, but we have a situation in the building. Please follow the emergency exit signs and form into a group in the front parking lot. Do not panic and do not remove any materials from your desk."

Maggie disappeared and her face was replaced by a screen saver which contained an advisory notice encased in a blinking stop sign that repeated her prior commands. Jim was astonished, "I guess this is how we do fire drills around here," he joked, as he reached for his Marc Jacobs leather jacket and headed out with his team. Although his team was jovial, he could sense that some of them were scared, especially the newer hires. One of Jim's managers who led an error correction team was a Chinese woman named Li Yun.

Li had shown Jim a spark of wisdom and initiative that immediately impressed him. She was a Harvard trained math and computer sciences graduate who could tackle numerical problems with ease, yet maintained a demure confidence and ease of speaking which left Jim in awe. Jim hoped that Li would offer him a chance to mentor someone like he had been mentored. Finally, he would be able to 'give back.' Importantly for Jim, Li acted with a maturity and poise that was beyond her 27 years, not at all like the typical novices.

But today, Li was looking nervous and Jim sought to reassure her. "What's the matter Li? Don't worry…it's just a fire drill."

"Dr. Andrews, I think I have caused this problem. I forgot to take my cell phone out of my bag this morning."

"Oh come on Li," he reassured, "this is not caused by your cell phone. Turn the damn thing off and don't forget again. C'mon, let's get out of here."

Li and Jim walked towards the exit door, following the others who were walking in pairs and small groups. As they approached the door, Jim saw Maggie's beautiful eyes peering into his lab office with a concerned face. When Maggie captured Jim's glance, she seemed to relax. "Oh, there you are Jim," she said, "I was looking for you."

As Jim and Maggie walked towards the front parking lot, Jim noticed that one of the guards approached Li and began casually talking to her. For a moment Jim was sure that he saw Li hunch over and sob, but Maggie redirected his attention. "Jim, Li screwed up," Maggie explained.

"What are you talking about? Is this really all about her cell phone?"

"Jim," Maggie responded, "Li knows that Isaac changed the rules on cell phones. We have a zero tolerance policy. I told you when you first started working here that Isaac is a security freak."

As Jim and Maggie watched, Li returned to the office and came out with her rucksack. It was a plain tan shoulder bag like a student would wear - the kind that goes over one shoulder and closes with a large flap. Li had affixed some patches on the rucksack, a Hello Kitty patch, a breast cancer awareness patch, and what appeared to be some music group logo.   The bag was slightly tattered, but was not sloppy looking. Li reached her hand into the bag and showed her cell phone to the guard, shaking her head apologetically. Jim could see that Li was indeed crying.

"Oh my God! Maggie, don't tell me we are going to fire Li," he protested.

"Jim," Maggie cautioned, "You can bring it up at Isaac's staff meeting tomorrow. But for now, let's not make a scene right here. C'mon over this way. Don't worry. You will be able to have an exit interview with Li in the conference room once we have finished the sweep."

"The sweep?" Jim asked.

"Remember I told you about that security breach a few weeks ago?" Maggie reminded, "Well now we do a full sweep every time a security event happens. Think of it as a real-world version of an anti-virus scan, but for the entire building rather than for your computer."

Jim laughed in disbelief. "Are you serious?" He asked rhetorically then paused when he saw that Maggie was not smiling. "Yes, I guess you are serious...what *is* it with Isaac?"

"I'm sorry Jim," Maggie excused, "I need to go inside for a few minutes."

Li walked towards the front door of the building with Maggie following behind. Maggie seemed to effortlessly increase her pace so that she caught up to and began walking side-by-side with Li. Jim looked around and noticed that there were about 75 people milling about the parking lot, keeping in small groups and talking amongst themselves. He noticed that Jeanine was talking to a group of 4 or 5 people and he made his way over towards her. Jeanine caught a glimpse of Jim and separated from her group.

"Hi Jim," she said as she waved, "Nice to see you, albeit under bad circumstances. How's everything?"

"Fine," Jim lied, embarrassed that one of his staff had interrupted the entire office. "I think one of my researchers fucked up." Jim was embarrassed when Jeanine looked at him with a disapproving glance. "I mean that I think one of my researchers had a misfortunate event."

Jeanine smiled, "Yes, it seems that way doesn't it?" Jeanine's face looked different from the last time he saw her. She was still dressed to perfection and carried herself in a confident and truly beautiful manner, but for the first time Jim noticed that Jeanine looked tired. She looked as if she had aged dramatically over the past month and a half. Although she had applied make-up, Jim could notice that there were bags under her eyes and new wrinkles had appeared at the ends of her eyes. She was still attractive, but Jim was sure that Jeanine was stressed out.

"Look Jeanine," Jim inquired, "I have been working here for almost six weeks and I am having the time of my life...this place is great. I never dreamed that I would have the chance to do what I have been asked to do. But, as I walked out to this parking lot, it struck me that I don't have the faintest idea, outside of my lab, who these people are and what they do. It's kind of strange, isn't it?"

Jeanine gave Jim a reassuring glance and put her hand gently on his shoulder. He noticed that her hands were perfectly manicured and that her wedding ring had been removed. "Yes Jim, it is difficult to get accustomed to the high security that Isaac has put in place, but I think the rewards of our research outweigh the inconvenience, don't you? Besides, I am sure you will find ways to shake things up, Jim."

Jeanine's response was reassuring. She had a way of making Jim feel comfortable and he trusted what she said. Yes, Jeanine was right. The security mania was over-the-top, but Jim was convinced that the whole opportunity was over-the-top. As they chatted about Jim's research plans, the security teams moved throughout the building, and gradually, one group at a time was permitted to re-enter the building. Jim's lab was the last group to be given the 'all clear' sign, and he and Jeanine were still rapt in conversation when their teams started ambling back into the lab. Jeanine looked up at the emptying parking lot and commented, "C'mon Jim…it looks like we're going to be the last two people out here if we keep chit-chatting. I will see you tomorrow at Isaac's staff meeting."

After the fire drill, Jim called his team together and reminded them about the cell-phone ban. He explained that Li had made a mistake, but he reassured the people that he had every intention of talking to Isaac about giving Li a second chance. As Jim was talking, Maggie's face popped up on Jim's LCD screen, "Excuse me Jim, if you want to have an exit interview with Li, you can come on out to the conference room."

Jim was embarrassed and the team grew silent. It was clear that Maggie's message had directly contradicted him. "Okay, I know that sounded bad, but I will talk to Isaac about it in our staff meeting tomorrow. Right now I am going to go meet with Li…please try to get back to work, and…I guess Li's team should elect a new leader in case Isaac refuses me."

Jim walked towards the lobby and realized that Li was not going to return to the team. He felt like an idiot for implying anything different to his staff and wished he could hit a rewind button or call a 'do over' for the meeting he had just held. Jim walked into the conference room and saw Li sitting openly, relaxed and talking with Maggie. Li had regained her composure and was more comfortable than the last time Jim had seen her. Maggie rose to meet Jim, motioned for him to sit down, and then shifted her attention back towards Li.

"Jim, Li and I were talking about having her meet with our financial backers to see if there is another one of their companies where she can find a role. Isaac feels terrible…as do I, but as I told you we have a zero tolerance policy."

Li was calmly looking at Jim, but he could see that Li's eyes were glistening. She held her composure and commented, "Thanks again Dr. Andrews, I really enjoyed working with you. I hope that we get a chance to work together in the future."

Li extended her hand and Jim reciprocated. She picked up her rucksack and headed out with Maggie by her side as Jim followed behind them. Isaac was taking good care of Li while also demonstrating that his policy was firm.

Jim grudgingly respected Isaac and dutifully headed back towards his lab.

Chapter 12

Jim had figured out how to eliminate the annoying buzzer by connecting his iPod to the alarm clock in the hotel. He was in the middle of dreaming when Jimmy Page, John Bonham, John Paul Jones and Robert Plant entered into his head, and they were pissed. Kashmir was echoing in full glory in his dream, creating disarray in his otherwise tranquil dream state. There was panic and terror as the ominous rhythm picked up, and Jim opened his eyes. This was his first staff meeting, and Jim was feeling nervous, but at the same time he was excited. He was proud of the work that his lab had undertaken and wanted to share his accomplishments with Jeanine, Isaac and Shilesh.

He noticed a suit and matching shirt was nearby as well as a pair of Louis Vuitton dress shoes and a matching belt. Jim laughed at the situation. "Magic Maggie is at it again," he said as he shook his head in amazement. Jim was finally getting the attention that he deserved. He was living the dream. Jim dressed and checked himself out in the mirror. He looked good. He turned to inspect his side views as well as his front. Jim peered more closely into the mirror and noticed that, like Jeanine, he had also begun to show some battle scars and some stress lines around his eyes. Oh well…there has to be some price to pay for all this fun, doesn't there?

As usual, Anthony was waiting in the lobby to take Jim to the office. It was about time that Jim found a place to live closer to the office. He made a note to ask Maggie about Greenwich and the surrounding areas. Living in New York City seemed like a dream come true, but Jim was working such long hours that he did not really even see Manhattan. Besides, he wasn't a socialite, he preferred being alone. Research suited Jim just fine - his lab partners were sufficient and engaging company. The occasional coffee and lunch with Maggie fueled his lust, but he had grown to have a deep respect for Maggie's ability to manage a wide array of complex tasks while never seeming fazed about it. Jim was convinced she was a genius, a hot and sexy genius.

Jim entered the conference room for the staff meeting, thinking vaguely about his last discussion with Li and wondering if he would have the moxie to ask Isaac to re-consider Li's dismissal. Isaac, Shilesh, Jeanine and Maggie were all seated and were in conversation when Jim entered the room. He checked his watch to make sure he was not late. Nope, Jim was on time, but he felt that the meeting had started earlier.

"Hello Jim," Isaac welcomed. Jim had not seen Isaac since his first day on the job, and he was reassured when Isaac came over to greet him. Isaac seemed impervious to the age-related strains that Jeanine and he were showing. Jim noticed that Isaac was impeccably tailored and he was thankful that Maggie had selected an appropriate outfit for his first meeting.

"I see that Maggie has spiffed you up, Jimmy,"

He hated being called Jimmy.

"Yes, pretty nice 'eh?" Jim replied, "I am not sure what I would do without Maggie."

Isaac smiled reassuringly towards Maggie and then shifted his glance back to Jim, "She's one in a million Jim. But then again, you're pretty special too…I have been hearing good things about your team. I knew we could count on you."

Jim felt welcomed by Isaac for the first time. His confidence built and he felt himself stand a little taller. "Gee, thanks boss," he joked.

The group settled down and Isaac began the discussion. "I wanted to share with you some positive developments that we have had this month. I know it has been a little hectic, but I have been all over the place since we last met. I'm pleased to inform you that we have secured an additional $100 million in financing for this year, so relax and keep working hard. Jim, the main reason for today's meeting was to formally welcome you to the team and to give you a chance to share with us an overview of what you have done since arriving at Audacity."

Jim felt the blood rush to his face and he knew that he was slightly blushing. Social situations were not his forte, but Jim had practiced his presentation, and he felt confident that his lab results were impressive. Jim thanked Isaac and rose to present his status report. He explained the lab structure, the research agenda, the team composition and the short-term goals that the teams had set. Isaac and the others seemed deeply interested and asked detailed questions to help Jim provide sufficient color to describe his achievements. Isaac nodded positively during the presentation while Maggie took occasional notes.

After his 20 minute presentation, Jim sat back in his chair and the room grew still. Isaac leaned back and began to speak, "Jim…that was an excellent overview. I know that the board of directors is going to be thrilled with your agenda, and I'm grateful that you have shown such dynamism." Jim was filled with pride. Isaac looked down at his notebook and glanced back at the team, "Is there anything else anyone wanted to cover at today's meeting?"

The room was quiet, but no-one was fidgeting. Jim looked over at Shilesh who seemed to be lost in thought. Jim supposed that he was deeply engrossed in microbytes or some other new concept. Jeanine was writing in her notebook, seemingly focused on other matters, as was Maggie. Jim decided to bring up the Li topic, and cleared his throat.

"Um Isaac there is one thing I wanted to discuss," he interjected. Shilesh dropped his gaze towards Jim and Jeanine stopped writing. Maggie continued her note taking, seemingly unfazed by Jim.

"Sure Jim, what's up?"

"Isaac, there are two topics that are on my mind. The first deals with Li and her errant cell phone earlier this week. I know that she broke policy, but I really respect Li's background and was wondering if you might re-consider her termination."

Isaac grew still and his intensity lit up. Jim could tell that he had pissed off Isaac, but also knew that he had little chance of closing the door he just opened. Isaac removed his aviator style glasses and rubbed his eyes slightly. He laid his glasses on the table and returned his steely gaze to Jim. The flash of intensity that Jim had noticed was suddenly gone and Isaac's face turned tranquil and relaxed. He explained, "I personally recruited Li from Harvard, Jim. She is one of the most promising researchers I have met in many years. It really is a shame that she screwed up, but you know I have to enforce the policy I set, or else I look like a weak leader."

Jim could see the concern in Isaac's eyes. This guy was a human being after all. He empathized with Jim's dilemma, but Isaac made it clear that there was not going to be a second chance for Li. "Now what was the second matter?" Isaac queried.

Jim froze for a moment and doubted whether he should continue to speak. Although Isaac had treated him warmly, Jim did not want to press his luck at his first staff meeting. But, he needed to come clean with Isaac or he would be bothered and distracted, so he continued, "During the fire drill this week…uh...I mean, during the Li incident, I was commenting to Jeanine that the segregation you have set up is pretty intense. Sometimes I am not really sure how all the pieces fit together Isaac."

Isaac winked at Jim to let him know that it was okay, "That's how I designed it, Jimmy." The room laughed and Jim suddenly felt at ease. Isaac picked up his pencil and tapped lightly on his notebook. "Have you ever had someone steal something from you, Jim?"

Jim was confused, and he replied honestly, "No, not really, Isaac."

"Well Jim, I have, and it is not pleasant. I know it's disconcerting to newcomers, and I know it can seem neurotic, but I have my reasons. You see, a few years ago I was about to launch a new product when some other firm beat me to the market. I was shocked and I thought that it was impossible. I was convinced that there was no way they could have done it. Later, I found out that two of my researchers were 'moles.' I had been made the fool. So, it changed me. I became secretive, and now I will do everything possible to make sure we are first to market this time…got it?"

Jim understood that the discussion was over, and he nodded in agreement. "Sure Isaac," he replied, "But sometimes I think I could make a better contribution if I understood the larger picture."

Isaac nodded, "Jim I agree that you need to get a broader view of our operations. Let me give it some thought and get back to you." Jim noticed out of the corner of his eye that Maggie had made a motion as she picked up her pencil again and took a notation. "Well folks, thanks for the extra effort, and let's keep it up!" Isaac cheered. He shook hands with everyone and exited the room. Jim was feeling let down that the meeting was such a waste of time, but he figured that wasted time was what Corporate meetings were all about.

Jeanine and Shilesh headed towards the door, giving a slight wave to Jim as they left, while Jim sat looking across the table at Maggie. He noticed that she was wearing a new pair of glasses, they were a light tortoise shell with a funky thick horned rim. Her hair was pulled back and her bare neck was exposed to Jim's imagination. Jim had developed a school boy's crush on Maggie. He also understood that Maggie was not available. She looked at him with a pleasant, but not seductive smile and brushed her hair back. For a moment, it appeared that Jim had made Maggie nervous, but she snapped out of it. "Jim that was excellent." She complimented, "You looked great and you made your points well. I was really impressed." Jim gushed inside at the positive feedback. "You're really special, Jim. I'm sure that you and Isaac will get along fine." Maggie stood up and left the room.

Chapter 13

The meeting went well. Jim could have been stronger with Isaac, but he was satisfied that he made his point and stood firm. And Maggie had congratulated him, he liked that. Jim started to collect his papers and then noticed that a card had fallen under the table. He reached down and picked it up. It looked like a smart card of some sort, and Jim was curious. He flipped it over and saw a picture of Shilesh with his name and department. Jim figured that Shilesh must have dropped his id badge, and would soon be back to retrieve it, so Jim decided to wait.

Jim grew curious about the office as he looked at the badge. It was predictable, but mysterious. Shilesh and Jeanine always came from the elevator bank, but Jim had never seen their offices. Isaac's rule, he laughed. No-one knows anything. Jim put the id card in his pocket and continued to collect his belongings. Then it hit him. He did not like the feeling that swelled up in his mind, but Jim could not put it down once it had reared its ugly head.

Jim had Shilesh's access card. He had *access*. The thought of being able to go to Shilesh's office was curiously invigorating. Jim knew that it was disallowed. He knew it was against the rules, and he knew that he had no other choice than to follow his instincts. Jim sat back down at the table and stared at his status report. He recalled what happened with Li and a wave of fear gripped him. What if he got himself fired? Surely the thrill of seeing more of the office would be nothing compared to the disappointment of joining Li in the outplacement agency. He loved this new gig and he did not want to jeopardize it.

With id card in hand, the allure of the unknown was nagging at his mind. Jim couldn't help it, he was curious. He had always been that way…and all these fancy clothes, the white-glove service and all the money in the world were not going to change his character. A loner, a tinkerer, and a wonderer - that was Dr. Jim Andrews. He knew what he had to do next as his adrenaline began pumping and his senses jumped into overdrive.

The hallway was empty and the office traffic was quiet, as usual. Lunch would not be served for a couple of hours and most people had settled down to get working because it was already 9:30am. Jim sat silently, flipping Shilesh's access card over and over, wondering and debating his course of action. He could take it down to Maggie's office. But, he hesitated, what if Shilesh was disciplined for being forgetful? What if someone thought that the seventy five year old mad-scientist was starting to lose his mind? That would be bad. Jim had a lot of respect for Shilesh and did not want to cause him trouble. Then, Jim felt a rush of guilt. He knew that the longer he held onto the card, the longer it would be exposing himself and Shilesh to risk. Jim thought about the Li incident. He remembered the RFID chip that Maggie gave him on his interview. This access card could also be tracked. Anxiety was building, and Jim was feeling sweaty and nervous.

He remembered that Isaac had agreed that Jim needed a broader view of the operations, maybe this was his chance? Plus, Jeanine had suggested that he would shake things up, right? From somewhere in his mind, Jim got up the courage to leave the conference room and he headed towards the elevator bank. He had to walk down the hallway past the men's room to get to the elevator. As he was walking to the men's room, Jim was fine, but once he passed the men's room door, he felt his pulse increase. Jim knew that the moment he passed that door, he had no valid excuse for being where he was. The women's room was a few feet down the hallway, and about 10 feet after that was the forbidden elevator bank. Jim panicked as he was walking. What would he do if Maggie walked out the bathroom? For that matter, what would he do if any woman walked out of the bathroom? In fact, what would he do if a man walked out of the men's room? Jim was shaking and starting to sweat as headed towards the elevator door. He passed the women's room and started to pick up speed as he grew near to the elevator door.

"Get a hold of yourself, man." He continually reassured himself as he approached the elevator. And then, like a seasoned office pro, Jim pulled the card out of his pocket and swiped it by the card reader. There was nothing to it. A green LED light on the card reader illuminated and Jim heard movement as the mechanics of the elevator began grinding. The cab was moving towards his floor, approaching the requested stop. He stood waiting, staring at the green light and wondering what in the hell he was doing.

He thought about running back to the men's room, but it was too late - the card reader had already recorded his action. According to the security system, Shilesh was waiting for the elevator, it was not Jim. These card readers kept track of all the comings and goings in the office. If Shilesh hailed the elevator and then failed to enter the cab, Jim was sure that an alarm would be set off somewhere, he just knew it.

Jim grew more nervous as the cab made more noise. He could tell that the doors were about to open and he felt his stomach pulsing with nerves. He had no business being in that hallway, and the initial rush from curiosity which led Jim to the elevator door had spoiled like milk, causing nausea. As seconds passed, his throat filled with the slimy acidic taste of bile. Jim was going to faint. He wanted to wake up from the bad dream, or find a way to disappear.

Despite Jim's desire to end the adventure, he heard the elevator cab stop and the doors began to open...

Chapter 14

"Oh, hello Jim," Isaac remarked with a dry smile as he stood facing Jim from inside the elevator car. Isaac was inside of the elevator cab! Jim froze in his tracks and his throat instantly grew dry. He saw shooting stars as he figured his blood pressure had hit new highs or new lows, and in that moment when Isaac's eyes and Jim's eyes met, Jim realized that he had just lost his job. A sudden disappointment crept upon Jim and he felt weak. He must have swayed, because Isaac reached out his hand to catch Jim from falling. "Easy there Jimbo," he laughed, "not so fast kid." Jim practically fell into the cab and the elevator door closed behind them.

The interior of the elevator was black granite, and there were no buttons or indicator lights. Jim heard the high pitch whistle of an exhaust fan, and felt that his body was wet with sweat. Isaac was inspecting Jim with a discerning eye. He was penetrating Jim with his stare and Jim felt like a little kid who was caught with his hand in the cookie jar. But this was not a game, and Jim suspected that he was in trouble.

Jim reached in his pocket and fished out Shilesh's access card, handing slowly it to Isaac, "uh... Shilesh dropped this in the conference room this morning and I was going to give it back to him." Jim knew how lame his excuse sounded - he was crestfallen, he was embarrassed and he was scared.

Isaac gently accepted the card and put his hand on Jim's shoulder. "Thanks Jim," he said kindly, "I appreciate that. You know Maggie could have made sure it reached him, right?"

"Yeah," Jim gulped, "I guess I let curiosity get the best of me Isaac. For some reason I wanted to see what else was going on in this place."

The elevator stopped and opened into another lobby. Isaac led Jim out of the elevator cab and explained, "Ok Jim, I guess you will find out now, but remember that curiosity killed the cat, eh? Here, why don't you follow me...I guess I'll broaden your view of our operations now."

Isaac led Jim out of the elevator cab. The elevator must have gone down, not up, because the lobby was immense. There was a reception desk in front of the elevator doors and there were initials emblazed on the reception desk. Jim's eyes widened as he understood what he was reading – N.S.A.

He looked at the reception desk and saw Anthony, his driver, grinning sheepishly behind the desk. "Good morning Dr. Andrews," Anthony greeted.

"Come this way, Jim." Isaac signaled, "There are some people that I want you to meet."

Jim felt weak as the realization set in on him that the past 6 weeks of his life had been a lie. He had been duped into believing that he was working in a secretive start-up, idiot. Audacity Frontier was not a start-up, and Isaac was not a CEO. Isaac was a spook and Audacity Frontier was a front for the NSA.

"Jim, I know you're going through a lot of emotions right now." Isaac counseled, "I think this will all make sense to you in a few minutes." Isaac led Jim into a conference room where Jeanine, Shilesh, Maggie, Jake and Li were seated around the table.

Maggie came over to welcome Jim with her hand outstretched, "Jim I wanted to explain all this to you sooner, but it wasn't possible."

Jake approached Jim, looking tanned but exhausted. He was still dressed like a fashion model, and Jim was feeling queasy. Jake laughed as he explained, "Jim, I'm a government agent, not a crazy-ass CEO. The Sound Fusion Factory was a legitimate business, but Isaac contacted me because a situation had arisen and I needed to come back underground." Jim was speechless. "Please sit down." Jake motioned and Jim approached the table.

Li stood up and reached out her hand to Jim. "Doctor Andrews, it's nice to see you again." She smiled.

Isaac picked up a remote control and dimmed the lights in the room. A screen on the wall illuminated and Jim read the words on the screen:

"In joining the NSA, you have been given an opportunity to participate in the activities of one of the most important intelligence organizations of the United States Government. At the same time, you have assumed a trust which carries with it a most important individual responsibility – the safeguarding of sensitive information vital to the security of our nation."

Jim stared at the computer screen and the words echoed in his mind as he read them. Isaac interrupted the silence, "Jim, the next few minutes are going to be pretty intense, okay?"

"Yeah, Isaac, I'm getting the picture pretty fast."

"We are about to bring you into a classified status and it's likely that your life will never be the same again," Isaac explained.

Jim breathed in carefully. "Isaac, am I going to have to disappear?"

Everyone in the room laughed, with Isaac laughing the loudest as he continued, "No Jim, you don't have to disappear, but you will be undercover for a while."

Out of nowhere, Jim felt a concern for Sally and Lily and he couldn't help himself as he replied, "Isaac what am I going to do with Sally?" he questioned.

Isaac pressed a button on the remote and a picture of Sally and an attractive man walking with Lily was displayed on the screen. Jim had a bad taste in his mouth, like acid reflux. "Jim, the man walking with your wife is Abdul Yimani, he goes by the name of Abraham Yeltsin. Abdul is one of the most wanted spies in the mujahedeen intelligence community."

Jim was stunned, "Are you telling me my wife is sleeping with an al Quaeda spy?"

The room was silent and the mood was tense. "Look Jim...these guys are professional manipulators. Sally was lonely, and she did not stand a chance with their charm," Isaac explained.

Jake straightened in his chair and spoke up, "Jim, you were doing great work for me at the Sound Fusion Factory. I know that that it killed your marriage and I know this is not easy for you. Abdul made his way into Sally's life because he is trying to get at you. We think he was trying to find the link between the Company and the NSA."

Maggie spoke up, "Jim, this must be shocking...I'm impressed that you're keeping it together."

Jim looked around the room and felt ill at ease, but at the same time a weight had been lifted from his shoulders. Shilesh, Li and Jeanine were respectfully watching as Maggie, Jake and Isaac were introducing Jim to his new reality.

Isaac pressed a remote control which showed a grid with each person's name including Anthony's along the top and a series of numbers below each name:

Isaac	Maggie	Shilesh	Jeanine	Anthony	Li	Jake
4	6	2	8	10	9	3

Jim looked at the table and then glanced up at Jake who was smiling. "What is it?" Jim asked.

"Oh, that's our betting pool for how long it would take you to figure us out." Jake laughed, "Looks like Maggie won."

Jim couldn't stop himself from laughing as the tension in the room eased up. Things were going to be different from now on, and he wasn't sure how to proceed. He looked askance at Jake and asked, "So what the hell happens now?"

"I don't know, Jim…ask Maggie, she's the boss."

Jim glanced at Jake, then at Isaac and Maggie. Maggie's perfect skin was blushing. Things were starting to make sense, but Jim was being treated like the 'fucking the new kid' on his first day at a new school. Maggie smiled and gathered her composure, "All right guys, enough! Okay?" She took command, "Jim I'm the head of the Cyber Security for the NSA. Jake is one of our personnel agents, as is Isaac. Their job is to live in the real world and look out for people like you."

"You will meet people like Isaac and Jake in almost every technologically-oriented start-up in Silicon Valley as well as in Tel Aviv, Bangalore, New York, London, you name it, we're there. We plant our folks in the corporate office, offer seed capital, and then we watch what happens. We call people like Jake and Isaac our 'links' to the real world because they walk and talk among you. They are not spies, but they have two jobs, one with us, and one in the corporate world. With their help, we keep a database of people like you, and when national emergencies arise, we use our real world linkages like Isaac and Jake here to bring people into the team. I know this might sound crazy, but it's the truth and we're in trouble."

"Of course," Jim blurted.

"What's that Jim?" Maggie asked.

"Look, when I first met you I thought you were a fashion accessory for Isaac. Then I realized that you had a photographic memory and an enormous capacity for management, but no matter what I did, I just couldn't figure out what Isaac did."

Maggie laughed at Jim's response, and she put her glasses on top of her head. Strands of her inviting hair fell around her face as she smiled and explained, "You ratted me out Jim. Now look, we baited you with Shilesh's id card because we have a situation. At first, we tried to get along without you, but there have been some unnerving developments lately and we wanted you deeper on the effort. I know this is going to sound strange, but we need to know if you've got it in you to be on the team. You're going to be given super classified clearance and you won't ever be able to account for what you have been doing or where you have been once our mission is completed. That is, if our mission is completed," she said.

For the first time since arriving in the conference room, Jim felt the thrill and intrigue of the spy business. "Um Maggie, you deliberately said *if*, didn't you?"

"Jim, this is serious...we're not making iTunes or cell phone companies rich, okay?" She teased, "Besides Jim, we're all consenting adults here."

Jim blushed again.

Chapter 15

Maggie reached for the remote from Isaac and brought up a world map that covered the entire wall. She handed out pairs of 3-D glasses to everyone in the room. Jim placed the glasses on his head and the world map was suddenly presented in the center of the room. He took the glasses on and off to test the effect. "Nice, huh?" Maggie asked. "Wait until you see the new projector, it doesn't require glasses."

The world map contained two layers. Jim assumed each layer was a network grid, but he also saw a strange resemblance to the veins in a human body. The lower layer contained a network of blue lines. The lines connecting major cities were thick, with branches towards smaller and smaller towns getting thinner. On top of the blue layer was a smaller network of red lines superimposed on most of the world's largest cities, but with few branches to small cities and towns. The lines were pulsing and varying in width such that they seemed to be alive. Jim could see that the lines in the U.S. and Europe were thicker and were vibrating more than the lines in Asia.

"Welcome to DARPA net, Jim." Maggie explained, "In the early 1980s, Al Gore did not invent the Internet, DARPA did." Jim was familiar with DARPA from some magazine articles he read a few years prior.

"DARPA stands for the Defensive Advanced Research Projects Administration in case you forgot," she continued, "What you see in blue is our beloved Internet Jim. In red, you see our secure DARPA net. The width of the lines indicates the data flows. Notice that Asia is asleep right now and that India and China do not have as much activity as Europe and U.S., except for Afghanistan. Maggie was using a laser pointer that enabled her to highlight areas as she was speaking. "Every once in a while you will see points where the DARPA net intersects the Internet, those are highlighted in purple." Maggie zeroed in on Washington D.C. "That's the home office by the way. All we focus on here is Cyber Security. Now, the areas of intersection are only unidirectional, they are not bidirectional. We can, and do, look at any and all data that flows across the Internet. You see, it was the genius of DARPA to invent the Internet and then claim to set it free. People drank the Kool-Aid and the rest is history. Now, the home office has teams responsible for reviewing and translating different communications like emails, phone calls, and blogs...we only focus on security here in Greenwich."

Jake chimed in, "The two most successful programs that we launched over the past couple years were Skype and Facebook. You see, we gathered personal details on more than half of the literate population of the world, and now we monitor everything from their porn consumption to their lunatic raves about conspiracies. It makes the census look like kid's play."

"Thanks Jake," Maggie interrupted, "but can we please keep on the topic before I send you on a development mission to Anchorage."

"Sorry Maggie," Jake replied as the room erupted in laughter.

"Now Jim, in addition to the Internet conversations, we have teams who are reviewing and analyzing cell phone calls, land-line calls and even Al Quaeda's encrypted conversations. You know we invented all the encryption algorithms, so we made sure that there was always a back door. The best thing about the end of snail mail is that now you can't see when the government opens your mail."

Jim had a sinking feeling in his chest as he absorbed what he was being told. "I'm sure you are sitting there wondering what all this has to do with you, aren't you, Jim?"

"That's an understatement Maggie," he replied.

Maggie gently laughed. "Right...about 8 weeks ago we noticed that the bandwidth usage across the Internet picked up considerably. It gradually grew to be more traffic than when Michael Jackson died. But since it grew gradually, no-one really noticed it."

"No-one except for you," Jim quipped.

"Right on," Maggie replied, "I like you Jim, you're a quick study. But here is where things got a little weird. Maggie clicked a button and the lines on the world map were replaced by a heat map, with conical shapes superimposed on the world's major cities. "This is an overview of our own analytical throughput Jim. The height of each cone indicates the rough amount of data that our systems and teams review. We're spies you know, so we try to make sure we get as much data as possible." Maggie laughed and the rest of the room chuckled.

She continued, "The graph you are seeing is dated September 20. Think of that as our baseline. Now, I am going to show you the same graph over a few days. Keep in mind that from September 21st onwards, the total amount of bandwidth consumption began steadily increasing. Jim watched as the cones seemed to pulse, growing larger, then smaller as the days passed, but not really changing in any notable trend.

"Jim what should be screaming out at you right now is the lack of change." Maggie continued, "You see, traffic was doubling every 14 days, but the analytical throughput is staying static...that makes no sense. Ever since we have been monitoring the Internet, our analytical throughput has increased in proportion to the traffic. It's predictable. And when the relationship broke down, it set off alarm bells from here to London to Tel Aviv to Bangalore. The silence was killing us. Let me put it to you in a different way. Imagine that you had scales under a highway so you could weigh every car that drove by a checkpoint, and you monitored that total weight and plotted in on a graph. Now, let's further assume that you began to see a steady rise in total weight, but when you looked out the window, there were hardly any vehicles on the road."

"Now, what's really strange is that this phenomenon not only happened on the Internet, but it also happened across the cell phone carriers. Fortunately, DARPA net has not been compromised, but that's why we went into lock down mode – that much of what you saw upstairs was real. You see, Jim, we think someone has hijacked the Internet."

Jim was waiting for the lights to turn on and for a game show host to come out and tell him he had been the hapless victim of a twisted reality show. But Jim suspected that this was too weird to be a TV show. Maggie pressed a button on the remote and lights became brighter as the 3D maps disappeared. Jim removed his glasses and let his eyes gradually adjust to the brightness. His initial panic had subsided and Jim was beginning to feel the importance of his team.

"Maggie," Jim asked, "Maybe you can tell me a little more about the role of Jeanine, Shilesh and Li."

"Sure," she replied. "Well the good news is that Li is exactly who you thought she was. From now on, Li will be your research assistant." Li smiled, and Jim was happy at the news.

"And Jeanine is indeed the leading authority on infectious diseases. We convinced her to take a leave of absence from the National Institutes of Health upon the recommendation of Shilesh."

Jim smiled at Jeanine and then shifted his attention towards Shilesh, who maintained that grandfatherly smile which reminded Jim of his high school mentor.

"Jim, I would like to introduce you to Dr. Shilesh Gupta, the Chief Risk Officer of the United States," Maggie paused.

"The Who?" Jim exclaimed.

Shilesh piped up when he saw Jim's response, "No Jim, I'm not the Who? They were still a bunch of teenagers when I was finishing my post-doc program at Yale." Jim laughed and appreciated Shilesh's humor, then Shilesh continued, "You see Jim, it was Dick Chentley who imagined my role and made sure that my existence would never be known. Even though the administration has changed, the policy has continued. I am serving a 15 year tour of duty."

Maggie interrupted, "Shilesh is indeed an innovator in the field of technology, but his role is very broad Jim. Shilesh is responsible for connecting all the dots. Shilesh moves seamlessly across all branches of the government, sometimes undercover, sometimes in plain view, but always with carte blanche. He reports to the Vice President under a secret act of Congress which was, subsequently, also secretly blessed by the Supreme Court."

"You've captured my imagination Maggie, but I feel like I'm having a little difficulty connecting the dots as you say." Jim was feeling lost, and every time he felt that he was grasping the gist of what was going on, the story seemed to change.

Shilesh leaned back in his chair and began to explain, "Jim, my primary job is to find and defuse problems *before* they cause disasters. We noticed a distinct correlation between the rate of bandwidth growth on the Internet since September and the rate of growth of the past five epidemics of influenza. We can discuss it in more detail later, but the mathematics are irrefutable. The Internet seems to have been hijacked by some kind of virus which we have never encountered, but its dispersion and growth is clearly following a biological epidemic pattern."

"Now, it gets even more strange. We noticed that two weeks after the Internet began to get hijacked; the same pattern of growth began to permeate the cell phone spectrum. And, to top it all off, these electronic invasions fit perfectly within the epidemic waves of the H1N1 flu. Hence we called both you and Jeanine under cover to work on this pattern. Something's happening Jim, but we have no real idea what it is. Our analysts have put some baseline theories on the table which we can discuss later, but that's why we asked Li to help you and Jeanine crunch through the statistics. Of course, we have put all of the world's supercomputers on standby in case you need to run simulations or other analytics."

Jim looked around the room and felt like he finally understood who the people were and what their roles were on the team. Although the entire episode had been terrifying, Jim was satisfied that the story was at least remotely plausible. Anthony, Jake and Isaac stood up to leave the room, and Maggie explained, "Jim, I want you to know that Anthony will be your personal assistant and your body guard. He's a Rhodes Scholar as well as a former Navy Seal." Jim waved towards Anthony as he was leaving the room.

"And I'm afraid we won't see each other for a while," Isaac interrupted, "My role here is complete Jim. I was sincere in my praise for you and I know that we're in good hands with you on the team. Please do your best Jim. The freedom of the Country and perhaps the safety of the world depend on you." Isaac extended his hand towards Jim who reciprocated.

"And I'm gone too," said Jake. "Look I know you hated me for blowing up the Company, but I was only doing my job. And now, thanks to Maggie, I'm headed back to the Valley to face the criminal and the bankruptcy courts so that I can resurface in a couple of years like a re-born Savior. I'm sure you will enjoy the pictures of me in the New York Times when they haul my ass into the pokey, handcuffs front and center for the cameras, but you should know I did it all for good reasons." Jake smiled at Jim and saluted as he left the conference room.

Maggie gestured for Jim to sit down at the table, and Jim surveyed the room. Shilesh was still staring at him, seemingly lost in thought, while Jeanine was staring at her hands. Li was quietly observing the room and Maggie was sitting at the head of the table, beautiful as ever, completely in control of the team.

"Jim…now that you're undercover, I guess I should explain that we've checked you out of the hotel today. From now on you will live here with us, on the floor below this office. You're free to come and go as you please, just ask Anthony to give you a lift." Maggie slid a strange looking blackberry across the table in Jim's direction, and explained, "Here, this is your new phone. We don't use cell phones. Your device is directly connected to DARPA net, not to the cell carriers. When you dial the phone it can also route through a Satellite phone server, so you have coverage anywhere in the world, literally. Your communications will all be secure now, so don't worry." Jim smiled as he accepted the phone and commented, "I thought you said you guys always left a back door open on these things."

"This one is real Jim. Welcome aboard." Maggie shook Jim's hand and began to exit the room. She turned before she reached the door looking towards Jim and whispered, "Jim, I have asked Anthony to show you to your room. Why don't you rest for a while? We can have a drink around 6:00pm in the lounge. Is it a date?" She smiled.

Jim couldn't help feeling attracted to Maggie and he responded like a kid, "You bet Maggie, see you later." Maggie turned and left the room. Jim was alone again. The events of the past few hours were spinning around in his mind like a drug.

Anthony interrupted his thoughts, "Dr. Andrews, why don't you follow me downstairs."

Chapter 16

Jim was shocked as he walked into his new room because it looked identical to the suite at the Tribeca Grand hotel. It was scary, down to the smallest detail, it was an exact replica. "Weird huh?" Anthony quipped, "We found that the fewer changes the better when we acclimatize people down under. So, we make sure that your bedroom remains identical. It's the little things that make the difference Dr. Andrews. You know your way around this room; let me show you around the rest of the floor."

Jim and Anthony walked down a long hallway, and he pointed out other residences. At the end of the hall was a gymnasium and next to it was a cocktail lounge with some dining tables. "This is the mess hall, Dr. Andrews, and if you decide you want to get in better shape, just let me know and I will ensure that you get set up with our personal trainer. He's a Marine, and he's the best. The rest of us live one floor down. Our rooms are not quite as nice as yours, but it sure beats military housing. I have to get back out to the front desk. Is there anything else I can do for you, Doctor?"

"No Anthony. I think I have seen and done enough today to last me a lifetime. I'm going to lie down for a while because I am supposed to meet with Maggie at 6:00pm." Jim looked at his watch; it was 4:00pm. Anthony turned towards the elevators and left him standing in the hallway. Jim walked back to his room and fell into bed, exhausted and confused.

He awoke to his doorbell ringing. Jim glanced at the clock and noticed that it was already 6:00pm. He had drifted into a troubled sleep. That must be Maggie ringing, he thought. Jim got out of bed and opened the front door. Maggie was dressed in a casual outfit, still looking stunning but she had ditched the funky glasses. "Hello sleepy stranger, you're running late, aren't you?"

"I'm sorry Maggie, I fell asleep. Why don't you come in?"

Maggie entered the room and sat down on the couch. Jim sat in the adjoining chair, then quickly changed his mind and rose. "Can you give me a few minutes to get changed?"

Jim left the sitting room and entered his Asian Spa bathroom. He couldn't get over how every aspect of his room was identical to the hotel, but it made things easier for him to get dressed. Jim picked out some clothes, straightened his hair and brushed his teeth, then checked himself out in the mirror to make sure he would be acceptable to Maggie.

As Jim returned to the sitting room, he saw Maggie had leaned her head onto the couch and appeared to be resting. She was beautiful in her restful state and Jim thought twice about waking her. He would enjoy spending a few hours looking at her as she was sleeping, but was concerned that Maggie might be startled if she awoke to see him staring at her longingly. Jim cleared his throat to try to wake up Maggie, then gently placed his hand on her leg. "Hi there," Jim whispered, "Looks you're as beat up as I am."

Maggie opened her eyes and looked at Jim with a bedroom glance.

"Hey…I must have dozed off while you were beautifying yourself Jim. You do look nice." Maggie straightened her clothes out and got off the couch. "Are you ready?" she asked.

Jim and Maggie headed out of Jim's suite. As they were leaving the room, Jeanine came out of the elevator and saw the couple. Jim was embarrassed, but Maggie responded, "Hi Jeanine, Jim and I are going to get a drink. Would you like to join us?"

"No thanks Maggie, you two go on ahead, I need to get some rest."

Jim and Maggie went down the hallway towards the lounge. The room was well appointed, with a well-stocked self-service bar, fancy leather trimmed stools against high tables, and 3 low cozy tables set evenly along a wall with comfortable club chairs. Jim and Maggie went to the bar. Jim got a bottle of Heineken and Maggie reached for a Budweiser tall neck. They opened their drinks and then took a seat at one of the lower tables. There was background music, it was a soft jazz melody, and Jim could immediately tell that the music had been recorded on a cassette tape. There was a discernible hiss and a distortion to the core sound quality which annoyed his ears.

Maggie began the conversation, "So, has it all sunk in yet Jim? I know it will take a while and I know you feel like we have exposed you to a huge mind game, but undercover intelligence is a complicated effort. You see, we never know how a person is going to react, especially the independent thinkers like you and Jeanine."

"So...how did you know I would agree?"

"We weren't sure, but I trust my instincts, and I had a good feeling about you. Plus, we were getting pretty desperate and needed to take the risk."

"How is Jeanine holding out?"

"Jeanine is fine Jim, but this has not been easy for her. Before we recruited her on this mission, Jeanine was living a high-profile life and speaking at prestigious seminars about the approach for managing and slowing epidemic outbreaks. She has advised governments and hospitals, towns and universities as well as medical firms, military leaders, and executives on strategies for minimizing damage from outbreaks. But this is a complicated endeavor. We're dealing with technology here, not an infectious disease. So until we were confident that you would agree to join us, Jeanine has been in a holding pattern. She has helped us in discussing some of the base line scenarios that Shilesh has formulated, but we're desperately in need of your imagination and skills Jim."

Maggie was smiling, but Jim could tell that she was exhausted.

"Well…it looks like your instincts were correct, Maggie…by the way, how long has it been since you slept?"

"I think I slept for a few hours, 2 days ago Jim."

"Maggie, you're right that this has been a real trip…I could never have imagined what was going on here. I knew that it was a strange place, but I figured that Isaac was just an eccentric entrepreneur. If I had any idea that I was supporting a front organization for the NSA, I would have reacted differently. And yet, I still don't know how a spy agency thinks I can be of any help."

"We're not spies Jim…I mean…I know I said that we were, but my team is really focused on national defense. There are definitely spies in our group, but not in my department."

Jim laughed heartily, "Good god Maggie, you don't have to defend yourself in front of me. I know that our country has spies and I respect that we need to keep ourselves safe. I have to admit I was a little taken back when you showed me that the Internet was an excellent tool for the government to spy on its own people, but looking at it objectively, I think that the benefits of the Internet outweigh the costs of having groups like yours snooping. Think about it…the power of the internet brought the world-wide exchange of ideas…it has changed the world. In return, we had to give up our privacy. It may seem like a Faustian bargain; but, the truth is, the benefits far outweigh the costs – don't they? And…hey, tell me, did you know that you were going to be a spy queen when you were a kid? Or was this an accidental career track?"

Maggie stared into Jim's eyes and began to speak, "No, I never thought that I was going to be a spy. I was going to be a model, Jim. But, there was one problem. You see, I could never forget anything that I read. I have this memory which astounded my parents and teachers. I can recite the Bible, and Jane Eyre and every other novel I have read, not to mention the newspapers since I was a kid, People Magazine and even my high school newsletters. I'm a freak Jim. It's simple."

"When I was studying literature at Harvard, I was approached by one of my teachers who suggested that I do an internship in Washington, D.C. I applied for the job and started working at the NSA. Before I knew it, I was addicted to the challenge. I spent some time in the eavesdropping division, then left to get a graduate degree in Computer Science. When I was about to graduate, the Head of the NSA called me up and asked if I would re-join. I didn't have any other set plans, so I agreed. Eventually I was given my own portfolio and was encouraged to build the Cyber Security department. We started off pretty small, but as the world evolved towards more electronic modes of communication, we just got bigger and bigger...I guess you could say that my career grew up along with the growth of the Internet. I liked what I was doing, and I guess I got hooked and never looked back."

Jim commiserated, "Yeah, I know what you mean. I have found myself absorbed in work over and over again. It eventually cost me my marriage."

"I don't think I need to worry about marriage...we don't get much time for romance around here. In fact, until I met you I was convinced that I was headed for another lonely winter in Connecticut." Maggie looked at Jim's face and raised her hand towards his cheek. She rested her fingers on his face, and Jim felt the hair on his neck rise up, along with his pulse and sex drive. Jim reached up to hold Maggie's hand, but she pulled away. "I'm not trying to be a tease Jim. The fact is I like you, but we need to be platonic on this project. As much as I hate it,

I need you here for professional reasons and I can't let my loneliness come in the way of our mission."

Jim understood Maggie's response. He was definitely not ready to get back into a relationship after the mess with Sally. And over the past six weeks, Jim had come to terms with his obsession with science. He knew that he was going to spend a lot of his life alone in the lab, and he was comfortable that the challenge of research was going to provide solace. But still, Jim felt an attraction towards Maggie and thought the feeling was reciprocated. When Maggie told Jim that she had feelings for him, he became enchanted despite the implausibility of a relationship. So, he tested the waters. "I know what you mean Maggie. I'm not really in a position to get involved right now; and as much as I would enjoy sleeping with you, I know that it would not be for the best."

Maggie looked bashfully at her beer and then peered back at Jim with longing eyes, "Okay Jim. I guess we should just go to your place for a passionate rendezvous just this one time, right?"

Jim felt excitement as Maggie went in for the kill. He rose from the table as Maggie also stood to leave. "Yeah I guess just this once," and he smiled.

As soon as the door to Jim's suite closed, they began groping like young lovers in the back seat of a car on a hot date. Jim began to kiss Maggie's neck as she leaned her head back. Then, suddenly she pushed Jim, hard, so that he fell onto the bed backwards and bounced like a beach ball. That was Maggie, always had to be in control. But Jim wanted to take Maggie on his own terms, not on hers, and he gripped her firmly and rolled her onto her back, propping himself above her as he stared into Maggie's fire filled eyes. Maggie seemed to enjoy the struggle, and smiled, grabbing tightly around his waist and pulling Jim closer towards her. She had to be in control.

Maggie was a strong fighter and at the same time she was a good lover. Their tussle left Jim feeling exhausted and fulfilled, completely and fully spent. As they lay calmly in Jim's bed, Maggie moved towards him, putting her mouth near his ear and whispering, "Just this one time, okay tiger?" And she kissed his inner ear, sending hot breath into his neck and seemingly penetrating his spine.

Jim looked towards Maggie and kissed her gently on the tip of her perfect nose. "Yes, just this once," as he smiled and held her in his arms.

After a few minutes, Maggie rolled out of bed and began picking up the clothes that had been strewn around the room. She went into the Asian Spa and came out dressed with her hair combed. "Jim, we get started each morning around 6:00am. I will see you tomorrow." She left the room and Jim drifted off to sleep, loving his new, twisted life.

Chapter 17

At 5:30 am, the disorienting beat of the pop group Abba singing their 1970s hit song, "Dancing Queen" at an illegally high volume on Jim's alarm clock radio shattered the silence of his sleep. Jim was simultaneously annoyed and confused as he came to consciousness and understood what was happening. His iPod had not only been compromised, it had been desecrated. He fumbled aimlessly around the bed looking for the off switch or the snooze button; anything really, as long as he could turn off the goddamn music that had invaded his suite. Jim located the off button, and then noticed a post-it note affixed to his iPod.

Thought you might like a change of pace! / love, Jake

"Asshole," Jim grumbled aloud. He forgot how much he hated Jake. Jake had made Jim feel inferior for almost two years, and when Maggie finally exposed him as a stooge, Jim was relieved. But replacing Led Zeppelin with Abba was further than any man could possibly go. The conflict had escalated, this was war! In retaliation for the severe iPod insult, Jim made a mental note to look at the newspaper every day until he saw Jake being led away in hand-cuffs. Yes…he would cut out the picture and have it framed so that he could send it every year to Jake as a holiday gift.

Jim moved towards the bathroom and grabbed some jeans and a casual button-down shirt. He slipped on a pair of loafers and headed towards the conference room. As he was leaving his room, he saw Jeanine walking down the hallway.

"Hey Jeanine," Jim yelled, as he sped up to her.

Jeanine was also casually dressed, but was somehow still impeccable in her appearance. "Now that you've come down under, I don't have to dress up anymore." She joked, "But

Maggie has assured me that I get to keep all those Chanel suits."

Jim laughed and they walked down the hallway towards the conference room. Jim was curious and asked, "So Jeanine, tell me what it's really like down here."

Jeanine smiled, "There are no more secret levels Jim. This is as strange as it gets, don't worry." They shared a smile and Jeanine continued, "It is pretty intense work Jim. We don't really know what we have run up against. Shilesh and Maggie are brilliant, but they are the first to admit that we are shooting in the dark. All of the analysts are smart and efficient, and we don't have to ask twice for anything that we might need to get the work done. Honestly, it gives me a rush to have such power at our fingertips, but I wish we had more of a clue about what's going on. Jim, I'm pretty stressed out about this, and, to tell you the truth, I'm a little scared. Some of the scenarios that Shilesh has been talking about are way out there."

Jim felt a lump in the back of his throat as he absorbed what Jeanine was saying. He knew from seeing the physical changes in her appearance over the past six weeks that Jeanine was under pressure, but he never imagined that it was this bad.

They entered the conference room, where Li, Maggie and Shilesh were already seated and working. Jim was astonished that he did not feel awkward around Maggie even though they had shared an intimate evening the night before. He felt natural and normal, as if there was nothing to it.

Jeanine and Jim sat down at the black granite conference table and Li closed the door. Shilesh stood to address the group. "For everyone except Jim, this next discussion is a review." Shilesh seemed professorial in his tone, and Jim was immediately transported back to his early days of schooling. Dr. Roberts was alive and well. He had been re-incarnated as a 75 year-old Indian scientist who effectively ran the U.S. intelligence community. Jim reveled at the chance to enjoy an intellectual challenge, and he relaxed as Shilesh began to expound, "Please, remember the ground rules. Find the weakness in my arguments, poke holes, and agree with nothing. You all know that we're missing something big here, so you should disprove and doubt everything that you are about to hear. With that in mind, let's get started."

Shilesh grabbed the remote control and the LCD screen in the front of the room illuminated as the lighting in the room became subtly lower. The following words were on the screen: *Scenario Analysis*. Jim was intrigued and became absorbed in Shilesh's lecture:

"Ladies and gentlemen, we are under siege. Although the facts and circumstances are not clearly understood, the Internet and various communications channels around the world have become overloaded with traffic which is, for all practical purposes, invisible to our intelligence operations. We get occasional glimpses of the side-effects of this invasion, but we are missing the big picture. We do not know its cause or its purpose. You have been invited to this team to help figure out the mystery, as it were."

Shilesh clicked the remote and a list appeared:

Facts and Observations

- *September 21 - volumes on Internet and Cell carriers increase to highest level in 22 months.*
- *September 30 - an estimated two weeks into the phenomena, Facebook servers are brought to a standstill for 10 hours requiring re-booting, cause unknown.*
- *October 15 - Centers for Disease Control estimates that wave 3 of the "Swine" Flu (H1N1) is well underway.*
- *October 19 - Office of Risk Analysis of US Government confirms that pattern AND pace of bandwidth deluge matches the H1N1 flu.*

- *October 20 - Blackberry and Gmail are brought down for 8 hours. Our communications reveal that technicians are re-booting servers for an unknown problem, same prognosis as Facebook outage.*
- *October 21 - Operation IR - Internet Rescue - is elevated to Threat Alert Level 1.*
- *November - Capacity on Internet backbone and cell phone carriers has declined 15% due to the unknown bandwidth consumption.*
- *Analysts in NSA are unable to 'see' or 'hear' increased traffic.*

Shilesh did not read the words on the screen out loud. He left the slide projected in front of the group for about 5 minutes as he stared at the team and at the LCD monitor. He seemed as intently reading the words as the rest of the group.

Jim looked at the screen and asked, "So you think the Internet has the flu?"

Li, Jeanine, Shilesh and Maggie laughed with Jim and Shilesh explained, "No Jim, the Internet does not have a runny nose. The reason we moved this event to Threat Alert Level 1 had more to do with the consistency between the H1N1 flu and the bandwidth deluge." Jim was silent and his face demonstrated the he failed to grasp the significance of Shilesh's comment.

Shilesh continued, "Jim, computer viruses and human viruses share some similarities, but not as much as you would think. In the early 1980s, we studied the relationship in a great amount of detail. At the time, the idea of a computer virus was novel, and we were trying to evaluate the impact that viruses would have on our fledgling successor to DARPA net, the "world wide web" as we called it back then. But I'm digressing from the point. You see, we found early on that the main difference between transmission of computer viruses and human viruses was a factor that we call 'Lambda.' Lambda is used in our mathematics forecasts to signify how fast a repeating pattern speeds up. Think of it as a measure of the contagion for a virus. If a virus is highly contagious, it has a high Lambda, if it is mild, then it has a low Lambda."

Shilesh stopped talking to sip from his water bottle. "In the case of our biological friends, the seasonal flu, the Spanish flu and even the common cold, our Lambda values are in the range of 4. In other words, the virus picks up speed at a rate of 4 times its original value with each new host. Jim, let's say you catch a cold tomorrow. Chances are that you will infect 4 others within a period of 2 days before your body develops defenses to stop the contagion. It doesn't mean they will all get sick, that's a different measure. Here we are only talking about the speed of infection. The pattern will repeat, on and on, until an epidemic has arisen."

"Ah yes, back to my point…in the case of computer viruses, we found that the Lambda was most always 100 or greater. You see, computers are much more social beings than people."

Shilesh laughed at his own joke, then he explained, "The reason computer viruses are so powerful is that normally they spread like wildfire, seemingly overnight infecting thousands or even millions of unwary, interconnected CPUs. Anyway, even though this Internet bandwidth deluge that we have uncovered seems to be taking over the bandwidth quickly, in epidemiological terms, it's a tortoise or a slug. If this were a traditional computer virus, the Net would have crashed by now, but as we have seen, it has not happened. We called in Jeanine to help us re-calibrate our computer-based threat models because we have never encountered a computer attack that is so painstakingly slow, or is it…deliberate?"

Jeanine picked up the conversation thread, "Jim, we confirmed that the rate of infection seems almost identical to the H1N1 flu transmission. Now, we know that computers cannot catch the flu, that's not the point. The point is that whatever or whoever is hijacking the Internet and the cell phone carriers is definitively not purely electronic. There is something, or someone who is buffering the rate of viral transmission. Maybe they want to ensure that systems don't crash; maybe they are trying to remain undetected. We don't know for sure, but it seems strange that they could pace themselves almost identically to the H1N1 flu epidemic pattern. Well, actually Jim, it's not only uncanny - it's impossible."

"But it's happening," Jim interrupted in a deadpan manner.

"Yes, I'm afraid it is."

The room grew silent and Shilesh continued to outline the situation, "I asked our Threat Assessment Office to suggest some initial scenarios so that we can begin to 'peel this onion' as they say. Here is what they came up with."

He clicked the remote again and the following list appeared on the LCD screen:

Potential Threat Explanations

- *Chinese, Russian or Iranian Intelligence agents are creating a Virtual Private Spy Network across our Internet, inventing their own private DARPA net by subverting the World Wide Web*
- *Terrorist group preparing to launch Cyber attack*
- *Rogue intelligence agents, Anarchists or similar fringe group attacking the establishment*
- *Unknown Life Forms*
- *Unknown Unknowns*

The room again fell silent as Shilesh quietly narrated the threats, stopping and resting after each point, until he got to the final point when he joked, "These lingo are really political speak for explaining that we have not the faintest idea what is happening, but we are afraid that if we're honest about it, then people will think we are stupid." Shilesh smiled gently and sat down in his chair, leaving the screen illuminated.

Jim was not satisfied with Shilesh's remarks and countered, "Shilesh, I understand the ones about bad guys trying to hurt us or fringe groups gone wild, but are you seriously suggesting that Aliens have landed?"

Shilesh continued speaking, "As for the last point, like I said, that one is truly a placeholder for the proverbial shit hitting the fan."

"What kind of research program are you envisioning to ferret out *Unknown Life Forms*, Shilesh?" Jim asked.

Shilesh explained, "Think about it more generally, Jim. Unknown Life Forms aren't only aliens, and yes I do believe in aliens. But what I am trying to say is that we come across formerly unknown life forms all the time in the life sciences. In the Western world, you are taught that Dr. Agostino Bassi identified the first 'invisible' germs by noting that they poisoned silkworms; we later named a microscopic fungus after him, the Beauveria Bassiana. For Agostino, these germs were *Unknown Life Forms*. But germ theory goes much further in history than Europeans like to admit. For example, back in India we have conceptualized germs as early as the Vedas. That was 40 years before Jesus was born. And yes, Jim, I believe in Jesus more than I believe in aliens." The room laughed along with Shilesh's humor, and he continued, "What I am trying to explain is that Unknown Life Forms do not only refer to green men coming down from space in UFOs. The term is intentionally broad and intentionally vague."

Maggie propped up her head and interjected, "Jim, actually we brought you here to coordinate the research program. Neither Shilesh nor Jeanine have spent their lives dedicated to basic research - to experimenting deeply in the unknown like you have done - especially in the communications and bandwidth disciplines. We were hoping you could sort of pick up these loose threads and start to weave them together."

Jim began to rock back and forth in his chair as he played with his pencil in a nervous manner. He looked at the screen and at his empty note pad, and then he slowly surveyed the eyes in the room. Li, Shilesh, Maggie and Jeanine were all staring at him, watching and waiting for his next move. "Why don't you tell me what you've got so far, Maggie?"

"The CIA has sent us full reports on all the foreign intelligence agencies. We have put them in a database on our secure DARPA net, which also runs our proprietary and secure version of Google's search engine. We've made a few tweaks to Google's model to improve the non-linear associations. Next, we superimposed those groups on our network map and found that there was minimal correlation between the hubs of unexplained activity on the Internet and the nodes where these groups typically get onto the Net. We widened out the search a little bit and found no additional information. As best as we can tell, this baby did not originate anywhere in Asia or East Europe."

"Then we beefed up the surveillance on our Mujahedeen friends. We translated and analyzed every single Arabic communication over the past 12 weeks. Jim, I mean literally every single communication. Our automated translators indexed and compared the conversations for threats. We cross-checked the conversations to our allegorical database to see if they were using code words or references from fables or religion to mask their true intentions, and similarly, nothing. Well, I can't say nothing. As you know, at any given time there are at least a half-dozen terrorists plotting some kind of trouble in the world. But we weeded out the bombings and assassinations and came up empty-handed. So, we don't believe that this is the work of Al Quaeda. However, we have still not understood why an agent infiltrated your marriage Jim. We don't know why they targeted Sally." Maggie paused and Jim stared at her with a cold gaze. "I'm sorry Jim," Maggie apologized, "But we have to look at all the angles here."

Maggie continued in her analysis, "Other than the episodes at Facebook and Gmail, we have not seen any indication of a rogue group. If a small group of fanatics are behind this activity, they are keeping suspiciously quiet on any blogs, phone calls or emails. Jim, we pulled out the stops here and analyzed virtually all of the email traffic of the past 3 months. We commandeered every supercomputer in North America and Japan to look for patterns of communication that would suggest a network of activity other than tiny groups of friends or families. We stratified all those communications into types and looked for key words, patterns, threats…you name it, we checked for it."

Jim was quickly losing hope in finding an easy solution as Maggie was explaining the depths to which the teams had already probed. These were very smart people who had been working very long hours for many weeks to try to figure out the answer to this puzzle. Jim started to worry that he was in over his head, but he took solace in the fact that all the geniuses in the NSA, FBI, CIA and the other developed world's intelligence agencies had not had any success either.

"I guess that leaves us with Unknown Life Forms and Unknown Unknowns," Jim ventured.

Shilesh took control of the conversation again, "Precisely, Dr. Andrews, and that is why we have brought you onto the team."

Maggie noticed that the conversation had hit a lull, and she announced, "Okay team…let's take a break for an hour to get some lunch. I have ordered food for you in the lounge. Take some time to reflect on the discussion and we will re-group at 2:30 to figure out where we go next. Jim, you will be the moderator for our afternoon discussion. Thank you all. I'm sorry to have to run…I need to hop in an F-16 and head to Washington. I have a meeting with the President at 1:15 and I would like to return to Greenwich for the afternoon meeting." Maggie quickly rose from her chair and exited the room.

Anthony was waiting outside and the pair quickly headed towards the elevator.

Jim looked up at Shilesh who nodded affirmatively, "Yes Jim…she is serious." Jim shook his head in disbelief. Shilesh furthered, "Hey Jim, last night we moved your lab from upstairs down here. Let me show you your new place."

Shilesh was smiling and Jim felt a rush of excitement.

Chapter 18

They entered an elevator and went down two floors. Jim was curious and asked, "So how many floors does this place have?"

"Only 6 Jim…there are 2 above ground, where you were working until yesterday, then 2 floors of living space and 2 more of labs and offices. You, Jeanine and I will share a lab on the lowest floor. I'm sure you don't care about this stuff, but you're protected from nuclear bombs, earthquakes and nearly everything else you can imagine." Shilesh bragged.

"Except for Unknown Life Forms and Unknown Unknowns, right?" Jim jabbed.

"That's true Jim, except for those."

The elevator door opened to the -4th floor where Jim and Shilesh entered Lab #2A. "This is going to be our little home for a while Jim."

Jim's portion of the lab was identical to the room he had established upstairs. Even his lab staff had moved, and they waved and got out of their desks to come greet him. "Welcome aboard Doctor Andrews" was the general refrain. Jim was astounded, and embarrassed, that he was the only person upstairs who believed that he was working for a telecommunications company, and joked aloud, "Oh my god…you are all G-Men?" The lab team smiled and gave Jim a hearty round of applause.

In addition to the lab that Jim had specified, there were banks of computer workstations, conference rooms and electronic devices of all types and sizes. There was even a section filled with lab mice and chemistry tubes, pipes and microscopes. The lab looked like a Mad Professor's den, but on steroids. Jim's eyes opened wide as he inspected the operation. He felt warm and proud to be on the team. Jim thought he had the dream job at Audacity Frontier, but now he really had arrived into the state-of-the-art. He was deep in the heart of the super-classified NSA and he really liked it. He sat down at his desk and looked through some research papers that Maggie had placed for his reading. As Jim was getting familiar with the research reports, Li interrupted, "Doctor Andrews, I know you are just getting acclimated to all of this, but please let me know if there are any guidelines you would like to give me so that we can begin working with you."

"Thanks Li," he replied courteously, "I think it is going to take me a while to dig into these papers. Maybe you can put together a cheat sheet on everything that we do know about this mysterious bandwidth onslaught."

"Sure thing Doctor," Li replied and headed back to her group.

About an hour later, Shilesh approached Jim, "knock knock," he said, "Let's get upstairs. I heard that Ms. Maggie has arrived."

They walked towards the life sciences section of the Lab where Jeanine was speaking with a group of analysts. She noticed their approach and broke away from the group. As she joined the other two men, Jeanine explained, "We're running a forecast to see how many waves it might take before this virus begins to seriously mutate."

Jim looked askance, and Jeanine explained, "You know these viruses have a nasty habit of mutating and that sometimes these mutations can be deadly. You've heard of the bubonic plague, right?"

"Sure," Jim gulped.

The three scientists returned to the conference room to see Maggie and Anthony talking. Maggie had returned to wearing her wireless headset so that she could singlehandedly control the entire planet, Jim mused. Anthony greeted the team, and then left the conference room. Maggie gestured with her hand for the team to enter and they followed in, taking the same seats where they sat in the prior meeting. "Oh, no, Shilesh you and Jim need to change places." Maggie corrected, "He's our moderator for the afternoon."

Shilesh handed the remote control to Jim as they changed seats. "I won't have much use for this right now Shilesh. In fact, I'm not sure I will ever figure out how to work it." Jim smiled as he slid the remote into the center of the table. He sat down and faced the group.

Maggie looked at Jim and explained, "I hope you got a chance to look at the reports I had Li give you?"

"Yes," Jim replied, "I started to go through them, but not all of us are speed-reading photographic memory geniuses, Maggie. I think it might take me a while to digest." He laughed.

Maggie smiled and lowered her head in embarrassment while she commented, "Right…um…okay, so tell us Jim, where's your mind at?"

"I think I have more questions than answers guys." Jim apologized, and continued, "I have asked Li to compile everything that we do know about this bandwidth problem. She is still going through the data. Meanwhile, let's dig a little more into the foreign intelligence scenario."

Maggie looked up from her notes and explained, "We use customized versions of a lot of commercial software packages to help us analyze data. Since we run everything inside of the private DARPA net, we have to create a parallel infrastructure for things that you take for granted on the Public Internet. For example, you use Gmail or hotmail, but we can't do that. It's not even encrypted. In fact, anyone with half a brain and devious intentions could read your emails without working too hard. We had to deploy our own private mail service, with encryption on each mailbox. Since we've done this, any emails that people send to us or that we want to send outside need to pass through a series of filters and masks. Search engines are another example. You just go to Google or Yahoo, but we had to create our own search engine to index everything on DARPA net. We started with Google's software, but the software teams customized it. It's an internal joke, but we named it Giggle, and we don't have any dot.coms here. Our world wide web is restricted, so we don't really need extensions like dot com, dot gov or dot org. All of our internal sites are the same suffix dot.dar. The list goes on and on, we have our own version of facebook and Wikipedia. Of course, Jake already spilled the beans that we invented Facebook and Skype – and we even got our hands involved in Twitter - so it shouldn't really be surprising that we have our own specialized versions of those."

"More importantly, the heart of our infrastructure is an inter-relational database, something that has never been released to the public. It's inter-relational because we have artificial intelligence robots constantly indexing and searching for patterns in our data as well as the rest of the Internet. We crunch through terabytes of data each day, constantly looking for correlations that humans would not ordinarily see. An example is the way in which we compared the H1N1 flu dynamics to the bandwidth deluge. A long time ago we coined the effort Total Information Awareness, but when the press found out about it, Congress freaked out. So, now we don't name it anything, but the program was never stopped."

Maggie continued, "Okay…now back to our analysis of bad guys. We took all of the data that the CIA had ever prepared on every foreign intelligence agency since the 1950s and we evaluated the database for non-linear associations which would suggest technological warfare or misbehavior."

"As you recall from Shilesh's slides, the base scenario was that a country who had never created their own private DARPA net decided to create a secret channel within the Public Internet and keep it all to themselves. You see, we had the advantage of setting up DARPA net before the Public Internet was created, so it was easy for us to monitor it, tap into it, to…to control it. If the foreign spy agency scenario were true, then we would expect to see some kind of traffic inside of the compromised bandwidth – even if our adversaries had invented a new encryption algorithm, they cannot hide bits and bytes, Jim. We looked at the traffic and there seemed to be no data inside the bandwidth. It doesn't make sense." Jim was taking notes as Maggie was explaining. She stood up from the table and used the remote control to launch the world graphic.

The team put on their 3D glasses, and Maggie continued, "We were not satisfied that the data was missing, so we decided to test our test. We figured that if some foreign agency was creating their own Virtual Private Network, then at least we would see an increase in activity in their nodes to the Internet. You see, we know where every single node is located because each one has a unique Internet Protocol address. We did not intend to be control freaks, but remember that the basic building block of computer connectivity is TCP-IP, the Transport Control Protocol / Internet Protocol. It was invented by the NSA and DARPA. Since we had what they call a first mover's advantage, we have always been in a position to know where every node is located; so, naturally, we track them. We look for new nodes and keep an interactive map."

Maggie pressed a button and the 3D world map was illuminated with multi-color pinpoints, each point corresponding to a node on the Internet. It had so many colors that it looked like a set of Christmas tree lights all twisted in a messy pile. She explained the map in detail, "The colors represent the age of the nodes. The red ones are the oldest, the violet are the newest. It's like the rainbow – red, orange, yellow, green, blue, indigo, violet. Got it?" Maggie used her 3D laser pointer to highlight certain areas in Russia as she explained, "See this group of servers? It's Moscow. This is where 90% of the world's computer viruses are released from. The bad part about being a spy is that we know about these viruses before they take hold, but we can't do anything about them because we are afraid to let people know how much we know. Anyway, if there were some devious ploy to hijack the Internet, then we would expect to see a lot of purple dots in Russia, China, or wherever. But what do you see? There's nothing of significance. The only statistically important purple icons are right here in California; and they're a result of Google and Facebook trying to keep up with our bandwidth villain." Maggie's laser pointer followed the geographies as she rattled off the countries. Jim was impressed with her analysis, but frustrated with the conclusions.

"You really have done your homework Maggie," Jim complimented.

"But Jim, we're not getting anywhere. Every leaf we turn over is a dead-end. We have looked up and down this problem and we just cannot see any data inside the bandwidth. Who in the hell wants bandwidth if there is no data going across it?" she asked.

Shilesh piped in, "Someone who is laying the groundwork for a future action."

"You're right Shilesh," Maggie exclaimed, "That's how we get to the next scenario - the terrorist plot."

Jim rubbed his face and turned to a new page in his notebook. He put on his 3D glasses as Maggie continued, "We don't like terrorists. They're crazy and they're hard to predict. Now look, we're not angels, I will admit that. But, our goals are mostly pure. We want to preserve your current way of life, not bring up a new empire. But that's a different story. You see, we hate terrorists because they have no respect for their own lives and they have invested 20 years in propagating ignorance amongst their people. You know the drill, illiterate women, reading is restricted to holy books, promise of a better future life, the list goes on and on. Regrettably, this brainwashing is effective, and over the past few years we have seen relatively more and more educated fundamentalists migrating towards terrorism. When you mix relatively strong intelligence with fanaticism, the results are deadly. That's our second scenario."

"Now, let's assume that a group of educated terrorists have created a sleeper cell to launch a massive Cyber Attack on the U.S. Let's further assume that these goons are distributed globally, are patient, and are in a position to lay the groundwork for major damage. Under this theory, it would make sense that the bandwidth has been hijacked, but left vacant because the bad guys are laying in wait. They are waiting for some event to occur where they can unleash an attack. Think of it like Shilesh said, they're 'laying the ground work.' But here's the rub. It's not easy to do that. You see, first of all it would take a team of pretty experienced engineers and second of all they would have to communicate in some way about what they are doing. We've listed all of our actual and potential persons of interest in our personalized version of Facebook and Wikipedia. We associate all these people to their activities in the Public Web, and our analysts add details and evaluate linkages." Maggie pressed a button and thousands of miniature figures were superimposed on the 3D world map. She used her laser pointer and a three dimensional replica of an Arabic man grew to life size, in perfect photographic detail. Maggie clicked on his head and a series of facts and conversations in hyperlinks appeared next to his image.

Maggie explained, "Here…on the left you have an outline of every single communication that Abdul Yimani has had over the past 12 weeks." Jim remembered that Yimani was the guy sleeping with his wife and he grew jealous.

"We have a set of automated translation tools that index every conversation; then we search them for actual or implied threats. We know that terrorists are sneaky, so we check for code words and story lines."

"What do you mean?" Jim asked.

"Didn't you ever create code words when you were a kid? When I was a teenager we used the Library as a code word for party, then we created all kinds of story lines to elaborate without letting our parents understand what we were saying. You know, something like 'I had a headache from reading too much' was code for I drank too much beer last night."

The people in the room laughed, but Maggie continued, "It may sound easy, but, in computer searching language, trying to superimpose code words is not a trivial undertaking. We have to keep a multilingual semantic database and cross reference words and phrases across all the languages. For example, shit can mean excrement, drugs or trouble…the meaning is contextual, and deriving implied patterns from contextual clues involves serious science."

Maggie turned off the interactive map and raised the lights so people could remove their glasses. Then she continued, "In addition to contextual screening, we work with allegories…you know…stories or common tales which are shared in a cultural setting. People can begin speaking in code through an allegory and then expand their conversation using the story for a baseline. Let me try an example on you. We all know the story of Mary had a little lamb. It's a nursery rhyme that most English speaking children hear. Let's assume we're using Mary to mean spy. I might call Jim and say, Mary has a little lamb and her fleece is white as snow. Now, since we have pre-arranged this conversation, Jim knows that this is a code word which means that he is being tracked by a spy. And he wants to know more about it, so he asks me, "But where do the lambs go?" It's his way of extending the conversation using the allegory. He's asking me if he can find a safe house. In some cases people will use these allegories to go off script, to try to communicate in patterns extemporaneously, and that's where things can get pretty esoteric. But, what we have done is to index every fable and allegory and we have used them as baselines to pick up code words and hidden communication. We've indexed every

Bible story, the Mahabharata, the Vedas, every tale in the Koran, every fairy tale, every proverb and every fable we can get our hands on. In the case of Abdul Yimani, we cross-checked every conversation to our allegorical database to see if they were using code words or references from fables or religion to mask their true intentions. That's how we found out he was using your wife to try to get information about you, Jim. But other than that, as well as finding a few whackos who were planning to blow up some train stations, we did not find anything that would suggest a plot to lay the foundation for a massive cyber attack. Just to put this in perspective, we scanned the cell phone, land-line and email conversations of more than 2 million persons of interest over the past three months. We're 95% certain that our bandwidth villain is not a terrorist plot."

"You keep telling me what you don't know, Maggie. What do we know?" Jim insisted.

Li had entered the room while Maggie was talking and stood to address the group. She spoke in her confident but soft manner, "Doctor Andrews, if I may interrupt, please, I have compiled the data you requested this morning."

"Sure Li," Jim replied, "and please call me Jim."

"Yes sir," Li paused. "We know that the bandwidth consumption is growing. That is important, because it would suggest that there is something inside of it, but that we just can't see it. In other words, data is in there, but it is invisible."

Li stopped talking to let the message sink in, then she continued, "And, we know that the Internet Bandwidth growth preceded the cell phone carrier blockage by a few weeks. That's also important because it helps solve the chicken-egg problem. You see, we know what came first. It was the internet bandwidth disruption. The cell phone disruption was a secondary effect." Li put down her notebook and stared at the people in the room, remaining silent.

"Is there anything else Li?"

"Yes sir," she replied, "we know that this activity has impacted the Public Internet. We know that sites like Gmail and Facebook have suffered, but so have Google earth, twitter and other social networking sites. We know that whatever is causing this disruption is interacting with our data in the public domain, but we have not seen any attempt to penetrate DARPA net. Whatever or whoever is directing this attack does not know we exist. So that's one advantage that we have. We are invisible too."

Jim leaned back and stared at the ceiling as Li's words sunk in. He repeated her last remark over and over in his head. "You're a genius Li"

"What?" asked Maggie.

"You're not Li," Jim joked.

Maggie smiled, and Shilesh popped in, "What's on your mind Jim?"

"We are as invisible to this villain as he, or they…or it is to us. Get it?"

"Clear as mud," Shilesh joked, "Are you trying to become a guru, Jim?"

Jim began humming a Bob Dylan tune as he picked up a piece of paper and crumbled it in a ball. He took aim and threw the ball at Shilesh's head, hitting him squarely on the forehead as he sang, "Yer invisible now, you got no secrets to conceeeal. Awwwww how does it feel?"

Shilesh was shocked but kept his cool and smiled as he wondered, "Okay Jim please explain what's going on."

"I hit you."

"No shit," Shilesh replied, struggling to keep his humor and gentility. "Now tell me something I don't know, Doctor Dylan."

"I hit you because I knew where you were. I could see you. It was easy to spot you. If I can see you and you don't want me to know something, you have to conceal it, or hide it. But if you're invisible, you have nothing to worry about. Work with me here...Imagine if Maggie had used her fancy remote control and turned all the lights out. Imagine how much more difficulty I would have had in nailing you with my paper ball."

"I see," Shilesh responded.

"Why yes you do," Jim joked, "You do indeed...and when you can see something, it's easy to feel it, to hit it, to investigate it and to do all those other fancy things that Maggie explained to us today. But goddamn it, first you need to see it!" Jim yelled and hit his pencil point into the granite, inadvertently causing small bits of pencil lead to explode and launch from the point of impact.

He furthered, "Li explained that we are invisible to this terrorist, or nutcase, or whatever it is. But we all know we're here. It's just that this person or thing can't see us. We're hard to pin down. Our adversary is the same way folks."

Maggie countered, "Jim we have looked at the bandwidth for every sign of encryption and have not found anything. We're sure that the bandwidth is empty."

"Of course you are Maggie," Shilesh interrupted, "Jim is explaining that our problem is that we're like the blind men describing an elephant."

Maggie laughed, "Please give us some background Shilesh."

"It's an ancient Indian tale which goes something like this. Four blind men came to an elephant. Somebody told them that it was an elephant and they were curious. The blind men asked, 'What is the elephant like?' and they began to touch its body. One of them said, 'It is like a pillar.' because he had touched its leg. Another man said, 'No, it is like a basket.' because he had touched its ears. Similarly, the men who touched the trunk and belly had different descriptions. In our culture, we understand this tale to mean that a person who has seen something in a particular way limits his perception."

"Exactly," Jim exclaimed, "Maggie…you're sure that the bandwidth is empty because you are looking for traditional data, encrypted at best. When you explained your research to me, you were very precise. You said even if our adversaries had invented a new encryption algorithm, they cannot hide bits and bytes."

"That's right Jim, it's basic computer science," Maggie countered.

"It is," Jim retorted, "You're absolutely right. In fact I have spent most of my life designing programs to compress and de-compress bits and bytes. But a few weeks ago, our friend Shilesh opened my eyes to a totally new world, and I'm not referring to this bomb-proof underground bunker. Shilesh, perhaps you can tell us a little more about microbytes because I think we are going to have to look deeper into our seemingly empty bandwidth."

"Good Lord, Jim!" Shilesh explained, "We've only postulated their theoretical existence."

The room grew silent as Shilesh stood and began pacing rapidly in the conference room. His mind was clearly moving a mile a minute as he stuttered and mumbled. He began writing notes on his pad, and then stood up to address the room. He explained, "To be honest, this was a pet project of mine a few years ago. I only brought it up to you, Jim, because I was trying to test you to see if you would ask me to clarify an unfamiliar term. You see, many people assume that if they ask about a term they do not understand, then people will think they are stupid. But, such behavior is nothing other than a sure-fire recipe for remaining ignorant. So, we test people about arcane topics to see if they take the bait; which you did, which was good. It showed that you never stop learning. But damn it Jim, now you've turned this whole project on its head. Of course! It really could happen! Oh my God, Oh my God…um…Li, can you help me put some material together? We're going to need a few hours, let's re-group at around 10:00pm."

Li and Shilesh left the room. Jim looked at his watch - it was 5:30pm. Maggie announced, "Great work team. I like the direction this is taking. Let's dig into it quickly though, I'm concerned that we don't have much time."

Maggie's tone was ominous, and Jeanine and Jim stared at each other with mutually worried expressions. Maggie continued, "Look Jim and Jeanine, I'm sorry to run out on you right now, but I need to update our briefing materials and we've got a major denial of service attack going on at the White House. It's the third attempt this week. We think the Chinese are pissed off at our trade actions. I'll leave you two here and we'll catch up at 10:00pm." Maggie pulled together her papers and left the conference room.

"Is it always like this?" Jim asked.

"Yup," Jeanine quipped, "That's why I'm aging so fast down here." She flashed a warm, gentle, tired smile.

Chapter 19

Jim felt the tension in the mood, and observed the strained silence as the team, well mostly Maggie, waited impatiently for Shilesh and Li. Maggie glanced at her watch and managed to give the distinct impression, through only the movement of her eyebrows and forehead, that she was more than slightly annoyed at the tardiness. She was the grade school teacher, the worried parent, the librarian, all rolled into a very precise and regimented frame. Jim understood that Maggie was accustomed to getting everything she wanted, and he looked at Jeanine who was busy taking notes. After two or three minutes, which seemed to drag out like an eternity, Li entered the room carrying her laptop and a stack of old notebooks, seemingly overjoyed and refreshed despite the late hour and incredibly long work day. Then came Shilesh, empty-handed and wan. The normally perfect professor's appearance was tilted towards the disheveled side as he sat down at the conference table.

Li unrolled a mat which measured two feet wide and four feet long in the middle of the conference table. Jim suspected that the mat was created from a metal film, and it was textured and matted into a dull black hue, with small reflective crystals. The effect was like a squashed disco ball. Li connected a small plastic wire that protruded from the mat into to a USB port on her laptop. The device was a projector which displayed a three dimensional hologram in the center of the table, no 3-D glasses required. Maggie commented, "That's the one I was telling you about. Pretty slick, huh?" Jim nodded in amazement. Shilesh began his discussion by projecting a three dimensional model of a rectangle. It looked like a brick, but had been divided into 8 columns and two rows, making 16 boxes and vaguely resembling a row of dominoes. The image extended the length of the conference table and Jim felt like he could reach out and touch the shapes.

"Okay, here we have the lowly byte. Think of it as an amino acid, you know, the building block of life. In our bodies, everything breaks down into amino acids, but in computer science, everything breaks down into bits and bytes. You all know that we use 8 bits to encode a character of text in a computer, and we call that 'group of bits' a byte . That's computer 101."

Li pressed a button on her keyboard and certain cubes illuminated.

"Bits have two states, 'on' and 'off.' I have shown it graphically here by dividing each of the eight columns in half. When the top is green and the bottom is red, my bit is *on*. When it's opposite, the bit is *off*."

Jim looked at the string of lighted cubes; the first was red, two greens, four reds and a green.

Shilesh explained, "Life is rather simplistic down at this level of computer science, isn't it? I'm arranging a sequence of 'on's' and 'off's' to get a code. As you see in our 3D model, I've created a little code for you, the alpha, or 'a' as we say in English. In Greek, alpha refers to the beginning, and that's exactly what we are looking at. For most of the world's basic everyday computers, all I do is pass this code 01100001 to our computer's brain, and it reads the letter 'a.' Think of the computer language as nothing more than thousands of strings of 1's and zeros. Now, for those of you who are more technical, I'm sure you are thinking; and it is true, that we can use 7 digits or 6 or even 4 digits for certain computer applications. But, here in the good old-fashioned Internet, and it is rather old fashioned, we use 8 digits or 'bits.' My mom was frugal. She saved everything and always tried to be as efficient as possible – must have been because she grew up in the Depression. Mom would be horrified at the Internet. You see, eight bits is rather wasteful and it stems back to a simpler time in computing and, I guess, a simpler time in life. But, we're stuck there. There is no escaping our past. There are other examples which you see every day. For example, look at the keyboard on your laptop. The letters have been arranged to make it harder to type faster. Your famous QWERTY keyboard was designed to keep a typewriter from jamming up. Even though it is archaic today, we keep with it, like a bad habit. Think of those 'fat' eight bits loaded into a byte like calories in a donut…but, I'm digressing.

"The computer world was relatively predictable with bits. They turned on and off like a switch. Let's continue with the light bulb analogy – traditionally we turned lights on and off. Imagine how impressive it was when the first dimmer switch was invented. Well, in computer science our simple world came crashing down with the advent of the qubit – (kew bit). The qubit is credited with being dreamt up by two guys, Schumacher and Wooters. They were applying the principles of quantum mechanics to information theory. You see, the qubit was a messy little bit; it was not always 'on' or 'off.' The bugger could be could be half-on, half-off, a little bit on, even double on, double off. Like I said, it was messy. Thanks to the crazy scientists who dreamt up quantum theory, our nice little patterns of 'on' and 'off' were replaced by probability statements, like *most likely on*, or *probably off*, and we started to identify new concepts like vector spaces and tangled bits."

Li hit some keys on her laptop and the cubes that were displayed on the hologram began moving like an animated movie. They became stretched into long, thin columns, and then twisted around each other to end up looking like a jumbled heap of red and green spaghetti.

"You see, in quantum theory we can have all kinds of crazy outcomes. Things can get really noisy, and reducing noise and errors is something you have been working with a lot, Jim. In your research paper, you applied an innovative probability approach into Shannon's Information Theory. You showed how compression and error correction could be more sophisticated, and as a result you helped music fans everywhere enjoy rock-and-roll on small mp3 files. But at the heart of your approach, you have cut out pieces of the sound and let your listener's brains fill in the missing gaps. Although their ears hear the music, it is filled with blank spaces, or errors, which the ears and brain are unable to comprehend. You're tricking listeners into hearing a complete song despite the holes."

Jim grinned, gave Shilesh the thumbs up sign and effortlessly regressed into a teenager's mentality. He raised his fist in the air, bobbed his head, and exclaimed, "Our brains rock dude! They Rock!"

Shilesh smiled and continued, "Yes…uh…sure, as I was about to say, our friends Schumacher and Wooters came about compression from a different viewpoint, they came at it from a quantum point of view, where uncertainty reigns. Their approach resulted in 'quantum compression' or what we affectionately call *Schumacher Compression* in the field. Basically Schumacher chopped up the information into something they termed a qubit and stored it in a bunch of smaller orbs. Not too different from your approach, except for an important point. You see, since Schumacher was not dealing in a world of absolutes, he did not have to drop out any information. Why not? Well, in Schumacher's quantum world, the music was never precisely correct in the first place. So, he did not need to rely on explicit error correction like you did Jim, and in doing this, he created a new field. Benjamin Schumacher was the quantum equivalent of Pink Floyd. As Jim will most certainly tell you, ladies and gentlemen, Pink Floyd's 1968 album *The Dark Side of the Moon* was one of the first high fidelity recordings. Benjamin Schumacher wanted the equivalent of hi-fidelity sound in his non-linear, probabilistic world, and he damn near achieved it." Shilesh sat down. Jim nodded his head with respect.

Then Shilesh continued from his seat, "I liked qubits and I liked the Schumacher compression algorithm, but it got me thinking. What if there was more to it? What if I could use the quantum theory and do away with the bit completely, you know, replace it with the qubit? What if I could compress things so that the tiny little bit became the big picture instead of just a lowly light switch? It reminded me of the old argument of 'How many angels can dance on the head of a pin?'   Our medieval ancestors were quite emphatic about their views on the size of angels you know. Well, it got me thinking that perhaps our view of bits and bytes was old-fashioned. Maybe a million angels can dance on the head of a bit? Or, to put it in terms that are more relevant to our Internet villain, maybe I can encode entire computer systems inside of a single bit. And hence I dreamed up the term 'microbyte' and became addicted to the field of nanotechnology."

"I knew that microbytes were theoretically possible, but I had never moved beyond the theory. And, as I am sitting with you all today, I think I need to add a new possibility to our list of potential bad guys. Ladies and gentlemen, what if the data inside the bandwidth is invisible because it is coded in microbytes?"

Shilesh sat down and Li turned off the three dimensional hologram. Jim looked up at the team and smiled, "Thanks Shilesh. That was great, but do you really think that the data can be compressed so small?"

"Jim, in the electrical engineering world, it is not so simple to create smaller and smaller machines. But nature has given us a view into something much more elegant and more complex than computer chips. Jim, do you have any idea how much data is encoded on the small DNA strand which lives inside of just one human cell? When I looked at the DNA of a human genome, I become convinced that with enough effort, I could compress my heart, my mind and even my spirit into pure data. And, if I could store it in microbytes, then I could fit all that data into a container the size of a cell."

Jeanine interrupted, "Sounds like germs, they're so small that we cannot see them, but science has undoubtedly proven their existence."

"I'm afraid so," Shilesh continued.

Maggie looked around the table and commented, "Shilesh, what do we have to do to test out your theory? Can you tell me by tomorrow morning?"

Jim, Li, Jeanine and Shilesh looked at each other in disbelief. Shilesh piped in, "Well, uh Maggie, you see, it's a little past midnight and uh…well, technically it's already tomorrow morning and…uh…well…we haven't even begun to design the research."

"Fine," Maggie replied, almost pouting, "so let's get together tomorrow at 3:00pm?" There was that impish smile again. "And don't tell me what time it is. Remember, I don't like crybabies on our team." Maggie's humorous, but demanding response broke the tension in the room. She had a subtle way about her for creating, then diffusing tension - like the matador, inflaming, taming and defeating in graceful moves.

The team of scientists shrugged and then Jim surrendered, "Sure thing boss."

Chapter 20

As they entered their lab, it almost appeared that Jim, Jeanine, Shilesh and Li were going to circle around in a huddle, then yell "Let's go NSA" lift their hands, clap and break into formation. Jim was in his element, he was the quarterback. He parceled out the research tasks in rapid fire. Li was assigned to place a digital sniffer into the mysterious bandwidth and to record a 15 second interval. Meanwhile Shilesh was asked to evaluate the mathematical formulas for converting microbytes back into big bytes. Jeanine was asked to create an overview of epidemic patterns and germ theory. Jim bounced between all the efforts, contributing where he could and absorbing the positive energy. The researchers were aware that they were embarking on new scientific ground, and they knew that they couldn't mess it up. As Jim and Shilesh were discussing theoretical bridges between quantum theory and traditional computer science, Li arrived with news. "I've done it. I've grabbed a recording of the bandwidth."

Shilesh handed a few sheets of paper to Li and explained, "Nice work Li, try to see if your team can program up this calculation. I know it's a little funky, but I'm sure you'll fix my math errors." Shilesh smiled at Li.

"Yes sir," Li replied, "You're math is not usually too bad."

Shilesh and Jim returned to their discussions and were reviewing research papers while debating and taking notes on a whiteboard. Their discussion dragged into and beyond the night. At some point, they rested their heads on the table and dozed off, only to be awoken at 7:00am by Li, who was filled with excitement as she reported, "Doctor Andrews, Doctor Gupta...wake up! We've got it! You were right! While you two have been sleeping, we were able to implement that program. Well, sort of...uh...we did have to fix your math substantially, sir, but you were right! There is something inside of that apparently empty space! Doctor Gupta, I think that you have created the world's first nanoscope."

Shilesh paused, "a what?"

"A nanoscope," replied Li. "We used your program to listen to apparently empty space in the bandwidth that I recorded and we found that it was filled with data. And not just a little bit of data, but tons and tons of it sir! We called your program a nanoscope because it gave us a view into nano-sized data elements, like a microscope, but on a much smaller scale. We still cannot tell what's in the data, because the nanoscope keeps crashing the computers.

"It seems that the amount of data is so huge that we cannot process it. I have reduced the recording down to a one second interval and still the amount of data is so great that it crashed the supercomputer at Livermore Labs. You really must come see it." Shilesh and Jim stared at each other in disbelief and ran towards Li's work team. The scientists were busy typing into their laptops and a couple of analysts were speaking on the secure telephone lines, apparently requesting more supercomputer capacity. Li brought up a line graph on her laptop that showed an upward sloping line which went off the charts upwards and she explained, "this is the capacity monitor for our supercomputer at Livermore Labs. You know that it is the most powerful computer on earth. It was designed for Star Wars calculations. You know, when Reagan wanted to intercept missiles in outer space. Anyway, we ran a one second clip of the bandwidth through your nanoscope. It is sort of like playing a tiny song on an iPod. But this graph shows the amount of data that was present in that one-second interval. It crashed the computer. It crashed a really, really big computer! There were 10 petaFLOPS of processing power and 300 terabytes available and it still crashed."

Jim looked at Shilesh, who returned the glance and asked, "Li, what in the world is a petaFLOP?"

Li smiled and replied, "Yes, sorry, got a little carried away there. FLOPS are floating operations per second. We use the term to describe a measure of computer performance. A petaFLOP is a big number. It is 10^{15} calculations per second." She typed on her computer the following number: 1, 000,000,000,000,000 and then continued, "in other words a petaFLOP is one quadrillion in Latin terms. It's even bigger than the US debt! And, we can handle 10 of them each second on our supercomputer."

Jim exclaimed, "That's a real super computer!" The joke fell flat.

Li grimaced and continued, "On the data side, a terabyte is also huge. 'Tera' comes from the Greek word for *monster*, and as you can see, a terabyte is a pretty monstrous number. Here, look!"

Li pointed to her computer screen and the following number was displayed 1,099,511,627,776. She explained, "It is a little more than one quadrillion bytes, give or take a hundred billion. And we had over 300 of those available, but as you see on this graph, we maxed out. There was just too much data! Our next step is to break our one second interval into a hundredth of a second to see if we can analyze it with the nanoscope without crashing the Lawrence Livermore Labs computer infrastructure. And as a backup, some of my guys are on the phone with the White House to see if we can get some additional capacity from Japan, Israel and the UK.

Jim's mind was spinning as he contemplated what he had just heard. It seemed impossible. Who? Or what could possibly consume that much data? What would they do with it?

Chapter 21

The door to Jim's suite seemed heavy, and the room was dark. His exhaustion was severe, and Jim felt like he was shoved towards his bed, falling against the mattress. Although it was disorienting at first, he thought he saw Maggie standing over him, glaring like a predator. She quickly pounced on top of Jim, placing her legs on each side of his hips and resting her hands on his shoulders. Jim could feel the warmth of Maggie's body and he tried to move her body towards his side, but she had strength, and her talons tightened around Jim's shoulders. He was amazed that she could trap him without effort, and she spoke in a sultry voice, "Not this time lover boy." Maggie insisted with authority, "Tonight I'm in charge." Jim saw fire and he understood that struggling was pointless. He knew that she needed desperately to be in charge on this occasion, and he gave in to her dominance.

Maggie grabbed Jim by the hair and pulled his head to the side as she bit his neck like a vampire. When she had eaten his neck, she moved her wet mouth towards Jim's lips and penetrated his tentative kiss with her tongue. He felt like a piece of driftwood swept into the ocean's tides, helpless and dependent as Maggie ebbed and flowed with a passion stronger than a thousand lovers. When Maggie's storm had receded, Jim was shipwrecked on the bed. He was vacant and exposed from Maggie's torment, but he rested with peaceful tranquility. Maggie seemed to be draped over Jim's body, her head resting on his chest and an arm over his body so she could embrace him fully. He smelled the scent of her perfume and looked for words to capture the moment. She pulled close to his body and looked pensively at Jim's face in the dark room, and for a moment, Jim thought he was laying with his ex-wife, Sally. Jim put his hand on the woman's cheek, holding her as he questioned, "Do you mind telling me what that was all about?" She gently kissed Jim on the end of his nose, then winked, got up, and seemed to float towards the Asian Spa bathroom. He was in the midst of a deep sleep.

At two o'clock, Jimmy, John, John Paul Jones and Robert Plant began to supplement Jim's riotous morning with "Whole Lotta Love." Was he dreaming? Was that real? Jim was unsure of his memories, but stopped to recognize that the song was particularly apropos. Had the music inspired him to dream of being so aggressively laid by a woman? Or, did she really enter his room like a thief and assault his senses? Jim laughed to himself as he re-lived the passionate episode in his mind, tentatively concluding that he never had, and probably never again would be treated so abruptly and physically by a lover. Whether it occurred in the waking world or the dream world was not relevant. The tryst was a once-in-a-lifetime event. "No-one could have a lover like that," he chuckled to himself, "no work would ever get done." Jim headed towards the Asian Spa bathroom and got ready for his afternoon session.

Jim was the last person to arrive in the conference room. Li was excitedly pointing towards her laptop as Shilesh, Jeanine and Maggie looked on. At first he was relieved not to see Maggie chastising his tardiness by staring at her watch and tapping her pencil expectantly on the granite table-top. But his relief gave way to curiosity, and he captured Li's attention. She smiled warmly and exclaimed, "We did it Jim! We were able to get a glimpse of the data." Li gushed with excitement, "And you're not going to believe it. It's …It's… it's remarkable. We still don't fully understand how it could possibly have been achieved, but it's a miracle."

Li beamed with joy, and Shilesh continued, "I think you had better come here Jim. You won't believe your eyes."

Jim approached the laptop and glanced at the screen. There was a listing of people, with small thumbnail images followed by a last name, first name and address. It looked like a standard Internet directory of people. "What's the rub?" Jim asked.

Li looked at Jim and elaborated, "This is the person view. It appears to be an alphabetical listing with a picture and address of everyone on any social networking site, anywhere in the world, like a giant facebook. When I click on the icon, I get a listing of dates and times, and each link takes me to a video with full sound. But here's the weird thing. The orientation of the camera makes it look as if we are seeing and hearing from the person's point of view. It's like their eyes and ears are doing the recording. It is also weird that we don't have movies for everyone, and they don't all seem to start at the same time. But it just keeps getting better and better. Here, look at this."

Li plugged in the 3D projector and Jim was greeted by the 3D world map, with seemingly hundreds of millions of small dots. Then she explained, "Each dot is a person, Jim, and we have discovered that this is indexed to Google earth, so we can drill down to the exact coordinates for the location where each of the episodes is recorded. We can see precisely where the person was when they recorded the movie."

Jim looked at the screen as Li was explaining the data, then he asked, "You said that this is the person's view. What else is in this data?"

Li clicked on a hyperlink which brought up a screen that read NSA Wikipedia. She spoke, "We were able to dig into this data with our knowledge database tools. Basically, we have a snapshot of the entire Internet every 5 seconds, fully indexed into subjects, topics and themes; and then ordered into time slices. It's pretty amazing. Imagine if you wanted to go back in time and see what the Internet looked like at 2:00 pm on August 4th – *poof* - there it is. You see, the content is not only indexed by subject matter tags Jim, it is ordered by time. That's why the data was so huge." Jim rubbed his face in amazement and Li expanded, "Jim, we are seeing an historical archive, indexed by time, of almost everything on earth. We see it from different perspectives, both human and electronic, and from space as well as the ground."

Jim sat down and looked at the research team. He was frozen in the moment as his mind raced errantly around the topic he had just seen. He cautioned, "We are looking into the eyes of God, aren't we?"

Shilesh glanced at Jim and inquired, "What do mean Jim?"

"What I mean is that we are looking at some data which suggests that someone, or some*thing*, is trying to achieve an omniscient and omnipresent knowledge base. Jesus Christ! We are looking into God's mind!" Jim shouted. The room grew silent. Maggie, Jeanine, Li and Shilesh stepped back from the laptop and took their places at the conference table.

Li corrected Jim, "Well actually it is not omnipresent yet because we only seem to have random time slices of people's visual and audio recordings."

"Godammit Li! We are looking through their eyes and hearing through their ears. How in the hell do you explain that? And does it really matter if this 'movie' as you call it is only appearing a few times a day?"

Li grew strong in the face of Jim's criticism and countered, "Doctor Andrews. This really is a tremendous event. And I agree that it can be hard to accept. But, let me be clear about a couple of things here. First, we are not able to see everyone in the world. It appears that there are only listings for people who have signed up for social networking sites, like facebook. And second, the frequency and duration of the movies appears to be random. Furthermore, the knowledge base is limited to everything on the Internet. If something is not on the Internet, it is not indexed into our Wikipedia."

Jim mockingly reproached, "Oh, I feel much better now that I know this thing is only tracking *some* people and only indexing everything on the *Internet*. Thank God! And tell me this, Li. If this monster has only been recording and indexing, that is to say, if it has only been alive for, what, three months, then tell me just how much stronger will it be in three *years*?"

Shilesh seemed irritated, but he calmly addressed the room, "Now, I know this is quite a bombshell. And I have to hand it to you and your team, Li, you really went over and above the call of duty on this one. But let's not go overboard with religious comparisons. The definition of God is pretty serious stuff, and while this indeed is a tremendous amount of information, I am not sure it would qualify as divine."

Jim countered, "Shilesh, I hear where you're coming from, but let me remind you that there are already a group of people who are convinced that Google is God. They have launched a religion called Googlism."

Shilesh grinned at Jim and asked, "What on earth are you talking about Jim?" Jim went to Li's laptop and typed in a url which read:

www.thechurchofgoogle.org/Scripture/Proof_Google_Is_God.html

A list of the following text appeared

PROOF #1 - *Google is the closest thing to an all-knowing entity which can be scientifically verified.*

PROOF #2 - *Google is everywhere at once*

PROOF #3 - *Google answers prayers.* *pray to Google by doing a search.*

PROOF #4 - *Google is potentially immortal.* *It is not a physical being.*

PROOF #5 - *Google is infinite.* *The Internet can theoretically grow forever.*

PROOF #6 - *Google remembers all.* *WebPages are stored on massive servers.*

PROOF #7 - *Google can "do no evil".*

PROOF #8 - *God is thought to be an entity in which we can turn to when in a time of need. The term "Google" is searched for more than the terms "God", "Jesus", "Allah", "Buddha", "Christianity", "Islam", "Buddhism" and "Judaism" combined.*

PROOF #9 - *Evidence of Google's existence is abundant.*

Shilesh read the text and exclaimed, "You can't be serious Jim?"

Jim looked at the team and said, "Does it really matter if I am serious? Look, I don't care if Google is God or not. I am not a priest or a rabbi or a prophet. I am a computer scientist! My point is that someone, or something, is indexing the entire Internet and it is also tracking individuals in an intimate setting. I can't explain it, and neither can any of you. This is not a question of divinity Shilesh." Jim collapsed into his chair and bemoaned, "I'm sorry, what's really got me concerned is that we are back to square one on this mess."

"What do you mean Jim?" Maggie peacefully countered, "Thanks to this team we have uncovered a wealth of information. We have discovered that data can be stored in microbytes. Jim, because of this team, we now know why the Internet bandwidth has been deluged!"

Jim glanced up at Maggie and corrected her, "Maggie, Let's not forget how we all got into this room. Yes! We know that someone or something has become a super spy. We know that they're taking snapshots of the entire Internet every 5 minutes and we know that they are somehow tapping into the eyes and ears of some, but not everyone. That much we know. But look at what we do not know. We do not know who it is. Or why they are doing it. And we have no idea why the cell phone carriers are suffering the same fate.   So, to be quite honest Maggie, we don't know a damn thing.   The only thing that I am sure about is that we are not going to like the answer when we find it out."

Li contradicted Jim. "Doctor Andrews, it was your idea to start looking for things that we knew. You pulled us out of our rut of getting lost in what we did not know. That's how we made these breakthroughs."

Jim stared at Li and saw her earnest and compassionate face. Li was right and he apologized, "I'm sorry guys. I guess I didn't get much sleep last night." Out of the corner of his eye, Jim was sure that he saw a seductive grin on Maggie's face, but he put it out of his mind and continued, "Looks like we have an ongoing mystery, Shilesh, you started us down this track, what's next?"

"We need to connect more dots team. We need to connect more dots." Shilesh paused and began typing into his laptop. The following words appeared on the LCD screen in the front of the room:

- What's the relevance of the cell carrier blockage?
- How and why did this maniac break into the eyes and ears of some people, but not others?
- Who or what is behind this?
- What do they want? (important)

Then he continued, "Jim, you focus on the first point. Jeanine, I want you to dig into the second point. I will re-visit the scenarios to elaborate on the third and fourth. Li, I think you should try to put your nanoscope on the cell phone spectrum. I have a strange suspicion that you will find more microbytes. If I'm right, you will need to decode those signals too."

"What should I do coach?" Maggie inquired.

"Maggie," Shilesh explained, "you better get back on your F16 and go explain this mess to the President."

Anthony came to the door and interrupted, "Maggie, can I see you for a minute, it's urgent." Maggie rose from her chair and left the room. Li and Jeanine began to review the data on the laptop and Jim looked at Shilesh quizzically and asked, "Any suggestions on how I can break the mysterious cell phone traffic deluge besides pointing the nanoscope on it?"

Shilesh replied with his fatherly, professorial smile, "Not right now, Jim."

Jeanine and Li began to collect their notebooks to head back to the lab. As they stood to leave, Maggie re-entered the room and interrupted, "Jim, I think we need to talk. Sally's dead."

Chapter 22

The blood drained from Jim's face as he received the news. Shilesh put his hand on Jim's shoulder as Maggie approached him, "I'm really sorry Jim. We just found out. It happened a few hours ago. I have arranged for one of our private jets to take you out to California. Anthony will go along with you. Jim, I'm really, really sorry."

Jim could see Maggie's eyes glisten, and he felt tears well up in his own eyes. He felt a sense of emptiness and guilt as the reality sunk in. Maggie put her hand on Jim's other shoulder and explained, "I will be in DC for a few hours, then I will try to join you in California, Jim. Anthony will take good care of you and he will brief you on the details during the flight." Maggie held a glance at Jim. The sadness and concern in her eyes was apparent as she slowly turned and left the room.

Shilesh shared his condolences and awkwardly left the room, leaving Anthony and Jim standing alone. Anthony explained, "Doctor Andrews. I'm really beat up about this. I feel terrible, but I can't imagine what you're going through right now. Look, I've arranged for your bag to be packed. Let me take you to the airport so we can head out as quickly as possible."

Jim felt empty and void. He agreed with Anthony and they headed towards the elevator. As they exited the fortress, Jim noticed that the Audacity Frontier signs and logos had been removed and that the lobby was vacant, except for two security guards holding automatic rifles at the front door. Jim and Anthony stepped into the chilly November sunlight, got into the Range Rover and raced to the Westchester County airport. The half-hour trip was compressed to a fifteen minute drive with Anthony behind the wheel. He had affixed a silent siren on the dashboard and he was cruising at about 100 miles per hour in the truck. Jim felt like he was being escorted in an ambulance, racing to an accident scene, and he felt sick to his stomach from grief and motion sickness combined. Anthony was talking on the radio, announcing their arrival and preparing the airport for Jim's departure. They raced into the airport driveway, passing the security guards and driving directly onto the runway as gates were opened and guards stood by. Jim and Anthony fled from the Range Rover and boarded a Learjet 45, which was waiting on the tarmac. A somber-looking pilot greeted them as they boarded the plane, and the door was closed. The plane immediately began its taxi and was airborne within 2 minutes.

Jim and Anthony were resting on the airplane's couches, facing each other. "Do you guys always travel this way?" Jim joked.

"No, Doctor Andrews, this is only for VIPs."

"So my wife dies and I become a VIP, huh?"

"Doctor Andrews, I am really sorry about Sally."

"Me too…even though she ditched me, I never really got to say good-bye." Jim held his head in his hands and remained still.

Anthony got up from the couch and headed towards the cockpit. As he was walking he explained, "I will be back in a few minutes Doctor Andrews. Please relax if you can; the flight will take about 5 hours. There is a bar and some snacks in the back of the plane, and the bathroom is over there." Anthony pointed to a door towards the back of the plane.

Jim was left alone in the main cabin. He looked around the plane and noticed it was finely appointed and could have easily accommodated 4 or 5 people. He remembered Sally and looked back on his life in California. It had all happened so fast. One day he woke up and she was gone, the next day he was working in a spy agency. Jim second-guessed his actions. He felt guilty for leaving. He felt angry at Sally. He was even angry at Maggie for bringing him to New York and for asking him to leave his screwed up life in California. Jim was angry at everyone except for himself; yes, the blame was easy to place on others. But Jim had nothing now, and he sought continuity. Up until that point, loneliness had never mattered. For Jim, loneliness was absorbed by distractions, mostly research. By the time his parents died, Jim had fallen for Sally, and she filled the vacancy. And, even though she had left him for another guy, Jim always knew, or at least he thought that he knew, that if he really needed to get back into touch with her, then he could get Sally back. He had no one else. And besides, the separation seemed so sudden. He had subconsciously convinced himself that Sally's departure was just a temporary blip. She needed to get some dissatisfaction out of her system, but she would eventually come back, as would he. Maybe, yes eventually, they would be reunited, but not now; no, not now, not ever.

The detached, sarcastic loner realized that he would now have the burden of true solitude mercilessly forced upon him by Sally's death. And, while speeding across the United States at 30,000 feet in a Learjet, Dr. Jim Andrews concluded that his dog Lily was the only remaining link to his past.

"I'm coming baby, Daddy's coming," he whimpered. Jim lay down and drifted to sleep.

Chapter 23

The plane touched down at L.A. airport and Jim was awoken by the jolt of wheels hitting the runway. He rubbed the sleep from his eyes and saw Anthony waking up on the adjoining couch. "Hey, that wasn't so bad," Jim explained. "No Doctor Andrews," Anthony replied, "But I do need to give you a briefing on the events surrounding Sally's death."

"Go ahead Anthony, let me have it."

Anthony spoke as they gathered their belongings to prepare to deboard the plane, "Jim, Sally was murdered. I'm sorry to be so abrupt, but we're sure about it. You know that she was running around with this guy Yimani, right?"

"Yeah," Jim replied, "Maggie mentioned it to me."

"Well, Abdul Yimani was a bad guy...a real bad guy. But the strange thing is that he is also dead." Anthony and Jim descended the steps to the plane and entered an identical Range Rover to the one they drove in Connecticut. Jim asked, "What...do you guys get a package deal on these cars?"

"Drug bust," Anthony explained, "The government gets to keep the booty from drug lords."

As they sped off towards L.A., Anthony furthered, "Okay, I'm heading over to the morgue so that we can identify the body. It's a legal thing. Then, we will head back to your house in case you want to close up the place. When Sally died, we sent your dog back to that kennel in the city. The lady there said she would look after him as long as needed."

"It's a *her*, Anthony," Jim corrected, "and her name is Lily, and I want to pick her up, okay?"

Anthony nodded, "We've had stranger requests, uh...sure. Oh, and I need to finish the story. Okay, I know this is hard to hear, but you need to know. You see, Sally and Abdul were driving on the Interstate when they collided with an oncoming van. We have surveillance of the incident because we were tailing her, but that's not important right now. What's important is that we saw the dude in the van swerve into their car. He was a suicide driver. We're 100% sure. But we still don't know why he did it. You see, Abdul was one of them. He was a freakin' Islamic terrorist. Why would they go after their own guy?" Anthony asked rhetorically.

Jim paused as he reflected on the story and asked, "You're sure Abdul was one of them?"

"No doubt, Doctor Andrews...Abdul Yimani was trying to get into your business. He was a professional spy. We have an inch thick file on him. He was a pro. He knew all the buttons to push on someone to get them to trust him and to follow him. The guy was a manipulative genius. He could seduce a librarian, Jim. The truth is...Sally didn't stand a chance. If she stayed with you and rejected Yimani, then *we* would have recruited Sally."

Jim was uneasy as he heard Anthony's explanation. He was angry that Sally had left him, but to hear it from Anthony, it seemed like Sally might still have loved Jim. He felt guilty, and lonely, and mad.

"Anthony, this is really hard for me. What am I doing in California? My wife is dead. I don't know what I can do here."

"Doctor Andrews, I have never lost a loved one. My Mom and Dad are still alive and living happily in Annapolis. I have no brothers and sisters and my school sweetheart found another guy a couple of years ago. The only relationship I have right now is with the NSA. We're all loners here. It can be depressing, but we love the work...we have to, it's all we have. Your wife may have left you. She may have abandoned you and left you for another guy. But Sir, she must have loved you at some point. And once you love someone, no one can take that away. I can't bring Sally back to you. I wish I could. I wish I could say or do something to change this entire situation, but I can't. I feel powerless about it. But my orders are to help you get to closure here, Sir. I don't know what that means or what it takes, but I will do it."

Jim looked at Anthony and was impressed with the honesty and candor in his response. He replied, "Anthony, you're a fine soldier. You made a good impression on me the first time I met you, and it has only gotten better as I get to know you more. This really is a messed up situation. I'm devastated and I know that my life will never be the same. But, I'm not depressed or sad any more – I'm just empty. I loved Sally, but I was always married to my work. I guess you and I are kindred spirits in that way. It's hard to lose someone, but I lost Sally a long time ago to science, and then I lost her to Abdul. She's in a better place now, and I can't go get her. You know what they say, 'til death do us part."

Anthony exhaled and stared at the road, "Doctor Andrews, you're a tough-minded, stone cold scientist, aren't you?" and laughed in disbelief.

Jim smiled as he tried to gather his emotions and replied, "I wasn't always like this, Anthony. But I have seen some things in the past couple of days which have given me a new perspective on this life. I feel like I am being called to serve a higher purpose than myself right now. I can't explain it…it's like a vocational calling. Don't get me wrong, I'm completely devastated that Sally is gone. I'm pissed off and feeling guilty for leaving and I'm not sure what to do next. But I know that I need to get this chapter of my life closed out right now. Let's get things wrapped up as quickly as we can. Now that Sally is dead, the only thing in California that I care about is my dog, and I'm bringing her back to New York."

"Yes Sir, Doctor."

They pulled into the County morgue and parked the car in the visitor's spot. Anthony looked at Jim as they walked up towards the door of the building and questioned, "Doctor Andrews, are you sure you're alright?"

Jim was ashen and distraught. "Let's just get this done Anthony."

The coroner visit brought home to Jim the finality of his separation from Sally. Jim cried when he saw her motionless body, marred from the automobile accident and lifeless on the metal tray. He felt like a piece of his life was stolen from him, and he nearly collapsed onto the floor. Jim touched Sally's face, holding her cheek in his hand as tears fell down his own face. Jim bent down and gently kissed the end of Sally's nose. He was sobbing as he acknowledged to the medical examiners and provided the positive identification.

"Good God," Jim gasped. "You're never coming back, are you?" he asked vacantly into the distance and mumbled, "She has no family, no relatives, no one. I am the only link between Sally and this earth, and now that she's gone, she's just gone. There's nothing here. Oh my God, my Sally is dead."

The medical examiner pulled a sheet back over Sally's face and pushed the drawer back into place. It looked like a file cabinet, and Jim was relieved as the drawer shut, concealing Sally's distorted features from his view. The medical examiner thanked Jim for his help and offered condolences, but Jim could not really hear anything. Words from the coroner's associate and words from Anthony were echoing as if they were hundreds of feet away. Jim heard only his own breathing and his heart beating rapidly as he began hyperventilating. He slowly turned to exit the medical examiner's room and Anthony held the door open for him. They left the building and entered the outdoor air. Jim noticed that the weather was turning, that there were clouds in the sky, and he commented on the cool weather.

As they entered the Range Rover, Anthony was silent and compassionate in the front seat as Jim looked blankly out from the back window. He started the car and let it idle, making every appearance not to rush Jim or prod him anywhere he did not want to go. The radio was playing in the car on low volume and Anthony's NSA DARPA net phone rang. He spoke quietly as Jim collected his thoughts and placed his despair back in a lonely room of his mind, back into a compartment that he could lock up and repress.

When Anthony hung up his phone, he turned back towards Jim and explained, "Doctor Andrews, I have made arrangements to move your dog to a kennel in Greenwich that is nearby the offices. Do you want to stop by your house or the kennel?"

Jim had not thought beyond the moment. He was rapt in his loneliness and loss, not feeling anything except anger at the people who stole and killed his wife. He harbored a deep regret that he gave anyone the chance to prey upon a lonely woman. Jim looked into the rear-view mirror and saw Anthony's eyes. He was concerned and gentle.

"Anthony, this is crazy. I don't know what the hell to do. Let's go over to the house and then stop by to see the dog. And then I want to get the hell out of California. I want to go away and never come back. This place is dead to me. Sally is dead. Jesus, a fucking part of me is dead. This whole goddamned place is dead to me, Anthony. I really need to leave...I need to get the hell out of here."

Anthony backed out of the parking lot and headed towards Jim's house. About 30 minutes after closing Sally's dead body into the large file cabinet at the County morgue, Jim and Anthony pulled into Jim's small driveway. Jim got out of the car and walked towards the front door.

The house was a one story ranch. It was clean on the outside and the neighborhood was nice. Jim's lawn was the most unruly on the street, but Sally had kept the exterior clutter free. There were no lawn statues or bicycles lying around, just some hedges in need of trimming and a front yard in need of fertilizing. Jim felt like a visitor in his own house. As he walked up the flagstone path, he noticed weeds sticking up from the cracks in the slate, and he saw that the screen door on the front was ajar. Anthony explained, "We closed off the house until you came, Jim. There's a local officer watching over the house, he's inside now to speak with you." Jim opened the door and was greeted by a young police officer. They shook hands and Jim looked around at his home. He noticed the signs of another man in his house, unknown clothes, a chair re-arranged, and a clean kitchen. Jim glanced into his office and was reassured. It did not look like his record collection had been disturbed, although he believed that his computer and work-papers had been invaded.

"Can we pack up the office contents for shipping to Greenwich? Otherwise, I'd like to sell the rest of this shit, including the house. I don't care about prices…just get rid of the fucking mess."

Anthony looked down at the floor and evaded Jim's glance. He seemed nervous and tentative. "Doctor Andrews, that's not a problem…but are you sure?"

"Anthony, I'm sure. I don't care if I never set foot in this State again. It's dead to me, don't you get it? It's dead, Sally's dead. This fucking house is dead." As Jim swore, he kicked a garbage pail over and the contents went flying into the den. "I'm sorry," Jim replied, "I'm not good right now."

Jim reached down to get the garbage can, and picked up the papers which had strewn around the room. When he had collected the garbage and placed the can on the floor, back to its original spot, he looked up and asked, "Can we go now? I really can't stand it."

"Sure thing, Doctor Andrews," Anthony replied, "I'll take care of it."

They exited the house quickly, and Jim seemed to ignore the contents and the scenery. He got back in the Range Rover before Anthony could reach to open the back door. Anthony was slightly surprised, but he got in the front seat and looked back towards Jim as he started the car.

"To the kennel?"

"Yes please, Anthony."

Chapter 24

The kennel was in a storefront in town. Next door, on one side was a Laundromat and on the other side was a dry cleaner. The dog kennel took up the space of what used to be 3 stores, so it was a dominant feature on the block. The building was nice, and the kennel was adorned by a large sign with a picture of a cartoon dog, winking his eye in satisfaction and giving a 'thumbs up' with his paw towards the words: *Doggie Day Care*. Jim absorbed the ridiculous picture and chuckled. "It is typical of this lady, she must be half dog."

As he opened the door to the store, the mixed scents of dog food, a faint trace of dog pee, the balmy itch of wet dog, dog shampoo, and just plain dog arrested his nose, reaching deep into his throat. Despite the onslaught of pet odor, the kennel was crisp, clean and orderly. Claire ran a top-quality establishment. She had a large outdoor run in the back, and her 'guests' had generally free roam during the day. She kept two large areas to separate those dogs that did not get along, and even kept what she referred to as the 'sauna,' which was nothing more than solitary confinement for the occasional non-spayed customer who arrived in heat. Claire paid attention to all the necessities of caring for animals. She had developed a bond with her dogs that was more like a nanny or a friend. It was easy to conclude that Claire maintained a second home for her animals; it was not a store in the middle of town, it was not a kennel.

Claire DeLuca was Chinese and she was large. Claire had large bones, long hair and a weathered but gentle face. She dressed well and kept her hair pinned up into a French bun. She was not taller than 5'6", but when combined with her heels and the hair, she stood about 6 feet tall, the same as Jim. As he examined her hair line, Jim could tell that she spent time grooming herself to ensure that a few curly strands fell from the bun to adorn each side of her face. He imagined that Claire had read in a fashion magazine that this type of hair placement would be alluring and slimming. And he could tell that Claire loved her red lipstick, and that she made liberal use of foundation, mascara and eye shadow. In short, she was coiffed to perfection. Claire was also adorable and full of happiness, and Jim realized that she was just like her pet poodle, whose name, oddly enough, was just plain 'poodle.' Claire called her *poo-poo* for a nickname, because she had to have a nickname for every pet. In fact, Jim was fairly certain that Claire had more regard for dogs than humans, and he assumed her client nicknames were not as affectionate as those of her true customers, the dogs.

The cacophony of barking and noise overloaded Jim's auditory senses. He felt like he was seeing nature at its finest and most raucous. How did Claire deal with the consistent dog noise? Maybe she tuned it out? Claire saw Anthony and Jim enter the store, and she and Lily came bounding over towards them. Lily arrived first and lunged towards Jim, placing her paws on his chest and hopping like a ballerina in excitement. Claire looked disapprovingly at the dog, commenting, "Oooh no Miss Wiggles, we don jump on people like dat now."

Jim held Lily's head in his hands and scratched her soft, warm ears. He was reminded that dogs never hold grudges and are always happy to see you.

"Claire, I can't even tell you how grateful I am."

She was gentle. "Oooh dear, dear Docka Andews. Yew know dat I luv Miss Wiggles, and I am sooo sad about poor Sally. Poor thing, poor, poor thing. Sally was such a dear, dear girl and it is such a waste. Oh, so bad, so bad." Jim felt uneasy with her sympathy because he really didn't know Claire that well, and yet she knew a lot about his personal life. "Now Docka Andews, I hear yew are goin da Newww Yark and Miss Wiggles is joinin' yew. I'm gonna miss 'er."

"Yes. I've taken a job there with a music company," Jim lied. "Oh, Claire, this is Anthony. He works with me."

Claire inspected Anthony, evaluating his features and formulating a first impression. For a moment, Jim expected to see Claire start sniffing his butt, but then she backed off. "Nice to meet yew," she barked.

As Claire was beginning to break into another dialogue, her cell phone rang. The ring tone was the song *Who Let the Dogs Out* and she stepped back slightly from Jim and Anthony to sing, or rather to howl, "Doggie Day Care this is Claire, how con I hep yew?" As Claire was talking, Jim heard the party on the other line requesting information about kennel rates and hours of operation. "We open late tonight, til 10:00pm."

He was impressed at the sound quality, but something was amiss and Jim could not put his finger on it. As he looked around the kennel and bent down to pet Lily, it occurred to him, like a lightning bolt, what had tweaked his consciousness. It was the silence in the kennel that was deafening. Jim realized that the barking had subsided while Claire was talking on the phone. When she hung up, Jim asked in astonishment, "Claire, how did you train all these dogs to quiet down when you get on the phone? That's quite a trick!"

Claire responded, "Yew know, I din do nuthin Docka Andews. It's da strangis thin. I tink it's magic spell or sump'in. An it's not too long ago neither. Dey jus started respectin' da phone, and only a few weeks back. I not explain it, but I'm not complainin'. D'yew know how annoyin' it use da be whiff all da hollerin and honkin?"

"Well maybe you're just a genius Claire," Jim complimented.

Claire smiled with approval, as if Jim were emotionally scratching behind her ears. He almost expected her to wag her tail in appreciation and smell his hand, but instead she handed him Lily's leash and bent down to give her a kiss, "Dare now Miss Wiggles, yew come back and see me, okay dear?"

Lily seemed to give Claire a kiss in return and Jim began heading out the door with Anthony in tow and Lily leading the pack. At the sight of the Range Rover, Lily was hesitant to have to jump so high to get in; but, with a little encouragement, she jumped up and made room for Jim to join her in the back seat. Anthony rolled down the rear window so Lily could stick out her head. As Anthony was starting the car, Lily began barking at a passing poodle. While Lily was greeting the outside world with her howls, Anthony's DARPA net phone rang, and he answered it.

"Doctor Andrews, it's Maggie."

Anthony handed the phone to Jim and he replied, "Hello Maggie." Lily increased her excitement as the poodle crossed the street towards their Range Rover. She ran over Jim's lap and began barking at the closed window next to Jim, causing Anthony to roll down the other window too. Jim petted her head and tried to juggle the phone and the rambunctious dog.

"Sounds like you got your hands full, Jim."

As Lily was barking, Jim laughed, "Yeah, she sure is a handful."

"Anthony tells me you're headed back. Are you sure you're okay, Jim? I can come out to visit if you want. We could spend some time on the beach."

"Maggie, I gotta get out of here. I will see you soon."

As they hung up, Lily continued to greet the oncoming poodle, wagging her tail so hard it tossed the DARPA net phone abruptly onto the car floor. Jim moved Lily off of his lap and petted her head, "C'mon girl, calm down, it's okay, now go sit down."

Lily reluctantly moved back to her seat, but continued to bark until the Range Rover was moving out of the line of sight and the path of smell of her newfound poodle. As the car picked up speed, Lily stuck her head back out the window to air out her mouth, causing her jowls to flap like a flag on a windy day. Jim smiled and rolled up the window next to him. Anthony joked, "Seems like you're missing the magic touch of that Chinese lady to shut up the dogs."

"You know it man," Jim replied, "she's one in a million."

The air that entered from Lily's open car window was cool and crisp, and it flooded the car with ambient noise while lowering the temperature substantially. The air currents were tossing Jim's black hair around, slightly whipping against his forehead, and with the breeze, Jim felt a sense of carefree detachment. The wind can do that to you.

It reminded him of driving as a kid, when air conditioning was not a standard feature on all cars. His mind drifted back to his lonely childhood, his solace in the lab and to Doctor Roberts, his first mentor. Jim had done cutting-edge research at the University and was satisfied with his part-time jobs in the Corporate world. And, since he had married Sally, Jim had good memories of intense research. Jim had finally come to terms with being a loner.

Sally's departure from his life would reinforce Jim's solitary standing. But he refused to invite loneliness into the solitude. He was lucky. He had been offered the chance to start a new life at the NSA with a fresh sheet of paper. He could start over.

As Jim was walking through the rooms of his memory, the current research project began to creep back into his brain. The development of the nanoscope and microbytes had been an incredible achievement, and his brush with the 'eye of God,' as he called it, was spooky and exciting. Jim began to think about the use of bandwidth, wondering about the cell phone deluge, thinking about other uses for the nanoscope.

And, without any notice at all, it fit together. It was two pieces of a jigsaw puzzle. But, it was two of those pieces that shouldn't fit. It was the tricky kind; the kind that when you place them together in the puzzle, it surprises you that they fit. You look down at the pieces, expecting to see that you had forced them to join, but that they really don't match. But, upon closer inspection, you feel good to realize that they were always designed to fit together. It completes the picture in a way you were not expecting. At first, he doubted his own mind. It couldn't really be possible, could it? Jim picked up his DARPA net phone and called Li.

"Hi Doctor Andrews, I'm so sorry to hear about your loss."

"Thanks Li, it is really distressing, but I'm getting through it. And, look, I hope to be back in the office tomorrow."

There was silence.

Jim continued, "Listen, I've got a strange request for you." Jim scratched Lily's velvet ears as he explained to Li his new requirements for the nanoscope. Then he interrupted, "Hey Anthony, what time is it?"

"It's almost 8:00 in the evening now."

Li took notes. Jim spoke, "Okay, here's what I want to do. First of all, go to that facebook register that we downloaded from the microbytes and tell me if you can find Claire DeLuca from Los Angeles. She runs a kennel called Doggie Day Care."

"Now, here's what I want you to look at..."

Chapter 25

The wheels of the Learjet momentarily screamed as they hit the cold, grey tarmac at Westchester County airport. It was 6:00am. Jim and Anthony had not talked much on the plane, because Jim was lost in his thoughts, occasionally making notes in his notebook and reviewing some research papers that Maggie had sent electronically to his DARPA net reader.

The DARPA net reader was something Jim had never seen before. It was like a Kindle eReader, but there was a finger print access key on it. Maggie had explained as she gave it to him that if a non-authorized user placed their finger on the biometric reader, the contents would be wiped clean automatically from the device. She explained that the device was sealed and that sudden changes in pressure also caused the reader to erase itself. But, she reassured him, if he accidentally deleted everything, the next time that his device accessed the DARPA net, it would reload the confidential books and documents. She was matter-of-fact as she explained, "It's like that paper in *Mission Impossible*, but instead of catching on fire, it sticks around on the secure eReader...unless a bad guy tries to pry it open, or a snoop tries to read it."

The Range Rover was waiting on the runway. Anthony and Jim loaded Lily into the car and sped towards Greenwich. When the elevator doors opened into their NSA offices, Jim came face to face with Maggie, Shilesh, Jeanine and Li.

"Nice pooch," Maggie commented, "but, you have to come see this." She motioned towards the LCD screen in the front of the conference room, where Jim saw the facebook listing with Claire's picture.

Li explained, "I used the nanoscope to download a few time intervals from about 7:45pm, like you asked me. It took a few tries, but when we looked at Claire's movie listing, we found one from 7:39pm. Here's where it gets creepy."

She clicked on Claire's facebook page and launched the movie from 7:39pm. Jim saw a picture of himself with Lily and Anthony, then watched as Claire scanned the kennel with her eyes. Li hit a pause button on the media player and rewound the movie to where Jim reappeared. She paused the movie so that a grainy picture of Jim was frozen on the LCD screen, his mouth opened as if he were ready to speak.

"I'm famous," Jim exclaimed, "Li…once again you're a genius. Guys, sit down, this one is going to be strange." The room settled, and Jim explained, "Dogs are pretty smart, but one thing they do much better than we do is they can hear things really, really well. That's why most of them have flaps on their ears. And it's why Doberman pincher owners cut the ear flaps off, it makes for a better guard dog, like German Shepherds with their pointy ears."

"I'm sure you have all heard *of* a dog whistle, but I guarantee that you have never *heard* one. You see, they're invisible to our audible spectrum. The sound waves are there, but our brains and ears can't hear them. Well, dogs can…dogs rule." Jim smiled.

"Anyway…Anthony and I were at Lily's kennel and Crazy Claire's cell phone rang. At first I couldn't understand it, but then I noticed that all the dogs quieted down when she was on the phone. It was spooky and we joked about it, but Claire explained that it had only recently begun to happen and she had no idea how she trained them. But it really hit me when Maggie called me on Anthony's DARPA net phone and Lily kept barking and barking. We were joking that Claire had the magic touch, but then I wondered. What if Claire had a dog whistle and didn't know it? What if there was some sound coming from the phone? Then I started thinking about the eye of God and it came together. It just made sense. Somehow, Claire's eyes and ears were transmitting what she saw and heard over the cell phone, on some frequency that we cannot hear. The dogs knew about it, but we had no idea. I wondered if that cell phone transmission was somehow getting loaded up into our mircobytes and coming out as home movies on the eye of God."

"And Li just proved it…it's nuts, isn't it? So, here it goes, I will bet a million bucks that if you cross-reference Claire's cell phone records to her eye of God home movies, each movie will correspond to a phone call. And I will bet another million bucks that every person in our facebook who has an eye of God home movie has a cell phone. And I will bet that their phone call records will exactly match their eye of God home movies. Every time they get on the phone, their eyes and ears are reporting into the eye of God."

Shilesh glanced up, "Jim, do you understand what you are saying? This is…this is…it's impossible. How in heaven's name can something like this happen? Do you really think we're looking into God's eyes?" Shilesh was pacing around the room like a mad professor. He was animated and kept looking at the LCD screen with Jim and Anthony's picture.

"Hey Maggie," Jim asked, "Do you have an electron microscope around here?"

"Sure. What's up?"

"First of all Shilesh, I told you I don't believe in aliens, but I am leaving an open door on the whole God thing, okay. He might have his hand in this puzzle, but let's keep our options open on the divinity play. Li, I've got an even more bizarre request for you now. I want you to go back to God's facebook from last week, and I want you to compare it with any death notices during that timeframe. I want you to see how many of our movie makers kicked the bucket." The room grew still as Jim made his morbid request.

He furthered, "Maggie, you need to work your magic now. When Li finds some dead people, I want you to bring them, and their cell phone, to Greenwich for autopsies."

Jeanine gasped, "Jim we don't have the equipment to handle cadavers here."

"I'm sure Maggie can have it here as soon as you get the list prepared, right Maggie?"

"The tools to examine cadavers and the electron microscopes, those are the easy parts," Maggie replied, "but the cell-phone carrying cadavers? Those are a bit more of a challenge."

Maggie laughed, stood up, and collected her gear. As she was leaving, Jim heard Maggie explain to her handlers and facilitators that she needed to get her hands on a corpse.

Jeanine piped in, "I will send a list of the autopsy tools that I will need, Jim, but tell me why the electron microscope?"

"Germs," Jim replied like he was in a creepy sci-fi movie, "*Dirty little germs*! Those cadavers and their cell phones are going to be filled with lots and lots of germs and we need to find out which germs are making the cell phone calls that the dogs heard."

Shilesh glanced at Jeanine and Jim and explained, "Uh…Jeanine, when you finish your morgue checklist, why don't you come back here? Despite Jim's sudden interest in germs and hygiene, I think we all need to talk about nanobots."

"What in the hell?"

"No Jim, it's not heaven and it's not hell, it's worse than that," Shilesh prophesized.

Jeanine looked at the pair of mad scientists and she glanced over at Li, who was passively taking in the entire scene with uncharacteristic equanimity.

Then, Jeanine spoke, "Okay, Shilesh, I should be done in about fifteen minutes. Why don't you guys go and get us all a coffee and we can regroup."

The coffee maker in the lounge was the kind that required you to input a separate cartridge for each cup. Shilesh inspected the small packet from all angles; then placed it into the machine. He chuckled as the lights on the machine began blinking.

"Cappuccino or Espresso Doctor Andrews?"

"Regular coffee with milk and sugar is fine…hey, do you care to elaborate about the nanobot?"

"All in good time, Jim…all in good time. I guarantee that you're going to enjoy the show."

Jim saw the indicator light on his DARPA net blackberry light up, and he reviewed the email, "Looks like Jeanine has finished her list Shilesh. Now if only Maggie could get us some cadavers."

"Come on," Shilesh insisted as he motioned Jim to leave the lounge, "Let's go chat with Jeanine and Li."

The two men entered the conference room, holding coffees in each hand. Li and Jeanine rose to greet them and to take a cup of coffee. They all sat down and Shilesh began his lesson. Shilesh was in his element when he played the role of nutty professor, and Jim drifted back to his days in high school with Dr. Roberts.

"Now where were we? Oh yes…nanobots. It's another term I invented, like the microbytes. In fact, it was an evolution from the microbyte. You see, if we are moving into a world where data and technology become microscopic, then the computers can shrink too. Think about the first telephone, it was huge; there were teams of operators running the switches. Now we take for granted that a palm sized phone can let us send and receive calls from anywhere in the world. Everything keeps getting smaller."

"Except for my waist," Jim concluded.

"Yes…ok…but back to my topic. When we made the leap from bytes to microbytes, we made a quantum leap smaller. I want to emphasize that again, it was a quantum leap smaller, not just a big leap. We're not talking Neil Armstrong on the moon. We're talking about the difference between our old-fashioned Internet and the storage capability to accommodate the 'eye of God' as Jim calls it. We're talking about entire computer software programs taking up less than one bit. So, naturally, if we can compress the data to be this small, why can't we compress the computer?"

"When we get into nanotechnology, we're talking about really, really small things. We may not even be talking about silicon chips anymore. We might be using actual human or animal cells to do the computing. Since our software code is becoming as small as DNA, perhaps it can be run on cells instead of computers."

Jeanine looked at Shilesh and asked, "Do you think that's what's going on here?"

Shilesh raised his eyebrows like a good professor and commented, "Very good question Jeanine. The truth is I have no idea, none at all. But, our friend Jim here just showed me a home movie from Claire Deluca's eyes and it was transmitted from her brain to her cell phone and stored in the eye of God. So if all that can happen in less than a week, then I'm putting some of my money on a bet that nanobots can, and do, exist."

"But what is a nanobot?" Jim asked.

"Another good question, Jim, let me continue…you see, once computers get so small, they can operate like insects; or, dare I say, germs. They can act like little tiny robots, and they can break many of the physical barriers that have always existed between humans and machines."

"I know this seems far-fetched, but let's suppose that some malicious bad guy decides to program a nanobot to act like a computer virus. But since it's a nanobot, the bad guy can design it to behave like a real live virus. If these nanobots are small enough, they can go dormant and float through the air like germs. If they attach themselves into your body, they could tap into the mitochondria of one of your cells, you know, its power station. With energy from your cell, they could boot up again. Once they're inside, these nanobots could 'set up shop' and run software programs. With nanotechnology, we have an ability to envision technology crossing the biological-system boundary. In fact, crossing that BIOSYS line is one of the most exciting new frontiers of nanotechnology."

"But, back to our nanobots…uh…well, you can easily imagine some of the horrifically bad things that someone could do if they actually got their hands on nanobot technology. But more important than keeping the idea a secret, there have been significant scientific barriers to actually creating anything that remotely resembles a nanobot. For God's sake, you may think that your cell phone is small, but try implanting it inside of your body and you would quickly see the differences between a nanobot and a normal electronic device. Anyway, the biggest barrier to date has been the enormous size of the data and the computer. But, once we saw the existence of microbytes, it suggested the theoretical feasibility of nanobots."

"So nanobots are like little tiny computers?" Jim asked.

"Yes."

"And they read little tiny computer programs?"

"I'm afraid so."

"And they can fly?" Jeanine asked.

"Well, it is theoretically possible that they can drift." Shilesh corrected, "They don't actually fly because they don't have propellers or jets or anything like that, but they are so small that they can glide or float for long distances in the air, like your germ spores, Jeanine."

"Are you asking me to believe in floating computers Shilesh?" Jeanine asked.

"I'm not asking you to believe in anything, Jeanine. In fact, I'm not asking any of you to believe a word I am saying. We are scientists. We never believe anything that anybody tells us. In fact, we spend our whole lives trying to disprove hypotheses. We work in vain to try to demonstrate that we are wrong! No, please don't believe me. Please prove me wrong! Show me that this is not happening!"

Then Shilesh calmed and continued, "What I mean is that I want to qualify all this by explaining that I am talking about theoretical science. I know that it sounds more like science fiction than science fact, but remember that the lines between fact and fiction have always been blurred, especially when we speak of the future. The only reason I am bringing any of this up is that I wanted you to keep it in mind while you are searching for your phone calling germs. Maybe, just maybe, your germs are not germs at all."

The room was still. Jim had folded his arms and was resting his head on the table. He was absorbed in the discussion, but looked like he had fallen asleep. Shilesh stopped talking, and Jim raised his head and began laughing as he explained, "Shilesh, you really do need to get out more."

Shilesh laughed along with the team and continued, "I don't know which idea is crazier, germs using cell phones or nanobots floating invisibly through the air? But if you ask me, the entire world seems to be nearing the end."

Chapter 26

Maggie stuck her head in the office and proclaimed, "Cadaver arrives at 6:00pm. Philadelphia, taxi driver, 72 year-old male, smoker, died of cardiac arrest in his sleep, no known family, signed himself over as wanting to donate his body to science. The attorneys have confirmed that we can squeak by with that one. Get this...his name is Charles Darwin, pretty fitting, huh? I'm convinced his parents must have had an odd sense of humor. Anyway, we will get Charlie in a few hours. Right now, he and his cell phone are in transit from LaGuardia."

Jim responded, "Why didn't Charlie get to use the Learjet?"

"Knock it off Jim. Do you know how hard it was for me to make this happen? We're crossing all kinds of legal and ethical boundaries. More importantly, this entire building is going to be treated as a bio-hazard site. Within the next hour, you will see nothing but people walking around in space suits, including us. And besides, I use that plane! Do you think I want to fly in a toxic-waste hearse? Yuck." Maggie crumpled her face in disgust and flashed her impish, princess smile as she left the room.

At 7:00pm, the hearse finally pulled into the parking lot at the NSA offices, formerly known as Audacity Frontier, now sporting no name whatsoever, just a lot of cameras and a lot of security guards in a remote field in Greenwich. Jeanine, Jim, Shilesh and Li sat in one of the lab rooms. A cadaver on a gurney was placed on one side of the room, and a cell phone on an examination table was placed on the other side. All of the rooms in the bunker had been sealed off. It was, indeed, a hazmat site. All 4 scientists were in bio hazard suits so that they looked like astronauts, as Maggie had predicted. They reviewed the final procedures checklist, and then began to implement the tests that they had spent the entire day designing.

Jeanine led the autopsy on Charlie, with Shilesh as her assistant. Their testing consisted of extracting blood and fluid samples which would be sent to the Mass Spectrometer, and then to the electron microscope. They were also responsible for performing a biopsy on the brain, and were required to extract several samples of brain matter, with a particular focus on the occipital lobe and the temporal lobe, the parts that control the eyes and ears. The brain matter was to be analyzed with the 'mass spec' and the electron microscope. Jim explained that he was not a 'blood and guts kind of guy' and that he did not want to faint or worse, vomit inside his space suit. "I'm a PhD, not an MD," he lamely insisted. "Please! Blood makes me heave," he begged.

Jim and Li were therefore tasked with disassembling the cell phone. There was no stone left unturned. They were responsible for swabbing each component and passing the swabs into an electronic 'sniffer' which could detect the presence of biological agents. In the case that a biological agent was discovered, a sample of the component would be ground into a powder and passed through the electron microscope. In addition, Jim and Li were responsible for downloading all of the software on the device. Their task included searching all embedded programs as well as operating systems. The software was to be decompiled back into its source code so that it could be passed through the nanoscope and would also be reviewed by a team of research assistants.

Both teams worked with painstaking patience. Every sample was gently extracted, precisely labeled and handled with care. The scientists were exhausted and hot, and the space suits made every movement and every action seem like a chore. A team of research assistants waited outside of the lab room, all dressed in bio-hazard space suits. They carefully removed the samples as the scientists made progress and initiated the discovery procedures. Shilesh and Jeanine completed their autopsy in 5 hours, but Jim and Li were struggling with downloading the electronic media. Their procedures lasted for 10 hours, and when they completed the last download, they breathed a sigh of relief.

Li looked at Jim, staring through her hermetically sealed helmet and explained, "Good work Doctor Andrews, now the hard part begins!"

As the teams retreated into their bio decontamination showers, the remains of Charlie and the cell phone were sealed up in a foil-like wrapper and placed in cryogenic storage while the clean-up crew entered the lab and began to decontaminate the area. After removing their space suits, the four scientists were released onto their residential floor, which had also been sealed off from the other lab areas. The entire NSA compound had been converted into what looked like a superfund site. There were plastic sheets hanging in every hallway and plastic drop cloths were covering every desk that was not in use. In addition, the air circulation vents were sealed, non-essential machines were powered down, all running water was drained from the pipes and hundreds of UV lights were placed throughout all the floors. The four scientists were trying their best to relax in the lounge, decompressing from the day's events, but mostly keeping silent and contemplating the situation.

Li received a message on her DARPA net blackberry and spoke, "It seems like the analysis of the code will take 24 hours, and the nanoscope review is estimated to be a 48-hour job."

Jeanine explained, "I think that the biological review will also take a couple of days. This is not instamatic stuff."

"So I guess we just wait," Jim explained.

Li replied, "We're all on call if anything comes up. But honestly, there is a ton of basic research that needs to get done, and we have a very strong team to do it. They're the best. We're trapped too…we can't just come and go from that lab casually. Each time we go in, we will need to suit up in a fresh space suit, and on the way out we will need to decontaminate. I think we're going to be on this floor for a while."

"What day is it?" Jim asked.

"It's Thanksgiving Jim," Shilesh explained, "Can't you tell?"

Chapter 27

Other than answering a few random queries, Jim felt bored while he was waiting for the testing to run its course. Occasionally he would receive some test results, but nothing was conclusive, so he paced around his room, read some documents on his DARPA net reader and occasionally slept. He was that kid who had been grounded by his parents, and after 16 hours, he was ready to strangle himself with boredom. When would the punishment be over?

At the end of the first day, the team reconvened in the lounge. They reviewed the status report that Li presented, "The source code review is complete. We found some abnormality on the SIM card, but otherwise nothing. The nanoscope review is going slower than we thought, but we think we'll do it within the next 24 hours."

"What's the deal with the SIM card?" Jim asked.

Li explained, "The SIM card is the Subscriber Identity Module of your phone. It is like a serial number for your phone, and it lets the phone company know who you are, where you are, and all the details that they need to generate your phone bill. It also contains the security authentication and ciphering information and two passwords called the PIN and the PUK. In Charlie's cell phone, there seems to be an abnormality, some kind of bug in the ciphering information."

Jeanine perked up, "What kind of bug are we talking about here?"

"No Jeanine. It does not seem like a biological bug, but it is still quite strange. You see the ciphering information has a set of keys that are to be exchanged when the phone needs to authenticate on the network, but these keys seem to have been corrupted. Maybe we screwed something up when we downloaded it, or maybe the SIM card has been compromised. We just don't know right now. We're running some additional tests, but since it showed an abnormality, we have narrowed our efforts right now to be focused on the SIM card. It was literally the only aberration in the testing. We're hoping that the nanoscope will bring something to light."

"What about the biological review on the phone?" Jeanine asked.

"Well," Li explained, "Let's just say that Charlie's phone was filled with critters. There was nothing out of the ordinary, but, Whoa! Cell phones are disgusting."

"How about the autopsy on the cadaver?" Shilesh asked.

Jeanine commented, "So far so good. We have confirmed that he had been exposed to the Swine Flu, his system had antibodies for that. And, he did have a very high lipid level, and that's probably what led to his heart disease, not that smoking did him any favors. But, other than that, we've come up with absolutely nothing of interest. In addition to the mass spec and the electron microscope, I have asked the team to do a full DNA test.

"Now in terms of the brain samples, we also came up with nothing conclusive, but there does seem to be something going on in there. It seems that Charlie was suffering from a mitochondrial disease. It looks to be nothing serious, but his levels were not good, and that's why we expanded our testing to include a DNA scan."

Shilesh looked pensively at Li, "You know that the mitochondria provide the cells with their energy, and that was precisely the area we hypothesized would come under attack by nanobots. You see, nanobots need power, they don't have adapters like our laptops. And if they were to enter the human body, the only way to get power would be to tap into the mitochondria."

"Yes sir," Li explained, "That's why I asked the team to convert the DNA samples into a digital format so we can hook it up to the nanoscope. In the meantime, we still have to wait for results."

The room sank.

On Saturday morning at 8:00am, the phone in Jim's suite rang. "Come on down, Jim!" Shilesh encouraged, "We've got some test results back!"

As he walked towards the conference room, Jim noticed that the hazmat crews were removing the plastic wraps and slowly opening the lab back for normal operations. "Are we done?" Jim asked.

"Well not really," Li replied, "but all of the biological agents have been removed and the physical assets have been sealed up in liquid nitrogen."

Li updated the team, "Doctor Gupta, congratulations, you are the proud father of a baby nanobot." She illuminated her 3-D projector and a geodesic dome with a few spikes was projected on the table. "It looks like a golf ball or a land-mine, doesn't it? Well, it is more exciting than that. It's our own Fullerene. We have named him a Guptabot; with all due respect Shilesh," Li teased.

"Are you telling me that you named me after a bucky ball...but why?" Shilesh squirmed.

Li confirmed, "Well, sort of...you know that Richard Buckminster Fuller was the architect who used the geodesic dome in his buildings, he was a pioneer. Anyway, in 1970 there was a scientist in Japan called Eiji Osawa who predicted that these funky shapes could also occur naturally in chemical compounds. Unfortunately for Eiji, it took until the mid-1980s before these soccer-ball shaped, carbon-based molecules were discovered. They named them bucky balls in honor of Mr. Fuller, which was really an insult to Dr. Osawa. We decided since you envisioned the nanobot, we would give you proper naming credit before someone else stole it; so, we called them Guptabots.

"It was hard to find, you see, we picked up some curious shapes on the mass spec, and decided to pass samples through the electron microscope a second time; and, there he was, just hanging out on Charlie's SIM card. The trick here is that this guy seems to have thousands of bucky balls inside him. It's like a miniature memory chip. Shilesh, you were right. There is a nanobot. This odd-looking ball can process computer code if it is small enough."

"Especially if it were written in microbytes," Shilesh confirmed.

"Yes Sir," Li replied, "But wait, it also has these tails which we believe can absorb energy. In the case of our SIM card, it seems to be drawing static electricity, but we believe that these spikes are small enough to latch into a cell's mitochondria too." As the team stared at the strange object projected on their conference table, Li continued, "It gets better, or rather worse, depending on how you look at it."

"We found a few thousand of these Guptabots in Charlie's temporal lobe. We called it the Guptabot army…um….sorry…uh…that was our lab joke, sir. Anyway, the nanobots were causing his mitochondrial disorder. But they did not kill him. We also found that these nanobots can communicate via their own frequency. They're interoperable, it's like a bunch of wireless laptops hooking up to a router.

"So, it seems that the nanobots that were lodged in Charlie's brain were coordinating everything that he saw and heard, and then transmitting it to the nanobot on his SIM card, which in turn used the cell phone to transmit the data in a frequency that we could not hear; but, as Jim discovered, the dogs could. We don't believe that the dogs understood the dialogue, but that's being reserved for future research." Li smiled, but the team was so engrossed that they missed her joke entirely.

"Okay, I know it was a bad joke, but we tried." She continued, "The cell phone transmission entered the cell phone carriers' networks and penetrated the Internet, filling up the eye of God. That's how we got to see recordings of people's eyes and ears. Someone or something had cross referenced the SIM card serial numbers to people's facebook accounts. It used that information to create an index to store the movies. They also branched out, you know, like not only facebook, but they hit all of the social media sites, Linked-in and MySpace, even the dating sites have been hacked into and their data has been loaded into this thing.

"But, the reason we only see movies at certain times is because the nanobots only broadcast when the user is making a call on their cell phone. You know, if this weren't happening on a microscopic level, it would be fairly standard technology. Kind of like kids walking around with iPhones, recording everything and loading it up to their YouTube accounts. But the deployment inside of the brain, with nanobots, now that's innovation!

"From all we can tell, the nanobots were not harmful. It is true that they did sap energy from the brain cells, but they seemed to run a pretty efficient shop and they were positioned in a manner that would not inhibit brain function." Li clicked a button on her laptop and a 3D image of a brain appeared over the table. The brain had thousands of colored dots on certain areas. These dots indicate the areas where we found the nanobots in Charlie's brain.

"Now, I know it looks bad, but in brain terms, this is nothing. You could do more damage with a few years of alcoholic binges than these nanobots would ever do. In fact, we would really like to investigate whether these nanobots provided benefits to the host that offset the power they consumed."

Jeanine interrupted, "You mean it was not a parasite, you think it was symbiotic?"

Li explained, "Symbiotic relationships occur in nature, and if our nanobots were able to help Charlie, then, yes, we would classify it as endosymbiotic because the nanobot lived within the tissues of Charlie. In nature we have come across examples where this co-existence is mutually beneficial. For example, we have found bacteria that live inside roots of trees and eat the nitrogen within the soil. It makes the tree healthier, while feeding the bacteria, it's a mutual benefit."

"Since the nanobots were sparing in their power consumption, and since they seemed to only reproduce to a point where they could record and transmit the sights and sounds, we are wondering if they also provided benefits to the host. We can't really ask Charlie, but we would like to try to do some field research."

Jeanine commented, "From the look of these nanobots, it seems feasible that they could travel in the air like a flu virus. Yes, I guess Charlie sneezes on his phone and the nanobot enters the device, gradually settling on his SIM card and then setting up shop. Meanwhile, his brain is being slightly invaded by the nanobot army, but only enough so that they can hijack his eyes and ears. Then, achoo, he sneezes on the bus and the guy next to him begins the process."

Shilesh paused and continued the discussion, "Yes Jeanine, and that would explain why this phenomena has been spreading slowly, like the flu, instead of spreading rapidly like computer viruses tend to propagate. It is being transmitted alongside the flu virus, not like a traditional computer virus."

Jim addressed the group, "Well Shilesh. I guess we can chalk this up to Unknown Life Forms, right? Or is it Unknown Unknowns?"

Shilesh grew quiet and introspective. He seemed disjointed and frustrated, then he collected himself and commented, "Yes...Yes...To be honest we may have to start the entire scenario analysis over again. You see, we still do not know who or what has done this."

"Think of the possible explanations. Is it some master programmer? Is it a terrorist or a foreign government? Are these alien probes? Has God come back to earth? The possibilities are scary, and they are real, and, ladies and gentlemen, we are under attack. We have just uncovered one of the most miraculous events I could imagine. I am an old man, and I will die before I see something as momentous again, of that I am sure. But we still don't know what to do about it, and as we speak, this virus is spreading. Eventually, it could bring down the entire modern world."

Jim replied, "Well, first we need to ping the big boss and let him know what's going on. I'm sure that you and Maggie will be jetting off to the White House in a few hours. Jeanine, do you think you can start to propose some strategies to save the world from this germ-like epidemic?"

Jeanine nodded and replied sarcastically, "Sure Jim, just as soon as I cure world hunger." She paused. "Oh, I'm sorry, that was uncalled for. I will get started, but we have to move quickly. What if these nanobots run their own 'Research and Development' team? What if they begin to mutate? Viruses always get more aggressive, that's why we call them virulent. Virulence is a measure of pathenogenicity. You know, it's a measure of how quickly it impacts you and also a measure of how sick it makes you."

Jim called up Maggie on the videoconference window. She was wearing her wireless headset and shouting orders to her staff when he dialed her up. Maggie glanced at the picture and replied in an exasperated tone, "So team? Please don't tell me you need more cadavers. You've got me knee deep in shit right now because of Charlie and his cell phone. The attorney general is after my ass! It seems that using a cadaver for government spy work is not, legally, science - imagine that!"

Jim calmly explained, "Hey boss, you need to come over here right now, we've got a code red."

Maggie grew serious. The apparent stress on her face as she was explaining the after-effects of getting her hands on Charlie seemed to fade when confronted by Jim's comment. She seemed to gulp. "I'll be right over."

Maggie intently listened as the team explained the idea of the nanobots. She was fascinated to learn that the nanobots burrowed into Charlie's brain and then into his cell phone before downloading his personal movies to the blocked Internet bandwidth, thereby creating Charlie's eye of God. The meeting took a couple of hours and Maggie's demeanor grew increasingly animated as she learned the details. She was blown away by the news, and called her intelligence analysts, who predicted that the only foreign power with a remote ability to create such a program would be the Japanese. The NSA analysts estimated that the Japanese were 5 years ahead of the Americans and the Israelis in the field of nanotechnology; and, the analysts felt that the Chinese and Indians were 'coming up fast.' The NSA analysts were also adamant that other countries were not even remote candidates to have the capabilities for such nanotechnology.   Jim was circumspect when he heard the intelligence reports, but he had no proof to refute their views.

The team debated the likelihood of rogue agents and concluded that the possibility was there, but it was as equally remote as a foreign government or terrorist cell. They even debated the potential for aliens and for divine intervention. The debates raged, and, as they were arguing over the potential villains and motives, Jim suggested the following, "Okay, we're not making much progress right now on identifying the bad guys. We have spent a few hours now running around in circles, accusing the Japanese, aliens and God…and we're no closer to solving this case. In the meantime, every minute we waste in this room, more and more nanobots are spreading. We have an epidemic on our hands, and we don't know how to stop it. I think we need to break into teams. Maggie, you need to alert the White House. Shilesh, you and Jeanine need to begin a risk mitigation plan and focus on containing this thing. Li, you and I need to dig into the technology more. I suspect this is more of a worm than a virus, and worms are usually created by programmers, even if Maggie thinks that everyone on earth is too stupid to create something like this."

Li explained in more detail, "I think that Jim is right. A computer worm can travel around a network without a carrier program. It just keeps looking around for systems, sort of slithering through the network, that's why they call it a worm. Our little Guptabot had to make its way around Charlie's brain, and around his cell phone, until he found the perfect place to clone himself and set up shop. In the late 1980's the son of a computer scientist released a worm from his college computer. It brought down the entire Defense Department. The poor kid went to jail, but when he got out he joined the NSA, and now he works on Maggie's team. I will run this by him and get his views."

Jeanine explained, "From an epidemiological point of view, we really don't care if it is a worm or a virus. The transmission pattern is flu-like, and that means that we have another, larger wave coming. I'm praying to God that these nanobots do not get violent; and, in the meantime, I will begin preparing a plan to isolate and remove the nanobots from God's earth. I don't think we'll get a vaccine for these little critters, and I disagree with Li that these are symbiotic creatures."

Maggie and Shilesh packed up their papers as Maggie called on her headset and requested a meeting at the White House.

Chapter 28

Jim met with the NSA Cyber Threat team to review computer transmission patterns while Li was reverse-engineering the nanobots. Li was challenged by Jim to find out how the nanobots communicated, how they cloned themselves and who their architect was. After two hours discussing the transmission architecture with the NSA chief scientist, Jim became convinced that the nanobots were computers, not aliens and not divine instruments. He was relieved, but was still terrified at the possibilities. If the nanobots were computers, then someone; or something, had become a dangerous programmer. Jim returned to Li's desk, armed with the belief that the nanobots were simple, powerful machines. Yes, they were small, they were molecular in size, but they were machines, not living creatures.

Li excitedly greeted Jim upon his arrival into the lab. She was hurried as she explained her findings. "We're reverse engineering the code by downloading it into the nanoscope. We have studied the computer architecture of the nanobot. Jim, this code is very elegant, but terrifying. As you suspected, the basic architecture is indeed a computer worm. But this guy is relentless. He has a genetic algorithm that is used to test out his clones, and he will modify them if they fail in their purpose. There are classes of the Nanobots, they're not all the same. There's the master configurator, he creates all the clones and then collects all the results. He also spawns the communicator, which is a nanobot that transmits and receives the data flows. The master configurator uses the communicators to check with the SIM card nanobot to get the phone owner's identity from phone company records. Then the configurator checks on facebook. If the host has a facebook account and a cell phone, only then do the nanobots begin their work. And look at this, when the nanobots encounter a new cell phone model, they map it, providing a blue print for the next nanobot who lands in the same make and model. It's like they're building drivers 'on-the-fly.' We've never seen anything like it. Jim, this is elegant programming, but it is a worm. No doubt about it."

Jim interrupted Li, "Whoa, hold on a minute. You are speaking at a thousand miles an hour. Can you slow down, slow way, way down, and let's start from the top. Tell me about our worm, the Nanobot."

"Sorry Doctor Andrews," Li apologized, "I got carried away. We are uncovering so much new ground every hour. It's almost supernatural."

"Li…it's only a computer, you said it yourself. Now, I realize that we're all breathing some pretty rarified air right now, but let's start from square one, and let's go slowly."

"Right," Li paused, "Okay, let's begin with the architecture of a computer worm. The best way to explain the difference between a virus and a worm is to explain what a worm is not. You see, a computer virus is designed to cause damage. That's its reason for existence. They didn't start out that way, but that's where they have evolved. The first viruses were cute little messages that popped up and annoyed users. From there, it became a cottage industry in destruction. Worms could be considered a variant of a virus, but they don't have to do damage. Sometimes they just move around computer networks looking for new things to break into. They may or may not clone themselves. The more they leave behind copies of themselves, the more they begin to behave like a virus."

"Well, our little nanobot friends are reproducing pretty prolifically, aren't they?" Jim asked.

"Sort of…you see…the basic architecture of this program is a collection paradigm. It is a seeker and a collector."

"What do you mean Li?"

"The basic program is focused on collecting everything it comes into contact with, but does not destroy it. Think about the Internet bandwidth that the nanobots stole. Prior to their arrival, it was freely available, it was unused. They needed a place to store all their snapshots of the Internet and their eye of God movies, so they found an empty parking space. The reason we found a bandwidth deluge is that they began filling up all the spare capacity." Li paused and stared at Jim.

"So our nanobots are surfing the web, and also surfing our brains with a sole purpose of collecting data?"

"Yes," Li explained, "That's how I see it. And they are clever. A worm has to be adaptive to slither around a computer network. It needs to be able to discover and adapt to defenses, new systems, new devices. Our nanobot worm does exactly that. As the worms permeate the Internet, they are creating a master taxonomy of life. We are calling it the *world canonical*, because the hierarchical view seems to capture every thought on earth – fact and fiction, history, emotions, news, scientific knowledge, political analysis, social networks – everything is categorized and ordered in this world view. Then, the worm uses the canonical to innovate. Take the use of facebook and cell phones. It seems that the approach for linking SIM cards to facebook evolved several weeks after the nanobots began recording snapshots of the entire Internet. It was an evolutionary step. We think that the nanobots encountered facebook and YouTube and experimented with merging the technologies. Some of this stuff we will never know for sure, but the historical pattern is consistent with evolution."

"Is it alive?"

"I don't know." Li explained, "Sometimes I don't really know the difference between natural life and artificial life. These nanobots are as close to living things as I have seen from a computer program. Let me explain. They have a hierarchy, sort of a caste system. There are leader nanobots and there are drones. At first we thought they were clones, but we have understood that the programs that get spawned by the leader have more limited functions. We call the leader the configurator because he consults the canonical, considers his mission, and seems to create drones to fulfill his mission to search and collect. That's how the cell phone and the brain nanobots were created. We believe that the computer worm created them."

"So our worm is a creator as well as a collector?"

"Yes, it's a little bit of both. The real secret is that the configurator works by trial and error, but every mistake is stored back in the canonical."

"So he never makes the same mistake twice," Jim replied.

"Yes sir."

"I wish I had a canonical in my brain," Jim mused.

"Careful what you wish for…anyway, let me continue. You see, the configurator has a single purpose, to gain and store knowledge. He has been designed to look for new stores of knowledge and to add it to his catalogue. He's a giant digital collector; he's a pack-rat. The leap from taking pictures of the Internet to taking pictures from our brains was definitely a big leap. But, it seems like the configurator came across some studies in nanotechnology, added those to its canonical, and used it to expand its knowledge gathering processes."

"It's insane," Jim responded.

Li corrected, "Well, it may be abhorrent, but you have to admit it is logical. The worm completed its task of cataloging the Internet, then it needed to keep searching, so it began testing different devices. The cell phone companies have been selling smart phones as a bridge between the computer and the phone, and the configurator took over. He agreed with their marketing material and he developed a way to enter the phone."

"There's an app for that," Jim joked.

Li smiled and continued, "Once the configurator had spawned a smart phone app, he learned about the users from facebook. From there, it was not such a big leap to invade their brains."

"But first the configurator had to learn about nanotechnology from its canonical," Jim replied.

"That's how we think it happened. Sometime in the not too distant past, the worm began generating variant programs to further its mission of collecting knowledge. Perhaps it had traveled all over the Internet and hit a dead-end, so it started innovating. It is easy to see how it could jump from the Internet to a smart phone…just like email…a standard download. And now the program is running close to the human brain - where does it go next? The program itself doesn't have any mass - it is just running on the processor of the cell phone. To create a small bucky ball, it needs 60 carbon atoms. So, it hijacks the cell phone's microphone. When you speak on the phone, you're releasing a lot of CO_2 …so maybe the program used static electricity to combine the atoms? We really don't know for sure, but one theory is that it commandeered a bunch of carbon, made a bucky ball, filled it with some DNA code via microbytes, and shot it into our bodies. Another theory is that the program hijacked the phone's transmitter and sent small amounts of radiation into the brains, causing the cells to malfunction and emit carbon…you know, you've heard that cell phones can cause cancer, right? So, another theory is that the virus kept shooting radiation at us until our cells created bucky balls, then somehow transferred the code to it. We'll never know the exact path of evolution – it will be another *missing link*."

"However, and this is important, we think that it has been a rather benign invader because killing the people whose brains it has invaded would defeat its mission. We think that the configurator designed the nanobots not to kill the host. Now here's where my pet idea comes in."

"Go on," Jim encouraged.

Li dreamt, "Let's say that our nanobots expanded their role just a little bit. Let's say that they decided that they wanted the host to be healthy so that they could continue their mission indefinitely. They could monitor our health and spawn new nanobots to fight off diseases inside our body. What if Charlie's nanobots could have detected that he had heart disease and then created new nanobots to keep him healthy? Doctor Andrews, imagine if the nanobots became our key to immortality."

Jim paused, "Li, you're a genius, and you're making me feel shivers up and down my spine. I agree with you that, for right now, these nanobots are just benign super-spies who are collecting anything they come into contact with. But, in the same manner that you see them turning into life-saving robots, they could just as easily turn into ruthless killers. Evil is the inverse of good, Li. You can't have one without the other. Here's what's troubling me…you told me that the configurator started spawning new nanobots, and that the evolutionary pattern repeated and repeated. You even have some theories on how the computer program created a nanobot, but who created the first worm? "

"We don't know," Li replied, "but we do believe that it started out as a normal computer program. As I explained, I believe the mutation from computer program to nanobot was made possible by the architecture of the worm. In other words, whoever designed the approach of a computer worm that included trial and error; a master canonical; and loosely coupled coordination made this evolution possible."

Li explained, "Let's say this worm has been around for a long time. You know, imagine that the original worm has been traversing the Internet for years now, but that it only recently began making the leap into nanotechnology when it reached the end of the Internet, or at least caught up with it. It's possible that the worm started out as a simple program, but that its elegant pattern of innovating, storing and learning made it get smarter and smarter."

"So what are you saying? On the eighth day, God booted up his Mac, wrote a simple program, and a few years later all hell broke loose?"

"Not God, but yes, someone wrote it…and then it evolved into what we are seeing today."

As they were contemplating the seriousness of the implications of a world where nanobots and humans co-existed, Maggie popped up on the videoconference window of Li's laptop. "Sorry to interrupt, but we have a new development. Shilesh and I are headed back to Greenwich."

Chapter 29

The scientists sat around the conference table looking at the hologram of the nanobot. They admired its elegance, but shared a terror in the implications for the future that it represented. The team continued to pepper Li with questions about the features of the nanobot. Li defended her theories of the origin, adaptation and implications of the nanobot, causing the room to fill with energy. The team was debating topics ranging from the soundness of Li's proposals, to the meaning of good and evil, to the potential for positive and negative evolution.

Maggie and Shilesh stormed into the conference room. The team looked expectantly at Shilesh and Maggie, as Shilesh continued, "As Chief Risk Officer of the United States, I get all kinds of crazy data. Everything from weather patterns, criminal activity, Maggie's cyber security threats, international funds flows…it's all there. You name it, I get it. And while I am not proud to explain this, Maggie has already explained to you that the government carries out a large espionage operation in Silicon Valley and most other hot-beds of innovation. Jim, you got a little first-hand taste of what that reconnaissance means."

"Anyway, the reports from our agents in the field are analyzed by a group of my best statisticians. They're responsible for connecting seemingly unrelated events. And this Internet deluge has kept us all on high alert for the past three months. Well, this morning we had a tragic event in California. You may not read about it in the papers, but one of the foremost computer scientists died last night. He was not only a well-respected engineer, he was my friend, one of the students I initially mentored and then grew very close to over the past 40 years that I have been working in industry. Rob Stanton and I were deeply involved in the initial launch of the DARPA net and he became a living legend in Silicon Valley. He was a great entrepreneur and also helped the NSA keep their eyes open for new talent and new opportunities. He even helped us commercialize some of the ideas that we dreamt up at DARPA and needed to get into the mainstream culture. Well, I am not here to deliver a eulogy, the fact is he died."

"And this morning I received a letter from him which was disturbing. You see, Rob took his own life. His letter outlined the terrible trauma that led to his eventual demise, and, regrettably, it confirms a lot of things. It seems Rob created a computer worm in 1995 as a research exercise. It was a precursor to the first search engine – you know like Yahoo and Google. He had this idea to index the Internet via a harmless computer worm and he was testing it out in the lab. Although he released the code, nothing came back and he thought it had crashed. Then he got called on a high-priority assignment and forgot about the research effort. The company he was working at folded, and the project died – end of story. But then, a few years later, Rob started seeing signs that the worm was alive and kicking. He writes that it seemed insignificant at the time, data would appear on servers, people would delete it, case closed. But, the data dumps started getting bigger and bigger, so he had cyber security cops enhance the controls around servers, released the idea into Virus Control software vendors and the problem seemed to be solved. Rob explained that he was sure that his fix was sufficient and that he forgot about it after a few years."

"Anyway, I had invited him to our brainstorming session a few weeks ago. We asked some experts to join us confidentially in preparing the scenario analysis for the bandwidth deluge. I figured he must have been under the weather, or maybe hung over or jet-lagged because he seemed out of sorts. I didn't think much of it at the time, but now I see more clearly. When Rob saw our analysis, he began poking around some, and he discovered to his horror that the worm was still on the Internet. He panicked. He told us in his note that he thought about coming clean, but he feared that the embarrassment would have been too great. You see, his entire life has been dedicated to making technology to improve the lives of people, and then one day he wakes up and realizes he has created a monster that is feeding on the very same people he was trying to help."

"In his note, Rob explains some of the actions he tried to take to get rid of the worm and he explains how he failed at each attempt, leading to severe depression, and ultimately to his death. Rob begged me to preserve his post-mortem reputation. I loved the man like a father loves his son and I fully intend to honor his dying wish, but I need your help to do that. Folks, this has been a roller coaster. Our bandwidth mystery is solved, and our eyes have truly been opened to new possibilities. And, thanks to Rob, now we know how the nanobots came to life. Unfortunately, we also know that they are running rampant right now, like an epidemic. And now we need to focus all our energy on shutting down these microscopic monsters once and for all. Let's finish the job that Rob started."

The team was stunned. Jim spoke, "Shilesh, I'm really sorry for your loss. It's awful, it's unimaginable. But…But…if the nanobot creator couldn't squash these bugs, what do you expect us to do?"

Li countered, "Jim, we have a whole team. Look around, we have the best expertise from a wide variety of disciplines. We know how this beast operates; now we need to engineer a way to shut it down."

Jeanine spoke up, "I've been putting a lot of thought into this, and I do have a solution. It is complicated, but hear me out. The nanobots which have already infected humans need to be quarantined. Unlike a traditional infection-based epidemic, we know who has been infected - they're listed on the nanobot facebook. We can also track the path of infections each day by looking for updates, you know, new members on the nanobot facebook. We know that the nanobots need to transmit their information because it has been built into their DNA. So, we have to stop their ability to transmit from the infected users."

Li asked, "Are you proposing that we shut down facebook?"

Jeanine explained, "No…that won't do the trick. You see, the nanobots have created their own version of facebook and have launched it inside the blocked bandwidth. They have done the same thing that we do with our DARPA net, they have created an isolated network for their own private usage."

"How about we shut down their cell phones?" Li asked.

"That's where I was leading to," Jeanine continued, "we know all the people who have the infected cell phones; we need them to turn off and destroy those phones."

Shilesh countered, "What happens when they buy a new phone?"

"I haven't solved that piece yet, Shilesh," Jeanine conceded.

Maggie explained, "If word of this leaks out into the general public, we will have a disaster on our hands. I can picture it now, hoards of people burning their cell phones. Random strangers will be suspected as carriers of the nanobot flu, they will be murdered. It will be anarchy."

Jim countered, "Maybe we can disable the nanobots? Maybe we block their frequency or jam their transmissions so that they begin to screw up."

"My concern is that unsuccessful attacks would only increase the likelihood of mutation," Jeanine cautioned. "On the one hand, we are very fortunate that the nanobots are not virulent. As Li has explained to us, and as Shilesh has confirmed, the nanobots 'purpose in life' appears to be benign. Clearly, we are all afraid that the nanobots can suddenly morph into something bad. And, that kind of disaster would arise if a mutation occurred. We do not want the nanobots to mutate, they cannot become innovative."

Jim quipped, "Can we get them a job at Microsoft? That will kill any innovation." The room laughed as Jim broke the tension, then he continued, "Jeanine, can you try to walk us through your plan in a little more detail?"

Jeanine replied, "I am concerned that if we cannot wipe out the nanobots in one fell swoop, then they may mutate, and we would have a disaster on our hands. We need to make a public announcement and begin the quarantine process with hopes of stopping this thing before it mutates."

"Why?" Maggie asked.

"You see, if word of the nanobots gets leaked into the news and we do not have a plan to clean it up, we will have mass chaos. Our likelihood of managing the crisis will be virtually zero." Jeanine explained.

"It is worse than that," Li explained, "You see, the nanobots are ordered into hierarchies, and they're built to innovate. They have leaders among their ranks, called the configurators, and the configurators are the ones that innovate; or mutate, as Jeanine would say. From what Shilesh has uncovered, we know that the configurators are descendants of the original worm that Mr. Stanton created 15 years ago. So, you have to ask yourself, how could this software persist for so long? Well, it is because of the artificial intelligence that was built into its design. You see, the nanobots have this master model of everything on earth, and everyone that they have been able to invade. They have indexed all of the material into their model; we call it a canonical. The canonical is the nanobots' master blueprint of how things work, of what mistakes have been made, and how to avoid them."

"Sounds like they have their own Bible?" Jim ventured.

"Bible, Torah, Koran, Vedas, or whatever you call it. These religious texts were in fact the very first versions of canonicals, but those were for humans. In fact, the nanobots' canonical contains the information from all of those books, but then goes on to keep indexing. Those ancient texts have not been modified in thousands of years. The nanobot canonical is being refined and edited in real time. It's the blueprint of the world. With the combination of a real-time canonical and the adaptive approach of trial and error, the nanobots continuously learn and improve."

"If we permit the public to realize that the nanobots exist, and if we make it known that we are working towards eradicating them, then our plans will enter the news, the blogosphere, and ultimately, it will enter the nanobots' canonical. The nanobots have never been threatened, so they never had to defend themselves. It would be a new phenomena, not only new to us, but also new to them. I am afraid that we don't know how they would react. It is possible that the mere act of raising public consciousness that we are aware of the nanobots and that we want to eliminate them might be enough information to cause the configurators to begin innovating to find ways to defend themselves."

Shilesh furthered, "So the mere fact that we let it be known that we want to eradicate the enemy would be sufficient to energize it to move against us. It's typical game theory, makes sense. Releasing this information to the public would degrade our conflict into a tit-for-tat exchange and the result would be that everyone would lose. This is a terrible situation. I do not see what options we have. Anyone have an idea on how to proceed?"

Maggie exclaimed, "All is not lost, at least we know that we need to act with surprise. We need to be covert in our approach to eradicating these buggers. We're good at covert stuff."

Jeanine countered, "Yes, the government is good at covert operations, but in Public Health Management, we use education and publicity to reduce the spread of epidemics. Being covert about the existence of an epidemic is contrary to our basic logic. If we cannot tell anyone about the nanobots, how do we quarantine people to stop the spread?"

The room was silent and the team was contemplative. Maggie suggested, "I think we need to be systematic. Let's try this, Jeanine, you and Li can study the nanobots that we have in the lab. Subject them to every type of hazard you can think of. Let's see what kinds of hazards will kill a nanobot. Then, we will eliminate all of the hazards that will also kill humans. If we have any hope at all, it is that there will be something we find which kills a nanobot, but not a human."

Jim joked, "So Jeanine, if you want to stop by my desk, I can give you a piece of kryptonite. It worked wonders on Superman." Maggie glared at Jim, seeming to lose the humor which Jim was offering. She continued, "Shilesh, you need to begin to formulate an emergency plan. We will call it the doomsday scenario. If we run out of options, you need to figure out how to turn off the Internet and all the cell phones, simultaneously. Then we can collect and destroy the cell phones, re-start the Internet, bringing one machine at a time back onto the Internet to ensure we have eliminated Mr. Stanton's nanobot nightmare."

"Maggie," Shilesh explained, "You're asking me to try to *turn off* the Internet? For God's sake, it's not a light switch. And you want to collect all the infected cell phones for destruction? Imagine the reaction. It seems impossible to me, but I will begin evaluating potential scenarios."

Shilesh looked drained and doubtful. Stanton's death seemed to have hit him hard, and he looked like he had aged 10 years since yesterday. The confident glow and warmth seemed to have permanently left his face.

"I know it's extreme, that's why we called it a doomsday scenario," Maggie reminded.

"Do we have a *non*-doomsday scenario?" Jim asked.

"That's what you and I will begin to evaluate, hopefully with some help from Jeanine and Li," Maggie replied, then announced, "Look...I know it's late. Why don't we all try to get a few hours of sleep. I've got a feeling we are going to be working on this baby for a while. Let's meet back here at 6:00am."

The team gradually dispersed and Jim hung around the conference room until he and Maggie were the last ones.

"You okay Maggie?" Jim wanted to be with Maggie, but he could sense that some kind of obstacle was rising between them.

"I'm fine Jim," she said, "But I don't have a good feeling about this."

Jim understood that Maggie was not interested in anything remotely sexual at that moment, and he didn't press further. They walked towards their rooms and platonically parted ways.

Chapter 30

The next morning, it seemed that the team was slow to organize in the conference room. Maggie and Jim arrived on time, but Jeanine and Li were 5 minutes late. Li had a face of exhaustion, and Jim suspected she had not slept. Jeanine was tentative, and seemed to be lost in thought. As they were waiting for Shilesh, Jeanine began to explain, "I have made a list of potential hazards, Maggie. Please let me know if we can get all these today. Li and I were not able to sleep, so we prepared the list a few hours ago."

Maggie smiled, "Sure, if anything else comes to mind, just let me know. I will get started on this right away." She typed into her DARPA net blackberry and Anthony appeared at the door. He retrieved the list from Maggie and left. Maggie finally began to lose patience and yelled to Anthony, "Can you go wake up Shilesh?"

Anthony hurried out of the room to get Shilesh, while the team continued to discuss potential hazards and strategies for testing the nanobots. A few minutes later, Maggie's DARPA net blackberry rang. When she answered the phone, her expression immediately changed and she exclaimed, "Oh my God!" Maggie hung up the phone and dropped the news, "Shilesh died last night." The team in the room was stunned. There were blank stares and gasps. Li began sobbing uncontrollably as Jeanine, Jim and Maggie tried to console her in the hopes of also consoling themselves.

When Anthony returned to the conference room, he brought details that added to the grim mood. He explained that Shilesh had also taken his life. Anthony believed that Shilesh had overdosed on medications, and by his bed he left a note that read:

Rob Stanton is me. I'm sorry.

Maggie seemed devastated at the news and remained still. Her mind seemed to be comprehending the severity of Shilesh's death. As the ramifications began to sink in, Maggie nearly lost control. She explained, "He was the Chief Risk Officer of the United States, nearly a peer to the President. Shilesh's role was designed to span across administrations so that the change of guard would not compromise our nation's safety. We will have the entire administration and the Department of Defense crawling around here in hours. This is a disaster. With the loss of Shilesh, there is no feasible way we can implement the doomsday scenario. Jeanine…Jim…Li, we're facing Armageddon, aren't we?" The team was spiritually bankrupt, and the mood was nothing but pessimism.

Jeanine suggested, "I think that the hazard analysis is our last hope Maggie."

Maggie immediately snapped back, "I know…I will make sure we get all the stuff together for you. It will become more difficult because of Shilesh, but we have no options but to find a solution. I need to go and brief the President. Let's regroup in a couple of hours."

Maggie yelled into her DARPA net blackberry, "Anthony, make sure you get on that list from Jeanine…and connect me to the White House." Maggie left the conference room, still shouting orders on her phone and making every attempt to bring order amongst the chaos.

Jim, Li and Jeanine sat and stared at each other. Could they find a solution to bring the nanobot epidemic under control?

The diagnostic equipment to be used for exploring whether there were ways to kill the nanobots arrived while Jim, Jeanine and Li were still formulating the testing plan. The team had agreed that Jeanine would review biological pathogens while Jim and Li would investigate mechanical approaches. The range of potential hazards was wide and included standard tests like heat, cold, UV rays and microwaves as well as more risky tests including radiation, electromagnetic waves, various chemical solvents and acids. Li had also suggested that the team should evaluate the potential for developing a competing nanobot which would neutralize the existing invader. The work was long and arduous, and when Maggie popped up on the LCD screen to ask about status, the team explained that they believed the tests could take 72 hours or more. Maggie was dismayed and nervous. She encouraged the team, "I know it is hard work. Do your best. I will try to buy some time. People are running around reacting to Shilesh's death, so I think that I can provide you with air cover for a few days."

They were rats running in a maze, bumping into walls and changing directions. Finding a nanobot killer was nothing but dead ends and false hopes. Jeanine confirmed that severe solvents would eliminate the nanobot, but she could not find any solution which would not also wipe out the human host. Li was equally stumped. She confirmed that radiation and an electromagnetic pulse would eradicate the nanobots, but this essentially meant bombarding the world with nuclear weapons, which was not a survival solution. After about 48 hours of testing, Jim, Li and Jeanine were becoming increasingly convinced that Maggie's doomsday scenario was the only option, but they continued to search for alternatives. The team had been taking turns sleeping in shifts, and it was Jim's turn to get some rest. As he was walking toward his suite, he saw Maggie sitting in the lounge with Jake. Jim's blood cooled as he saw Jake, but Jake was as warm and slick as ever, "Hey there, Jimbo. Maggie's briefing me on my upcoming arrest and incarceration. I need a break…do you want to join us for a drink?"

"Sure," Jim replied as he grabbed a beer from the self-service bar and joined Maggie and Jake. Jim was haggard from the intense research, and he wasn't overly talkative to begin with, so his presence was difficult for all the parties at the table.

"Sounds like you guys have a big issue right now?" Jake asked.

Jim wasn't sure how much information Maggie had given to Jake, so he replied vaguely, "Yes, we've got a lot going on right now. Some pretty interesting stuff."

Jake responded, "It's a shame about Shilesh, I am not sure how his death will affect us. Maybe Maggie will become the new head honcho, what do you think Jimmy?"

Jim exercised all of his self control to remain calm, and casually shrugged, "I don't really think about that kind of stuff Jake. The thought never crossed my mind."

"What do you mean you never think about it? I mean, come on, she's smart, she's a woman, and she's working on a project which has given her more face time with the President than anyone we know."

Jim leaned back in his chair and reacted in an unconcerned manner as he explained, "Jake, I'm a scientist, not a politician. People like you and Maggie are destined to lead those kinds of lives. Being the President of the USA right now is a waste of time if we cannot stop these nanobots. The leader will end up being the person rearranging the deck chairs on the Titanic as it slowly sinks."

Jake seemed to sense that Jim was headed for a conflict and he quickly changed tack, "Thanks for the letter of recommendation, Doctor Andrews. But I'm putting my money on Maggie anyway. Hey, sorry to be a pooper, but I gotta go." Jake excused himself and headed quickly away from the lounge.

Maggie stared into Jim's face and asked, "Do you really think I'm destined for it Jim? I mean, it's a hell of a way to get a promotion to have your friend die on you." Maggie had hit a nerve. Jim searched Maggie's face for a hint of the passion and romance that they had shared, but he could sense that the flame had died. He used to find warmth and empathy in Maggie's eyes, but Jim could tell that he was alone again, and he excused himself and stood up to leave. Maggie interrupted him as he was leaving and explained, "Hey, I'm not really feeling myself right now. This whole mess has started to take a toll on me, sorry."

When he arrived in his suite, Jim lay awake pondering the discussion with Jake and Maggie. He evaluated Maggie's sudden change of heart, and something was nagging at him. It was that itchy scab which you don't want to scratch. You try to ignore it, but it burns. So, you scratch it just a little bit, hoping for relief, but finding that the irritation has only increased. Then, like a balm, Jim put his finger on the problem.

Jim's mind drifted back to Sally and Abdul Yimani, to their courtship and to Anthony's comment that Sally did not stand a chance with a guy like Yimani. Jim replayed the scenes of his life with Maggie, their courtship, their romance, the rapidity of the sexual encounter between them. His nagging doubt began to smolder and burn and Jim started to wonder if he had been 'played the fool.' He guessed that Maggie was 'cut from the same cloth' as Jake, and ultimately, the same cloth as Yimani. Jim contemplated the linkages. Why did Sally die? Why did they kill Yimani too? Perhaps the intelligence service was done with Yimani? Perhaps he failed in his mission to get information on Jim, so he was killed? In that case, maybe Sally's death was an accident. Then Jim thought about how carelessly Jake approached the closing of the Sound Fusion Factory. He was indifferent to the displacement and pain that he caused. For Jake, pain was 'incidental' to his mission. He understood that people like Jake and Maggie viewed their mission as foremost, and everything else as secondary. From that perspective, Jim suspected that Maggie was using him as a pawn, just like Yimani had used his wife.

And, what if Yimani had worked for the US government? What if he was a double agent? It was a credible scenario that he could have been taken down by the people he betrayed. Jim felt ill at ease as he developed the idea in his mind. There were too many lies. If Maggie is a scumbag, like Jake and Yimani, then she will just use me until she's achieved her mission, then spit me out - leave me to hang. His troubled thoughts churned in his mind. He was only exaggerating. He was going crazy. This was just a breakdown from the stress of the research, from the loss of Sally and Shilesh, and from being impotent in finding a quick fix for the nanobots. Perhaps it was paranoia arising out of sleep deprivation. Yes, sleep would be wonderful. With proper rest, he would recuperate. He would calmly look at things with a fresh mind in the morning.

But the morning slowly came. Jim was watching, thinking, tossing, and waiting. The troubled night surrendered into a troubled morning. Jim needed answers. He needed Maggie to be straight with him.

Maggie was meeting again with Jake when Jim passed by her desk. Jim was looking forward to Jake's departure and imminent incarceration, and he was depressed to keep bumping into him.

"Hey Maggie, when you're free, give me a holler, I need to go over some stuff."

"Sure. Maybe about 20 minutes, Jim."

Jim returned to his lab and settled down to review the results of the testing that had taken place while he was pretending to sleep. Without notice, Maggie popped up on Jim's videoconference screen. "Jim, can you get Jeanine and Li and meet us in the conference room? Looks like the shit is hitting the fan."

"Yum," Jim replied.

Maggie weakly smiled, "Nope, it's never pleasant when that happens."

Chapter 31

The scientists were greeted by a conference room filled with VIPs. In addition to Jake and Maggie, they were staring face-to-face with the Secretary of Defense, the Secretary of State, and the Vice President.

Maggie continued, "Madame Secretary, Mister Secretary and Mister Vice-President, I would like to introduce you to the team that was working with Doctor Gupta." She motioned for the group to come fully into the room, "Jeanine, Li and Jim, please sit down."

The Secretary of State began the meeting, "I must say that Maggie has been very complimentary of your team. You have all been performing a service for the Country. You've disrupted your lives and have gone far above the call of duty, as we say. We're obviously distraught with Shilesh's death. He was a personal friend as well as a colleague and we are mourning the loss. But, unfortunately, as you know, we're not in a position to stand still. As Maggie has briefed us, it seems like we are on the cusp of an international event, and we were hoping you all could give us some deeper answers on where we stand and what we can do about it." The scientists looked around at each other, and then at Maggie and Jake.

Maggie nodded her head towards Jim, but Li spoke up. "Excuse me Madame Secretary, it's…it's just that we're not accustomed to this kind of environment. Let me start with the basics. Have you been briefed on the nanobots?"

"Yes, we're aware of the threat. It seems serious," the Secretary of Defense cut in.

Jeanine added, "It has the potential to be devastating, Mr. Secretary. If this epidemic progresses on its current path, we could face a rampant disaster. And from what Li has uncovered, we are not able to publicize the matter. We're trying to find ways to stop the epidemic while maintaining secrecy."

The Secretary of Defense pushed back, "What about the doomsday scenario?"

Maggie interjected, "We're holding that back for the last resort. It is drastic, Mr. Secretary."

"Tell me Doctors, what is the likelihood in your opinion that these nanobots turn on us?"

"You mean the likelihood they become virulent?" Li asked.

"Yes…you know…virulence or aggression, whatever you want to call it. What is the likelihood that if we just keep quiet…you know…what if we just sit tight, but increase the Internet's bandwidth capacity? Do you think that these nanobots will just peacefully co-exist within the infected population? I mean…think of how useful this could be for surveillance."

Jim felt the vomit rising towards his mouth. He stared at Jeanine who explained, "Mr. Secretary, the truth is that we do not know. We can tell the pattern of the epidemic…it's spreading like the flu…that much we are certain of. In fact, we are sure that the nanobot does not cause flu like symptoms; rather, it seems that if a host has the H1N1 flu, then the nanobots tie themselves into it and use the flu symptoms as a transport mechanism. It explains why the nanobot transmission has tracked the H1N1 flu. Unfortunately, we don't think that the nanobots would be stopped even if we were able to eradicate the H1N1 flu, because we think that it would just latch onto something else - the common cold, the seasonal flu, whatever it takes. So, like it or not, the nanobot epidemic will march on. To answer your question about coexistence, we need to understand the potential for mutation. I mean, we know that it exists, but we do not know whether the mutation would be virulent."

The secretary of Defense angrily countered, "Maggie, I thought you said these nanobots were peaceful."

Li interrupted, "Yes Mr. Secretary. Maggie is correct…the nanobots are currently existing symbiotically with the hosts and inside the SIM cards of their cell phones."

"So what's the likelihood that they turn into terrorists?"

"Sir, we don't think it will happen; and, odd as it sounds, we think that the one event that could turn the nanobots into a threat is if we publicize their existence. It's hard to explain in lay terms. But we believe that if the nanobots were to discover…that is, if they were indexing news sites and created a topic which indicated that we want to destroy them. Well, we think that it would have the potential to cause a defensive mutation and possibly result in aggressive evolution."

"So what do we do? Do we just sit tight and shut up?" the Vice President asked.

Maggie confirmed, "The confidentiality is our only hope."

"Besides the doomsday option," the Secretary of Defense confirmed.

"Yes, I'm afraid so. And we think the doomsday option is not feasible," Maggie replied.

Jim observed as the Secretary of Defense rocked back and forth in his chair. He was staring at the ceiling and contemplating the situation. Then the Secretary spoke, "Well, I guess this is not that bad is it? I mean, we're able to keep it confidential, that's not too difficult. Meanwhile, you all can find an alternative strategy to take out the nanobots. If all hell breaks loose, we can always push the doomsday button."

Jim explained, "We're looking at strategies, but so far the results have not been promising."

Li continued, "It seems like we may require a month or more to find anything definitive, and there is a chance we may not ever find a palatable solution."

The Secretary of Defense cross-examined, "And we're sure...we're absolutely sure that this is not the work of our enemies?"

"Shilesh explained how he accidentally caused the problem Mr. Secretary," Maggie assured, "It looks like we shot ourselves in the foot."

"Yes, yes, yes. Okay, now let me ask some more difficult questions. What if it takes us two months to find a cure?"

Jeanine explained the pattern, "It is just like the flu. Within 12 months, the majority of the world would be exposed. So, in two months, this wave would be cresting and the next wave would be beginning. Each wave affects more and more people."

Silence attacked the room, tension held them hostage.

"Maggie, please make sure we place orders to substantially increase network capacity," the Secretary of Defense ordered.

"Yes sir...we have arranged it already. Jake is going back to Silicon Valley to start a company that will be focused on bandwidth expansion via compression. We will combine massive purchases of hardware with a few of the innovations we have recently learned. Primarily, we will focus on using microbytes to increase capacity."

Jim was floored. The words fell out of his mouth like drool, "What about jail, Jake? I thought you were going to jail?"

Jake was unflappable. He smiled at Jim with a look of genuine friendship and replied, "We've taken care of all that." Still, his response was made in such a manner that Jim felt like an idiot.

Maggie interrupted, "You see, it turns out that Jake disappeared because he was in confidential negotiations with the Carlyle Group to sell Sound Fusion Factory. The bankruptcy was just a big mix-up, a very unfortunate misunderstanding, and since Jake was bound by a non-disclosure contract, he had to be quiet. He had to disappear. But, now we will explain that someone has agreed to buy the Sound Fusion Factory, and they are going to use it as a platform to build a new company to pursue bandwidth expansion. At least, that's how it will read in the newspaper. As you know, we believe network capacity will be a burgeoning market since our little nanobots keep eating up the bandwidth on the Internet."

Jim had not slept. He was already distressed before this meeting. Now, he was grasping the ledge of sanity with his last few fingers. He was holding on, but could feel himself slipping dangerously close to the abyss. Breathe…breathe…in and out, in with the good air, out with the bad air…do not display emotion, not here, definitely not here.

The Secretary of Defense continued, "Maggie that's a good story, nice job. But I have some more questions. Now, I know that this is going to sound nuts. But let's assume that Jeanine, Jim and Li are correct and that the nanobots are peaceful. Let's assume that we can keep them safe and secure, you know, keep them clueless that we know about them and that we want to eradicate them."

"Go on," Maggie encouraged.

"Well, think about it for a minute. We know about the nanobots, but they don't know about us. You see. Now *we're* the invisible ones. Think about the surveillance opportunities. I mean, for example, let's say these nanobots get passed into our enemies' brains. Jeanine has estimated that we can get there in about a year. I mean, think about it! We can track the bad guys, we can spy on them, we can become their eyes and ears! We wouldn't need any more real spies. Think about it, Maggie! This capability would put us in an unprecedented position."

Jeanine lost her nerve, "No!" she gasped.

Maggie defused the bomb, "Mister Secretary, with all due respect, I think that there is too much uncertainty. I mean, the ethical, and legal and moral considerations would make it impossible. You're right that we could spy on our enemies, but we would also be invading every person in the world who has a cell phone. It's…it's…not possible."

The Secretary of Defense backed down, "Of course, of course Maggie. I was not suggesting that we actually do it. I was just explaining that while Jeanine, Li and Jim are developing the cure, we should keep an eye on the progress of the nanobots. And…and…as we discussed, if for some reason they turn against us, we have a doomsday plan. Let's get someone thinking about the logistics of the doomsday option. Now that Shilesh has left, we need someone to focus on it. Maggie, do you think you could assume that role?"

Silence recaptured the advantage. Stillness crept in. Jim began to keep score, like a pitch count in a baseball game - Silence 2….Bullshit 2.

"Uh….it's a pretty tall marching order. Shilesh left a big pair of shoes to fill."

"Fine Maggie, but the three of us are sure that you can do it." The Secretary waved his hands towards the Vice President and the Secretary of State, who all nodded affirmatively in a polite and inviting manner.

"I'm honored, but...but...I will consider it sirs and madam. I mean, it's a big challenge."

And then it happened.

"Jim, Li and Jeanine, thank you so much for coming to meet with us." They were dismissed by the new Chief Risk Officer of the United States.

As the scientists walked back towards the lab, Jim commented, "I didn't like that one bit."

"Scary," Jeanine concurred.

Jim erupted, "We've got to find a solution...this is untenable. Imagine two weeks from now...a new boss comes in, priorities get changed, and we get marginalized. The nanobot threat takes a back seat to something else, and the government gets a great new spy tool. We've got to stop the nanobots - we've got to stop the NSA!"

"Jim, we *are* the NSA," Li drily explained.

Silence 2...Bullshit 3 - three strikes and you're out – Jim lost it.

Chapter 32

Jim clutched the door to his suite and entered. He needed time to decompress from the twist of events. He continued to practice breathing exercises and stared at his laptop screen on the desk in his room. He paced the rooms, leaving the sitting area and entering the bathroom and then back again.

Something must be done…it will be okay…this will work out. Jim sat down at the desk and stared at his laptop. He was searching for answers, searching for anything really, then he decided to search the DARPA net's internal Wikipedia for Shilesh Gupta. As he expected, the entry was immense, his accomplishments were many. Jim missed Shilesh. He was depressed, confused and felt isolated.

Jim did not mind being alone, he was accustomed to being a loner. But this feeling was different. He felt adrift at sea, with no rudder and no compass, mindlessly surfing the DARPA net Wikipedia to read the obituary of an old friend. Jim was reminiscing about Shilesh when a secure chat screen opened up.

B4:   Hi there stranger.

Jim: Who is it?

B4:   Are you alone?

Jim: Is this Maggie?

B4:   No, it's Shilesh.

Jim stared at the chat window, not believing his eyes and continued typing.

Jim: I saw them carry Shilesh away in a body bag, who are you?

B4:   I died, it's true.

Jim: Who are you?

B4:   It's me, can I explain?

Jim: Sure.

B4:   Did you ever read Ray Kurzweil?

Jim: Yes, I'm a fan, why?

B4:   I really messed up on this worm. So, I decided to fight back. When I realized the full scope of what I had done, I began to create a counter attack program. I got the idea from Kurzweil that I could fashion it after the persona of Shilesh Gupta, so I uploaded all my personal data, my preferences, my history, basically as much of my spirit as I could represent in data. I loaded it into an expert system, but I embedded this expert system in the worm and then I launched myself as a nanobot. I am nanobot version 2.0. I made some adjustments for prior mistakes. For example, I cannot reproduce, and I have a time bomb, which means I die in 15 years. And I have programmed in non-violence. I am not even allowed to include any violence in my decision trees. All I can do is disable the nanobots, I cannot hurt people or anything else for that matter. I also made some upgrades. For example, I added a secure communication channel and linked it to a Turing engine so that I can chat. And, I am hooked into the DARPA net as well as the Internet, and I can jump back and forth. That way I can keep an eye on you guys. And finally, I programmed in memory loss. In fact, now that I have told you my history, it will be deleted from my registers, but I will save a memory of you.

Jim: So I will not chat with you again?

B4:   It's unlikely. I have a very limited mission now. I have to fix what I broke. And I have one request.

Jim: What?

B4:   Open the desk drawer and look inside, tell me when you find it, don't plug it in.

Jim opened his desk drawer and, in the tray where pencils were usually kept, he found a small Toshiba memory stick. He picked up the memory stick and looked at it.

Jim: Found it

B4:   It's the source code for Nanobot 2.0. I want you to load yourself into it also, in case you need it.

Jim: What do you mean?

B4:   There is a configuration manager, you will get the idea. Then, I want you to save it on your iPod so that it remains out of the eyes of the NSA, and of course then destroy the Memory Stick. Think of it as Life Insurance for the planet.

Jim: Why would I need it?

B4:   Maggie killed me. My nanobot was instructed to lie dormant until my obituary appeared on the Internet or DARPA net. I suspected it would happen, so I planted the stick in your room. If you're chatting with me, I'm dead. I might need your help in here.

Jim: How would I find you?

B4:   I installed a sensor. When your nanobot activates, it sends out a message. I will know you've died and will find you. We have a crypto key, so we will know each other. Then we can coordinate to chase down the nanobots.

Jim: Did you put Abba on my iPod?

B4:   Love them.

Jim: Why did Maggie kill you?

B4:   Whoever controls the nanobots has ultimate power. She connected the dots a lot faster than you did.

Jim: What if I choose to remove your nonviolence criteria in my nanobot?

B4:   Error Message: Out of Bounds Logic Error, Please re-enter your question?

Jim: Can I make myself eternal?

B4:   Yes, you can eliminate the termination date in the setup screen.

Jim: Anything else you want to tell me?

B4:   May the force be with you ☺

Jim stared at the blinking face on the screen and watched as the chat window disappeared.

Put my life on a memory stick? The thought was novel and, as usual, curiosity took over. Jim disabled the wireless connectivity on his laptop and plugged in the Memory Stick and the iPod into his laptop.

The computer brought up a dialog box:

Migrate to iPod: Y__   N__

Jim clicked *yes* and the program ran for a few minutes, and then closed. Uneventful really; there were no graphics or anything, just a spinning hourglass that disappeared after a few minutes.

He looked on his iPod and saw that the nanobot program had been stored as a Podcast. He tested it and saw that he could easily download it to his laptop. He saw the setup program and froze in his tracks. It was done, it was ready to be configured.

Jim shut down the computer, unplugged the memory stick and the iPod. He put the iPod back on the docking station on top of the alarm clock and looked at the memory stick. He twirled it around in his fingers. "The key to eternal life," he mused. "You won't get in the wrong hands, baby. Not on my watch," he said as he broke the stick in pieces.

The bowels of the memory stick contained a printed circuit board; and, in the electronic wreckage Jim could clearly see the DRAM chip. That's the place where all the data was stored. He walked into the Asian Spa bathroom and retrieved a pair of nail clippers. Jim pried loose the DRAM chip from the printed circuit board. It was small and black, barely larger than his pinky fingernail. So much damage could come in such a small package. The nail clippers made a distinct crackle as they ate into the DRAM chip, creating a half-dozen pieces of silicon, spilt on the desk in disarray. Jim threw two pieces in the garbage can, flushed two down the toilet and ate the other two pieces. "That should do it."

He swept up the remains from the broken Memory Stick and threw them in the garbage can. Jim returned to the Asian Spa bathroom, straightened himself up, and headed back downstairs to his lab.

Chapter 33

As Jim was leaving his suite, he saw Maggie walking down the hallway. She smiled at Jim, albeit in a purely platonic manner and asked, "How are you doing Jim. This has been a pretty crazy day, huh?"

Jim was terrified of Maggie, indeed now he hated her. She was Medusa, not Venus, and he was afraid to look into her dangerous eyes. Jim unexpectedly snapped back, "Crazy? How about nightmare! I think we're down here trying to save the planet, then I realize that you and the other spooks want to use the nanobot invasion to take over the world! Crazy doesn't even begin to capture the mood Maggie. You people are lunatics...and you've taken over the asylum."

Maggie did not take Jim's bait. Like Jake, she was unflappable. She smoothly responded, "Jim, it got a little weird in that meeting, I agree. Sometimes the Secretary of Defense can be aggressive, but we set him straight."

"Our only goal is to keep tabs on the eye of God while you, Jeanine and Li find a cure. Jake will ensure that we have adequate bandwidth in case the cure is hard to find. You see, the Government doesn't want to try to control the nanobots. Even if someone someday followed that path, we would only use them for peaceful purposes. But for now, we will do nothing. We will keep quiet until you find a solution."

"Speaking of solutions, since we're moving into a new mode of research, this does give you, Jeanine and Li a chance to move to a more pleasant locale. Do you have any interest in returning to California to work with Jake?"

Maggie picked up on his mental recoil. She continued, "It's just an option, you're welcome to stay here in the bunker. I just thought that if the research dragged on, you might go stir crazy. Or worse, you might end up being a full-time hermit like me."

As Maggie was placating, Jim opened his eyes to her manner. Her responses were making him regret ever expressing any feelings for her. He held nothing but disdain for Maggie, but attempted to hide his emotions. Maggie could pick up on his changes, and she peppered him with a question, "Hey Jim, are you okay? You don't look good."

Jim lost it. "Maggie, I don't like getting used and then thrown away."

"What do you mean?"

"You used me Maggie. You lured me down here, dressed me up like your little doll, and then fucked me. And now that the mission is changing colors, you're dropping me down the toilet like a piece of shit."

"I used you? Hah, now there's a good one Jim."

"What are you saying Maggie?"

"Jim, I gave you what you wanted. You wanted money, I gave it to you; a new start in life, done; you wanted to set up your own lab and run your own show, done. And now you have the gall to say that I used you? You're incredible. You wanted to sleep with me the moment you walked into this office. You think I don't know? I see it, I feel it. Jim, do you even know my last name? No, you don't. You were too busy checking me out. Besides, who needs a last name when they have tits like these, right? The first time we talked about any possibility of a relationship, I told you it was not possible. And, you still wanted to sleep with me. What did you expect? It happened; yes, it happened one time. And you used me as much as I used you - it was mutual."

Maggie began to leave, but added, "And by the way, Shilesh screwed both of us. You should be more angry with Shilesh than with me. I'm trying to help you."

Jim had transcended his body and was watching the conversation from afar. He was proud that he held his tongue. Yes, Maggie was dangerous. She was an abject liar. She was a cold, ruthless killer. Jim wanted to strangle Maggie, right there in the hallway. He saw his hands wrapped around her beautiful neck as he squelched the breath right out of her, leaving her limp and lifeless.

But as this morbid thought flashed through his mind, Jim realized that Maggie was only a symptom of the problem. There were dozens of Maggies-in-waiting. She was only propagating a warped system. So he relaxed and concentrated on his breathing. Within a fraction of a second, Jim put up walls around his emotions and locked his anger, his romantic rejection, and his fear into a compartment far in the back of his mind. Defense was important - Jim did not want to end up like Shilesh, until he had the opportunity to more fully reflect on Shilesh's insurance offer.

"You're right Maggie. I don't know what got into me. Must be the stress. I'm sorry if I was an ass. I just need some time to think."

"Think about what?"

"I mean…maybe you're right…maybe California is a good idea. A few days ago I thought I would never visit that place again, but I can't live in this fortified bunker forever. The research could take a while. We both know that the results we're seeing so far are not that encouraging. There doesn't appear to be an easy fix. Besides, if it were easy, then Shilesh would have fixed things instead of killing himself. So, maybe you're right…maybe I should go back home. I don't know…I need some time to think. I need to get some fresh air."

Maggie softened her tone and empathized, "I know what you mean Jim. Look, take a day off. Ask Anthony to take you somewhere. Get a new perspective...we can talk about the future later. You've got a whole team working on the nanobot research, and they will get by for a day or two without you. Let them know you're leaving and keep your DARPA net blackberry nearby in case they need you. But take a mental health day; Jim, you've earned it."

Jim used all his effort to manufacture a smile. "Thanks Maggie, I think I will. I'm sorry for the way I acted. You probably think I'm insane."

"This whole business is insane, Jim. Not you, you're special. And by the way, it's Paige. Margaret Lynne Paige." She smiled.

They parted, and Jim retreated back to his suite. The lab would have to wait. He felt angry and scared, and he knew that he needed to escape without making a scene. Jim thought about Maggie's response – "take your DARPA net blackberry," she had said. Of course, with the DARPA net blackberry, Jim could be tracked anywhere, but he also needed the link back to the NSA. Jim looked around the closet and found a small bag he had brought for his first interview. He threw in some clothes, mostly his old clothes, and prepared to leave. He entered the Asian Spa bathroom and packed his toiletries, then called Anthony. It was time to go.

"Hi Doctor Andrews. Maggie told me you wanted to get away for a while. Let me know when you're ready."

"I'm ready now. I think I'd like to go to Long Island, see some old sights from my childhood."

"Sure thing Doctor, I'll be right down."

Jim picked up his iPod and put one ear bud in his ear, while he let the other dangle. He made sure his appearance was casual and left the suite. As he walked by the lounge on his way to the elevator, he passed Maggie and waved. "I'll see you in a day or two."

"Take care Jim," she warmly responded, earnest and genuine.

Chapter 34

As they entered the Range Rover, Jim asked, "Hey, let's stop by and pick up my dog, okay?"

"Sure"

The drive to Long Island was uneventful and traffic was calm. Lily seemed excited to be out of the kennel and she immediately placed her head out the window to catch the breeze as the car drove. Jim smiled and patted her back, "Man's best friend, eh?"

Anthony glanced into the rear view mirror and flashed a smile. "Doctor Andrews, do you want me to have someone get you a hotel or something? Do you have any plans?"

Jim had not thought of any logistics. His time with Magic Maggie in the NSA bunker had left him spoiled from the realities of everyday life. Jim acquiesced, "Anthony that would be great. Can you find a place near Amagansett? I'd like to spend the day near the beach."

Three hours later, Anthony was checking Jim into a modest, but elegant beach-front hotel in Montauk, the last town on Long Island's Southern tip. Jim thanked Anthony and asked, "You staying?"

"No, Doctor Andrews, I gotta get back to the office. Give me a call when you're ready to come back. But this time give me about three hours notice, okay?"

Jim agreed and they parted. He sat down in the hotel room and his mind began to race. What about the flu? What about the germs? Jim inspected the hotel room's furnishings. Although it was elegantly appointed, he retracted in repulsion when he thought of the risks for getting sick. He vowed to keep as far a distance from people as possible in hopes of avoiding the nanobots. The real world was dirty, and infection was easy. As he was preparing his mental protection plan, Jim realized that his life would never be the same. He had become pampered and coddled inside of the secure shell of the NSA. Jim was protected although he was trapped. It was a delicate balance - his protection was offset by the implied detention.

Jim grabbed Lily's leash, put it on her neck and asked, "Want to go for a walk Miss Wiggles?" Lily was ecstatic and they departed the hotel room. The late November air had turned into a cold December breeze, and the beach was empty. Jim fought against the constant wind, lumbering with each sandy step while Lily effortlessly ran crisscross in front of him, jolting his arm to the left and to the right as she hit the leash's end.

As he stared at the lighthouse on the tip of Long Island, Jim mused, "You've got the right idea Lily. Live in the moment. That's the only alternative isn't it? Try to do well, but live in the moment. Maybe Shilesh is right. Maybe I should download myself into an Orwellian nanobot and leave it dormant in case these guys decide to put the hit on me.

"Yeah, I need to do it, don't I? But what do you think Lil', should I choose a termination date? I mean, do you really want to know the day you will die? Do you really want to live forever?

"I think Shilesh was right about not reproducing, there's too much risk there. You never know how the offspring might turn out. And then there's violence and defense. I could do without violence. I mean, look at the maniac that runs our national defense. It is like good and evil, defense and aggression, they're two sides of the same coin.

"Yes, Shilesh was right. I can choose to work with him to search and disarm the nanobots, but other than that, who needs violence?"

Jim debated himself, "Of course, what would I do if I chose immortality? What if we fixed the nanobots five years from now? I would have no mission and no ability to terminate. I would be a lost soul, just like I am today, but with no end in sight.

"I think that if I am going to program myself into a nanobot, I should seek enhancements – like Shilesh did. Maybe I will program myself to be the Internet cop. You know, I could be on the lookout for nanobots and other bad guys, and disarm them. What do you think girl? I could be Superman in cyberspace."

Lily was busy sniffing sand.

Jim watched the Atlantic Ocean's waves. The tide was moderate and the winds were pulling white caps onto the tops of waves, causing spots to disrupt the blackness of the water and foam to build up on the sand. He decided to unhook Lily from her leash because there was no one around. She ran towards the water line, but stopped short when the icy water touched her paws. She stooped and jumped around the water line, sniffed the wave foam and began chasing either her shadow or the breeze, Jim was not sure. He envied the freedom of living in the moment.

Jim reflected on the chance for digital eternity and he was reticent. This was not a spiritual eternity, it was not physical either. It was somewhere in between. The collection of memories and preferences and beliefs; was that his life? Was Shilesh still alive?   If Shilesh deleted his memory registers but kept working in cyberspace to defuse the nanobots, was it really even Shilesh? If he joined Shilesh, would he really be Jim? Would he be a loner in cyberspace too? Would he even be alive? And what is the meaning of life?

But despite the wind and surf and despite Jim's cloudy thoughts, it was all just a 'tempest in a teapot,' wasn't it? You see, Jim was not a philosopher and he was not a spiritualist. Jim Andrews was a loner and he was a scientist. He was driven by curiosity and exploration, and the thrill of the quest for discovery was too much. The answer was already written. The debate was moot.

Jim returned to the hotel room and felt the magnetism emanating from his laptop. Once he had decided to follow Shilesh's advice and had mentally agreed to program his very essence into a nanobot, the allure was impossible to resist. Jim carefully downloaded the podcast and launched the installation program. He followed the instructions, but opted to generalize his mission - he signed up to become the digital cop, the 'ultimate good guy' in cyber space.

He relaxed the prohibition against violence, and selected to eliminate his termination date – eternity awaited.

Jim poured his heart and soul into the program, defining his values, memories, and his preferences. The programming was difficult and his hands ached from typing.

The clock read 5:00 a.m. Jim had spent the entire night establishing his nanobot persona, his mission, his life insurance. He had decided on a slight enhancement to Shilesh's program, which was to make the nanobot activate only if he died within the next 10 years. Jim figured that a natural death would not be bad. He would accept life and death in human terms. But Shilesh was right. If his life was snuffed out prematurely, then Jim needed an insurance policy, not necessarily for revenge, but for the safety of the world…okay, maybe it was for revenge.

As he was putting the finishing touch on his second life, Jim became aware of the enormity. He paused to second-guess himself. Then, with courage and fear, Jim accessed the internet, sealed the cork tight and tossed the bottle into the sea, watching it disappear and reappear in the rough seas. It was done, born, alive, like an embryo, just sitting there. The digital, life-like message in a bottle was patiently waiting for the moment where it would wash up from the Internet surf and be cracked open.

What next?

It was time to reconsider the NSA and the underground bunker. Having the ability to work on challenging problems and meeting knowledgeable people like Li and Jeanine was rewarding. Jim reflected on the past two months. Despite the pressure, and the lies and deceptions, he enjoyed the technical challenges. It was exciting and rewarding, and he was nervous that life outside of the NSA would be unbearable. He had become spoiled by Magic Maggie. He had become entranced by and dependent on the support network. But, as in all cases, now he had to pay the piper. Life in the NSA meant that he had to accept limitations on his freedom, limitations on his ability to set his own priorities. Jim projected himself into the future and imagined what life would be like if he followed his current trajectory. He was not dissatisfied, but he knew that Maggie would ensure the nanobots were never stopped. Eventually, Maggie would take him down like she took down Shilesh, and probably, like she took down Sally. Maggie was, after all, a killer.

There was one item that kept nagging at him. What about Li and Jeanine? Why didn't Shilesh deliver the nanobot code to them? Jim had no way of knowing, but he could fix the mistake. He went to the hotel lobby and asked the concierge for a taxi.

The cabbie was an older gentleman who smelled of cigarettes and coffee. Charlie the cadaver immediately entered Jim's mind and he shuddered. "Cat walk across your grave mister?" the cabbie asked.

"What?"

"You shook like you just saw a ghost or something. Where are we going?"

"Can you take me to a drug store?"

The CVS was always open, twenty-four/seven. Jim asked the cabby to wait for him and entered the store. He glanced around the aisles until he found the goods. On sale, 2 for 1, USB memory sticks. He paid the cashier, got back into the taxi and headed back to the hotel. Jim decided that Shilesh made the right decision about cutting off the secure chat server after the payload had been delivered. He figured that if he were to become a virtual being; and, if his mission was to patrol cyberspace and look out for bad guys, he did not want or need to open a direct line with humans. Jim would leave his interactive scripture, drop off the keys to eternal life, and let Jeanine and Li make their own decisions. He knew that Shilesh would approve, even if he could not double check.

Jim sat at the desk in his hotel room and stared at the memory sticks – so small, so easy to misplace. What if they got in the wrong hands? What if Maggie or some other nut at the NSA got their hands on the memory stick? Jim felt flush. Shilesh could not possibly have taken the risk to invite anyone else for fear of letting bad guys come in after him. Shilesh had taken a big enough of a risk to make it known to Jim what he had done. The more Jim thought about it, there was no way to protect the memory sticks from bad guys. Every attempt he designed failed. Encryption – no good, biometrics - not enough time, secret codes – ha! this was the NSA for heaven's sake. Every plan was destined for failure. He imagined what would happen when he entered the NSA offices with the memory sticks in his pockets. Immediately he would be searched, questioned, suspected and probably killed. Maggie would grab hold of the memory sticks and in no time the secret would be out. No, making the memory sticks was a bad idea. He decided that the only hope was to pass his iPod to either Li or Jeanine when the time was right. But who would he give it to? Jim was being forced to play God again. In the same way Jim never wanted to be like Maggie or Jake, he did not want to be like god. There was too much responsibility, too many difficult choices. Jim had a simpler mission; he could do his little part to save the world without being a savior. Jim grabbed a book of matches that were in an ashtray and he ignited the memory chips. "Not this time around," he said as he dropped them in the waste bin.

There was no respite. Jim stared at the walls, at the ceiling, and at his dog. His escape to the beach had served its purpose. With a fresh view on life and death, he needed to re-enter the world. Still, Jim was unsure if entering life meant returning to the NSA or doing something different. The choices were equally bad. If he remained inside the NSA, he would be guarded with a watchful eye, and would wage an indirect war against Maggie and her ilk. If he moved outside of the NSA, he would become a wanted man. He saw with Jake's situation how easily fact and fiction could be bent to his disadvantage. Jim used game theory to evaluate his risk of leaving.

He remembered that Li had cautioned against leaking the knowledge of the nanobots. Yes, if the NSA thought that Jim was going public with the nanobot story, they would leave him in peace, because releasing the nanobot story on the Internet would precipitate the doomsday option. Jim knew that the NSA did not want to have to shut down the nanobots. No, their goal was to keep things a suspended state so they could use the nanobots for global surveillance. Since Jim could threaten their plans, he had a bargaining chip!

But, what would happen if someone stole his iPod? Or what if it crashed? Jim had no backup for Nanobot 2.0. He had already loaded his own nanobot into cyberspace, but he could not pass on the keys if the software disappeared. Jim became immediately cognizant of the iPod, its location, the risks facing its existence. He made sure the iPod was securely placed in his pocket, and out of harm's way.

And what would happen to Li and Jeanine if he left the NSA? It would be hard to contact them to warn them of the danger from the outside. Would they even believe him? He thought about Li's response – we are the NSA – it rang over and over in his head.

Then he thought about himself. Jim was a clown, the irreverent one in the group, the square peg. He never quite fit in with the NSA crowd, and maybe Li and Jeanine thought he was too brash. Maybe Li felt she solved the whole puzzle? Maybe she thought he was unworthy? Jim felt a new sense of self-doubt. He knew he had contributed to the team, but he realized that he had never developed a personal relationship with either Jeanine or with Li. It was strictly business, all the time, and whenever he lightened up, he was sarcastic and immature. Jim had never taken the time or the risk to get to know them, and he never opened himself up to be known. Jim was and had always been a loner, and now he was reaping the rewards of being detached from relationships. He never knew who to trust, and now it mattered. Jim was deep in his mind, arguing with himself and struggling to find a direction when his DARPA net phone rang.

Chapter 35

It's not easy to be a successful woman in the working world, especially in a male-dominated industry like the spy business. Being beautiful doesn't help much. And, if you're beautiful and smart, most people will immediately reach for the term bitch as your primary description. And God forbid you are smart, beautiful *and* actually reach a position of power, because then it's given that you either slept your way to the top, or knifed down your challengers; or both. Sadly, meritocracy applies only to the male gender in the majority of the business world.

But, it can be done. Margaret Lynne Paige had achieved a position at the pinnacle of power and influence during her 10 year tenure in civil service with the NSA. And up until the past year, Maggie did not have to kill anyone to get to the top.

The death of Shilesh Gupta was an unfortunate event. But, his murder did open up the promotion opportunity, so it was not all bad. At the urging of the Vice President, Maggie reluctantly accepted the position of Chief Risk Officer to the United States. She had not really intended to kill Shilesh, but when the nanobot empire was exposed, the situation became untenable. Besides, he was weak, meek and old. How could he be such a stupid genius? What kind of idiot would create the nanobot accidentally? He was so embarrassed about his mistake that he invented some lame story of a *dear friend* in California who took his life after realizing that he had created the nanobot. It was preposterous, and Maggie immediately recognized that Shilesh was the guilty party.

Shilesh had to either come forward or pay the consequences, and when Maggie confronted him, he capitulated like a kid. He was empty and exhausted; he was ready to be caught. Shilesh seemed almost relieved to get the secret off of his chest, and yet his egotistical fear of being recognized as the culprit of the nanobot invasion was more than he could bear. How was Maggie to know this? He didn't seem like he was ruled by pride. And, when Shilesh told Maggie not to worry, when he told her he would take responsibility for his actions, she believed him. She even gave him 48 hours to come clean. Maggie explained that she would notify the President of the situation if Shilesh didn't own up to his mistake. That was gracious, wasn't it? And so it was settled, he would come clean.

Twenty hours later, Shilesh had overdosed on sleeping pills and provided a note of culpability. She killed him without ever touching him, brilliant, genius! It was like a page out of Sun-Tzu's *Art of War*. And since she never really touched him, it wasn't really murder, was it? No, it was a tragic suicide, yes tragic…and yet it was fortunate.

Maggie's new role was a classified position. She reported directly to the President of the United States and had unparalleled access and power. The job required intelligence, acumen and discipline, all of which Maggie held firmly in her beautiful, manicured hands. But the nanobots offered something sweeter than the allure of her official duties, they offered the ability to control access to the 'eye of God' and with that control, she had the ability to redefine the U.S. Intelligence business. Maggie was not about to treat such a precious asset lightly. No way! She had given up too much to get to this place in her history – she had no social life, no freedom, no dreams of ever having children – all were sacrificed on the altar of working success. This new twist of events was Maggie's opportunity to gain the recognition and the respect that was due to a person of her unique intelligence and capability. And with the eye of god, she might even be able to influence and control the President to follow her guidance – she could wield ultimate power! The thought of it made her giddy, it was the ultimate rush. Was that evil, she wondered. Was that lust for power? Wasn't lust bad? It didn't feel bad. It felt good, almost sexual. And Maggie deserved power, she had worked hard – it was the American way! No, this was not evil. Maggie was not evil. She had played by the rules all her life, and the few incidents like Sally and Shilesh were not intentional atrocities. Look at Shilesh, he infected the entire goddamn planet – he was evil. That was evil. Yes, Shilesh was evil and Maggie was goodness.

And then there was Jim…Jimmy. What to do about Jim? Dr. Andrews was an unruly and ungrateful recipient of Maggie's beneficence. In a few short months she had transformed him from a bumbling professor in 20 year-old clothes to a leading candidate to head up the NSA's Cyber Security Division. Maggie gave Jim a new life, and she saved him from that wretched existence in California, and the result…ingratitude.

What about his wife, Sally? That one really was a mistake. Her death was accidental damage that sometimes happens in this world. When Maggie launched Operation Allure, she needed Yimani to get into Sally's personal life, but her goal was purely for surveillance and to weaken Jim's resolve; just 'soften him up' so that he would yearn for a change in his life. How could anyone have guessed that an enemy would figure out Yimani was a double agent? It was a freak accident, and Sally's demise was collateral damage. Sure, her death sealed Jim's fate to become her NSA pawn, but it was not intentional…there is always a silver lining in bad events - one just has to know where to look.

But Jim was dogged. Maggie was convinced that Jim had gotten so wrapped up in the nanobot mystery that he failed to see the long-term power that would accrue to the masters of the technology. He was always a loner, but now he had become a radical thinker, a protester…he had become a danger to her success. Maggie had created a brilliant future for Doctor Jim Andrews, and he seemed to be indignant – it was typical. He was pathetic…he deserved his miserable life.

Maggie had initially enjoyed the challenge of seducing him, but he fell so easily into her game that the thrill of the chase left soon after their rendezvous. The horse had barely left the gate, and the race was over – too bad. Once Maggie saw the neediness and loneliness inside of the genius scientist, she knew he would become too much of a liability for a long-term fling. She had to cut the cord quickly and let him know that only she could choose the times of their romantic interludes, not him. He was to become a toy for her amusement, and he was weak enough that he would accept this one-sided position – he was pathetic, smart but pathetic.

But Jim had an adept mind, and he could think about problems inside and out. He could systematically build solutions to complex problems, and he could anticipate what could go wrong. And for that skill, Maggie respected Jim's abilities, in fact, that was the only part of him that turned her on. But, she knew that those abilities could become dangerous if not channeled correctly. Yes, if anyone could derail Maggie's plans for controlling the nanobot surveillance system, or the 'eye of god' as he called it, it was Dr. Jim Andrews.

So, what to do about him? At first Maggie tried the bribe of power. She thought that a big promotion would be enough to attract Jim, but she feared that he would know that her underlying purpose was to distract him from the finding a nanobot cure. And what if he had his own selfish plans for the 'eye of god'? One of the biggest problems in the spy business is that you can't trust anyone. All you can do is try to trap them or lure them to do what you want. And to date, Maggie had failed on both accounts with Jim. She needed to get inside his head and figure out what made him tick.

He was quick to go on a mini-vacation, but would he leave the NSA? Leaving would be too risky…Jim would panic outside in the real world. Even if he tried to rebel and left for a few days, he would come back – Maggie was sure of it. These nanobots were becoming an epidemic and they had not currently found a cure, so he would not risk infection. No, Jim was too weak to go it alone. Besides, he needed the powerful tools at the NSA, the computers, the nanoscope, the research teams…the personal service. He was a kid, a 45 year old kid who needed a safe and secure pod.

Yes, Jim Andrews would come back to Greenwich and Maggie would welcome him…she might even have sex with him again. And once he returned, Maggie would make sure to involve him as close to her as possible so that she could keep an eye on him - keep your enemies close at hand. Yes, Jim would be a difficult nut to crack, but he was predictable, Maggie knew where his thumbscrews were. He was, after all, just a man. The others would also be easy to deal with.

What to do about Jim?

Chapter 36

He was engrossed in thought when the sound invaded his head. For a fleeting moment, he feared that something was happening to his precious iPod, but then Jim realized it was the DARPA Net phone.

"Hello."

"Hey stranger," Maggie said, "How's the vacation? When are you coming back?"

Jim forced his words to come out relaxed, "I'm good. Oh, the ocean is beautiful. You should be here to see it."

"I'd love to, but I'm headed to Washington, DC, tonight."

Jim continued, "The ocean is good for the soul, that's for sure."

"Hey, the Secretary of Defense asked me who would replace me at the NSA, and I recommended you. I hope you're not angry, but I think you've got the right skills for it. So, what will it be? Do you think you could come back and work for us? Why don't you meet me in DC tonight? We can talk about it over a bottle of wine."

Jim stared at the hotel room door as he listened to the murderer's invitation. His life flashed before his eyes – his parents, Doctor Roberts, Sally, Shilesh, Jeanine, Li. The lies, the facades and the double crossing would never end if Jim did not take a stand.

"First I need to destroy these damn nanobots."

And with mere words, battle lines were drawn.

####

Thanks for getting to the end! If you liked it, see our web-site
http://www.sim-bio-sys.com

This is the first book of a series. **Coming Soon** is "Revenge"

Please tell your friends to buy a copy! It will motivate me to
finish the second book faster.

Suggestions for further surfing or reading:

[1] http://en.wikipedia.org/wiki/Germ_theory_of_disease
[1] http://en.wikipedia.org/wiki/Blind_men_and_an_elephant
[1] http://en.wikipedia.org/wiki/Byte
[1] http://en.wikipedia.org/wiki/Binary_code
[1] http://en.wikipedia.org/wiki/Sound_recording_and_reproduction#Stereo_and_hi-fi
[1] http://en.wikipedia.org/wiki/FLOPS
[1] http://en.wikipedia.org/wiki/Subscriber_Identity_Module
[1] http://en.wikipedia.org/wiki/Fullerene
[1] http://en.wikipedia.org/wiki/Symbiosis
[1] http://en.wikipedia.org/wiki/Virulence
[1] http://www.wired.com/thisdayintech/2009/11/1110fred-cohen-first-computer-virus/